THE
GOOD
LIAR

Also by Denise Mina

THE GOOD LIAR

DENISE MINA

MULHOLLAND BOOKS

LITTLE, BROWN AND COMPANY

NEW YORK BOSTON LONDON

Mulholland Books / Little, Brown and Company
Hachette Book Group
1290 Avenue of the Americas, New York, NY 10104
littlebrown.com

First North American Edition: July 2025
Originally published in the United Kingdom by Harvill Secker: July 2025

Mulholland Books is an imprint of Little, Brown and Company, a division of Hachette Book Group, Inc. The Mulholland name and logo are trademarks of Hachette Book Group, Inc.

The publisher is not responsible for websites (or their content) that are not owned by the publisher.

The Hachette Speakers Bureau provides a wide range of authors for speaking events. To find out more, go to hachettespeakersbureau.com or email hachettespeakers@hbgusa.com.

Little, Brown and Company books may be purchased in bulk for business, educational, or promotional use. For information, please contact your local bookseller or the Hachette Book Group Special Markets Department at special.markets@hbgusa.com.

ISBN 978-0-316-24304-9
LCCN 2025938447

Printing 1, 2025

LSC-C

Printed in the United States of America

'It is difficult to get a man to understand something when his salary depends on his not understanding it.'

Upton Sinclair, 1935

THE
GOOD
LIAR

18:38

Professor Claudia Atkins O'Sheil, MBE, and Lord Philip Ardmore were taking the back stairs at the Royal College of Forensic Scientists in Regent's Park, heading down to the distant rumble of a party in the open courtyard.

Even here, in a little-used service area, the new building was elegant and understated. A handrail of pale ash spiralled seamlessly down from the third floor. A soft light from skylights tucked into the eaves made the concrete walls look like grey suede in the late January gloom.

In just twenty minutes Claudia was due on stage in front of an auspicious audience, being filmed and recorded as she gave a career-defining speech about her most famous criminal case. She would outline the facts of the murders at Chester Terrace and the subsequent investigation, explain how her scientific evidence had secured the conviction of a vicious murderer.

But Claudia was not going to give that speech. She was going to tell the truth tonight. It would ruin her life but she had to do it.

If certain people knew what she had planned they would do anything to stop her so she had been careful and secretive. To protect her sons from this act of social terrorism, she had tucked them somewhere safe and set up a bank account in their names. She'd handwritten the speech and burned her early drafts because she didn't trust the security on her computer or the sanctity of her bins.

Every minute of every day for the past few weeks she had been expecting to be found out, denounced and stopped. But it didn't happen. In twenty minutes she would blow her world apart.

Astonished to have got this close, the enormous consequences of what she was about to do began to weigh on her. Her staff would lose their jobs. Criminal cases the world over would have to be retried.

A lot of well-meaning people would be discredited. She would ruin her own career and that of the man walking with her now. Lord Philip Ardmore had asked her to speak tonight. He had sponsored her career in many ways, had been kind and supportive since she lost her husband. He had promoted and protected her.

Philip was quite proper and this would be a gross public humiliation for him.

Claudia was no great fan of drama but the theatrics were absolutely necessary. Having the courage to speak out was only half the issue. The real problem was getting people to listen.

Comfortable fictions versus awkward truths were not unheard of in forensic science.

A day after the first Shaken Baby Syndrome conviction the academic whose work it was based on gave several interviews to the press. The court had misunderstood his data, he said, the numbers didn't mean that. No one listened to him. For decades afterwards grieving parents had been accused of shaking their infant children to death. It was a fairly successful charge: many accused fathers pled guilty and confessed to the crime. Of course the authorities were not in the home at the time of the offence. They couldn't know which of the parents was to blame so both were charged. These couples often had other children. It occurred to no one that the fathers might plead guilty so that their partner was set free and allowed to raise the other kids. Shaken Baby Syndrome had a good conviction rate. It became an accepted charge.

And Claudia knew it was hard to listen to the contradiction of an established legal fact because reversals were so consequential. The serial killer Ted Bundy was convicted on the basis of Forensic Odontology, bite-mark-matching evidence, a science now discredited. If Bundy wasn't dead, he'd be out.

She was familiar with the stickiness of a comfortable lie, how hard it was to make people turn and face the truth, so her revelations had to be spectacular. She would make a fool of herself by saying these things. She'd much rather just keep quiet and collect her pension, but she might die of shame if she didn't do something. She was too angry to stay silent.

The man walking next to her wouldn't have let her out of the stairwell if he knew what she was planning. He was the living embodiment of the status quo.

Lord Philip Ardmore had organised this celebration. It was the first anniversary of the opening of the Royal College of Forensic Scientists building, a relaunch. Last year's actual opening party was ruined by the bloody events at Chester Terrace and it was important to Philip that tonight went well. He had steered the whole College project from design to completion and the building was a mirror to the man: clean, lean, considered and calming.

Ardmore, slim as a bookmark, was tall with thick silver hair. Though closing in on sixty, he still walked with a youthful bobbing gait, the eager lope of someone keen to get where he was going. This evening he was dressed in a classic but casual cream linen suit, the raspberry lining occasionally visible next to his crisp blue shirt. He wore no tie.

Professor Claudia O'Sheil, MBE, was a foot shorter and wide of hip, twenty years Philip's junior with skin that tanned at the opening of a fridge and glossy black hair that neither steam nor witchcraft could tame. She had dressed in a black silk shirt under an Yves St Laurent trouser suit in burnt orange velvet that was terrifyingly easy to stain.

Philip expected the night to go like this: a bit of mingling, sipping champagne, and then they'd all file into the auditorium. He'd introduce Claudia in glowing terms and then she would get up and tell the story of Jonty and Francesca's murders, finally putting that ghastly episode behind them all. The applause would be rapturous. Afterwards they would mill for a while, being congratulated, greeting old friends, before slipping out of a side door to a waiting car and being driven over to his club for a celebration dinner.

The Albemarle Club was so high table that it had only recently acknowledged the existence of women. Eight former Prime Ministers had been members and Beau Brummel was one of its founders. Members were limited to a few visitors per year and being invited to supper there was a step up on the golden ladder. Philip knew that Claudia loved a bit of upper-class nonsense, that's why he nominated her for her MBE. He'd hinted that, after this evening, a damehood could only be an honours list or two away.

But that was not the evening Claudia had planned.

She was going to get up on stage and, in full view of everyone, she was going to tell the truth about what happened. She was going to hit the fuck-it button and blow her life up. It would ruin her and they were roped together, these two. Only Claudia was braced for the fall though. Philip was defenceless.

Feeling a pang of conscience, she glanced at him and saw his nose twitching.

'Claudia, have you been smoking?'

She bristled. 'No, of course not.' But then she sniffed her sleeve, the soft velvet brushing her nose, and even she could smell the disgusting tang of smoke. 'Actually, I have.' She bit her bottom lip. 'I didn't notice the smell. Shit.'

Philip reached into his inside pocket. 'No, it's fine. Look.' He took out a tiny sample vial of scent. 'Shall I squit this cologne over you?' He held it above her head, his finger poised over the pump lid.

She nodded and he sprayed a tiny glittering cloud into the air. It settled on her head and shoulders.

Philip sniffed the air around her, 'You smell lovely now.'

But she didn't really smell lovely. She just smelled like him.

They continued down the stairs and Claudia autopsied her response: was it normal to deny she'd been smoking and then admit it? Did she sound anxious? She wasn't used to lying to anyone but herself.

If she sounded nervous the audience could dismiss what she said, say she was hysterical, a disappointing speaker, she'd had a terribly sad life what with her husband's awful death and everything. They'd say that she was past her best.

Their steps echoed in the empty stairwell. Claudia felt an anxious tremor deep in her stomach as they approached the fire exit that led out into the Botanical Courtyard. The party hummed warmly beyond the doors.

They took a moment, knowing that this was the last time they'd be alone until after her speech. Philip cleared his throat, Claudia flattened her hair and pulled her jacket straight.

They looked at one another in their splendid clothes. They looked powerful and authoritative and they both knew it.

He turned to the door. 'Ready?'

'Yup.'

On Philip's signal, they took a door each, pushed the bars down and made their entrance, swinging both doors wide into the party.

A roar of gaudy light hit Claudia's eyes and she flinched as a sudden backdraft of dry heat from the patio heaters billowed into the stairwell.

She was back, a year ago to the day, standing next to Philip when he got the phone call that would bring them to this point.

Gunshots in a grand house less than half a mile away, up on Chester Terrace.

Two dead.

Come at once.

We have the place surrounded.

I

The sweetness of the elderflower cordial and rising scent of daphne caught the back of Claudia's throat. She felt a little sick. This was her first party since she was widowed. She didn't want to come but was here to support her new boss at the forensic analysis company, ForSci Ltd. Sir Philip Ardmore had been so supportive of her since James died. Attending the opening ceremony of a building project he'd been instrumental in was the least she could do.

The warren of glass and concrete was on the edge of Regent's Park and something of a miracle in the Central London conservation area. Planning regulations had been circumvented somehow or other. She thought the sheer social heft of the board might have something to do with that. Tonight was the opening party and they were all there: all the MPs and MBEs, the landed and the lords. She would have been anxious about the company if she wasn't still a little numb. The lingering shock of James's sudden death lent her an air of disinterested sangfroid.

Her doctor refused to prescribe antidepressants. They won't work for you, he said, grief is a rational reaction to your husband dying. The depression is natural, not something that can be washed away with chemical sunshine. You'll just have to wait until the gnawing awareness of the frailty of life recedes, which it will. I'm sorry.

Claudia was sorry too but functioning in low mood gave her a new perspective. It wasn't insight so much as a world drained of colour, stripped back to clean lines with all the dissembling and distractions beyond her grasp. It had been four months and one week ago and Claudia had been absolutely still, watching the world move around her.

Her face still moved in expression-making ways. Her body went to work, came home, cooked, moved from their crappy cramped house in Battersea to an even shitter flat in Lambeth, attended meetings with pastoral care teachers concerned about her boys. But Claudia was frozen, watchful, waiting for the black to lift, to thin, for the shock to lessen. Adrenalin trilled through her body every waking moment. She felt as if she had woken up at the top of Nelson's Column and was expected to act as if nothing had changed.

All she wanted to do was sit and smoke and sob. But she didn't. She couldn't afford to.

Ironically, she had been steeply promoted during this time, achieving an income she'd never managed when James was alive. She wondered if her detachment looked like wisdom from the outside, if it was a precondition of her success and why Sir Philip supported her rapid advancement in an area she had so little experience in.

She was coping, she kept reminding herself, countering the voice in her head that insisted she couldn't cope. You are coping. Look at the evidence.

This evening she must have seemed less capable than usual though, because Philip had been following her around like an anxious nanny. That worried her. It didn't do to look weak.

They were in an open space at the heart of the building, the Botanical Courtyard where, according to the newspapers, ancient poisons and hallucinogens were being grown under government licence. This wasn't true. No one knew where the rumour started, but there had already been several attempted break-ins even before the official opening. Now brand-new cameras were trained on every corner.

A figure slid in front of Claudia, coming in from her blind spot, standing close, filling her field of vision with a large chest and broad shoulders. A woman with a domed forehead haloed by a velvet Alice band.

'Claudia?' Her head was tilted to the side, 'Dr Claudia Atkins O'Sheil? Remember me? I'm Dr Kirsty Parry.'

Claudia didn't think she did recall the woman but Kirsty was standing too close to focus on her face properly. 'I'm terribly sorry . . .'

'Organic Chemistry at Merton. Different year from you, two below, obviously you remember me.'

'Oh, yes,' lied Claudia, 'of course, yes.'

Kirsty looked around the courtyard and the groups of people clustered around the heaters, 'Odd time of year to have a party, isn't it?'

Claudia hadn't organised the party. 'Is it?'

'I mean *January*, really? People are barely back from skiing.'

'Oh, I suppose so. Quite nice to be outdoors with the heaters on, isn't it?'

Kirsty was looking down her nose at Claudia, sceptical, 'You really don't remember me, do you? We met at James's service.'

'His funeral?'

'Yeah, yeah,' Kirsty shook her head as though Claudia had said the wrong word and she wanted to shake it out of her ears. People unfamiliar with loss often behaved as if death was a vulgar mistake other people made.

'Sorry,' said Claudia, 'it was a fairly hectic day, I'm sure you appreciate . . .'

'Yeah yeah yeah. James and I, families knew each other. Ski school.' She widened her eyes with surprise as if astonished at herself.

There was an edge to Kirsty, as if she wanted something but resented asking. She was wearing the bad tribal outfit of James's class but she was a fine-looking woman underneath it, with a good long face, wide blue eyes and a poise that belied her head-girlishness. 'We were only thirteen, yeah?'

Claudia didn't know what she was being asked to affirm. The best she could come up with was, 'Gosh!'

James had told her about ski school. His parents were quite old and had sent him away over Christmas thinking it would be a treat to be with other young people. But James was too young to be away, read the trip as rejection and cried all week.

'Thirteen is so young! *Too* young,' said Kirsty, not specifying for what and trundling on, 'but, obviously, we knew each other since we were very little, kiddie parties and so on. Families . . .' She sipped her drink, blinked twice and looked away.

Claudia gave a non-committal hum and tried to sidle off but Kirsty followed her. 'Got kids, haven't you? Boys?'

'Yes.'

'Ages?'

'Thirteen and sixteen.'

'Yeah. I didn't work much when mine were little but I'm keen to get back into it.'

She stared at Claudia, unblinking, as if the ball was now in her court. 'Back into what?'

'Forensic reporting. D'you know of anything? I mean, I've got a doctorate from Oxford too, so . . .'

So juries will believe me, is what she meant, so judges will defer, so benefits-of-the-doubt will follow me all the days of my life.

'James used to say how sinister it was that the red-brick universities corralled all the most ambitious young people together and crammed tradition down their throats as if they were showing them that change is impossible.'

Kirsty blinked and a weak smile wavered on her face. 'Yes,' she said. 'And Merton *is* lovely.'

Claudia sighed. She missed James a lot.

She came from a lower-middle-class home in Glasgow and arrived here via Oxford and a good marriage. She sometimes felt like an anthropologist among the Maasai, deciphering gestures and measuring heads, comprehending only a fraction of what was said, but even she could see that there was a hierarchy of belonging and some, like Kirsty Parry, might be in the group but were very definitely at the bottom.

'Well,' said Claudia. 'I know Hamilton Analytics are looking for someone to run their low copy DNA lab. They've probably got work in other fields. What's your specialism?'

Kirsty answered quickly. 'That.'

They grinned at each other. Kirsty must want work badly enough to wing it and Claudia liked that.

'Hubby's between jobs at the moment, city . . . I'm feeling like I'd like to dip the toe . . .'

She was desperate for work. Claudia guessed that the husband had been sacked or had a breakdown, maybe their mortgage was overdue.

'Well, you could do reports on the low copy job or, hear me out, something you actually know about. Was your DPhil research or theoretical?'

'Research. Professor Dale's project on haemolymph clotting in caterpillars. But I did tutor on the Forensic Science Masters.'

'What did you tutor?'

'Ethics in ancestry DNA sampling, blood spatter analysis and probabilities, all that stuff.'

'Blood spatter? That's my area—'

'Oh, I'm *well* aware of that,' said Kirsty, as if Claudia had taken a job that had been promised to her. 'I tutored on the use of the O'Sheil Blood Spatter Probability Scale, actually. Specifically on your 3D reconstruction model.'

The Blood Spatter Probability Scale was Claudia's seminal work, partly developed during her DPhil but never properly monetised because the university owned part of the copyright for her thesis. Her system fed all the blood spatter information from a crime scene into a computer programme which then created a 3D model reconstruction of the events. It had been groundbreaking and she was proud of it. After James died, Philip showed Claudia how to separate out the parts owned by the university and use the rest. He helped her register a worldwide licence on the BSPS. The effort had started to pay off now: it was so persuasive that it was being used by defence lawyers in every case that could afford the technology.

'Well, Hamilton Analytics are always looking for analysists who can talk coherently on the stand. Believe it or not, most experts aren't great at public speaking.'

'Okay. Cheers for that. I saw Steve Hamilton earlier.'

'Oh, you know Steve?' Claudia had spotted him across the party. He had a distinctive head of hair that looked like a very expensive toupee but wasn't.

'Of course. Everyone knows everyone,' said Kirsty, looking around for him.

Kirsty was right, this was an unusually narrow social tranche. They were all born rich or, like Claudia, were as driven as Tam O'Shanter fleeing Old Nick, running twice as fast as everyone else to feel they were keeping up. In her own middle-class Catholic

Glaswegian background everyone knew each other, met at mass and attended the same schools, but the additional factor here was money and the worry that people who didn't have any were trying to get theirs. Fear made the bond hermetic.

Kirsty was looking at her. It was probably Claudia's turn to say something. 'Small world,' was the best she could come up with.

Kirsty was delighted by this. 'Oh!' she said, as if this was an earth-shattering observation, '*Terribly* small!'

Philip slid a shoulder in between the two women. 'Kirsty Parry . . .'

'*Sir* Philip Ardmore!' Kirsty brightened at his presence. 'We were just saying what a small world it was.'

Claudia could see that Kirsty found Philip terribly attractive. A lot of women did. He was tall and drole and always well dressed. Claudia liked small, angry men like James. It may have been her disinterest that made it possible for them to be friends.

He and Claudia were so closely associated that her assistant, Rob, had nicknamed them 'Mop 'n' Bucket'. They were as close as anyone could be with their boss: Philip confided sometimes, about work frustrations, how his divorce from his chaotic wife, Mary, was going, about his love life. He was cryptic about it. He currently had a crush on someone he called 'L.B.'. Claudia reciprocated the confidences a bit but always held a little back. He was her boss after all.

Kirsty wandered off, absorbed into another group nearby.

Philip shook his head, 'I knew I should come over when I saw you talking to Kirsty Parry.'

'*Doctor* Kirsty Parry,' corrected Claudia.

'Oh yeah, she's terribly keen on the titles. Called me 'Sir' eight times in one sentence earlier.' Philip was still a little queasy over his recent knighthood, granted in the last New Years Honours list.

'She said "everyone knows everyone" as if I was trespassing on the gene pool.'

'An odd fish,' he frowned. 'That hairband screams fifth place at the gymkhana. Oh God, look who she's talking to now.'

They looked over at Kirsty, now standing with a group of people listening to Sir Evan Evans murder an anecdote. Something about his shoes being Italian! From a little man in Perugia! Wooden lasts hanging up all over his teeny, tiny little shop! You had to go in sideways!

Evan Evans was the dullest man in London. He routinely began a story and forgot where he was going with it, not because he was old, but simply from the sheer habit of being listened to when he shouldn't have been. His money was as old as his face was red. Claudia thought people were so open in their dislike of him because he was what they feared they might be: rich and dull and only invited out of obligation because he donated to everything.

'I can't abide that braying fool.'

Claudia watched Kirsty nodding over Evan Evans' shoulder at his audience, as though he was delivering their conjoined thoughts. She quite liked Kirsty. She trusted people with clumsy social skills.

'Oh, my little stubby legs are aching.' Her stubby little legs were fine but she wanted to move the conversation on from bitching because it was a downer. 'Let's sit down, shall we?'

They looked around and found a bench.

It was a relief to get out of the rolling howls of heat from the mushroom heaters, nice to feel the crisp evening air wash across their faces. Darkness was falling softly and the lights from inside the building glowed upward, warm and flattering. She sat down and gave a little groan. Her shoes were formal and pinched.

'I must be getting old,' she said. 'Tonight has wiped me out.'

'Oh, for heaven's sake, you're not even forty,' said Philip, sitting down. 'Wait 'til you're my age. My knees pop so loudly they wake me up at night.'

He was trying to cheer her up, it was sweet, but she must have been looking miserable for him to try so hard.

'Anyway,' she tipped her glass at the lovely setting. 'Here's to a job well done, Philip, to getting this built, setting up ForSci and all the charity work you do. A knighthood well deserved.'

'Well,' he sighed. 'Here's the catch. I've been working up to telling you all night. I've been asked to chair the Forensic Ethics Committee. We're drawing up a protocol on what is and isn't admissible, stop phrenology and palm readings getting into court, but I'd have to divest myself from ForSci.'

That sounded ominous. 'And will you?'

'Thinking about it, yes. I have a buyer looking at the company. A conglomerate have been making increasingly wild offers for nearly a year. Will they be impressed? It's all going quite well?'

She said yes, they were getting lots of commissions, doing a high volume of court reports under the new system.

Forensic testing had recently been taken out of public ownership and privatised. Companies like ForSci and Hamilton Analytics commissioned tests and submitted a Streamlined Forensic Report to the court, bringing all the results together in a concise single page that was easy to digest. The defence could accept the test results in the report or dispute it, in whole or in part. Mostly they accepted the report and the case proceeded on an agreed set of scientific facts. It was saving the courts a lot of time.

ForSci Ltd were at the forefront of this new market and Claudia's Blood Spatter Probability Scale was their calling card. It was Claudia's idea to pay their staff commission for each bid submitted and work was flooding in.

'Want to buy my stake?' he said, serious for once.

He didn't know that Claudia's finances were still dire, that James had left nothing but debts. 'Still reeling from James, to be honest. I think I should avoid big decisions for a while.'

'All right, well, I have a potential buyer but I'll have to step aside as Clinical Director. Would you take the position? It's a lot more money and there's a house because the director has to live in central London.'

'A *house*?'

'It's draughty but a nice part of Belgravia.'

'You're joking?'

'No. It belonged to my grandma, actually, but it was sitting empty. I signed it off to the company as a tax write off.'

James was a lawyer. He would have asked more about that but James was gone.

'Is that usual?'

'Oh, yes. The office needs to be near the courts, you need to live near the office. Perfectly usual. You're a great asset.'

A house. She was currently roaring through her savings paying the rent on a cramped ex-council flat in Lambeth.

'Let me think about it?' But she was going to say yes. 'I'll let you know tomorrow. How's L.B.?'

He was having an affair with someone, possibly married, definitely secret.

'Oh, you know,' Philip smiled and a soft blush broke high on his cheeks, 'little evenings here and there. Christmas is always difficult.'

A mobile phone rang out, muffled.

Panicked at vague thoughts of her boys falling, fleeing, fighting, Claudia flattened her hand on her handbag to feel for vibrations. Nothing. Relieved it wasn't hers, she looked at Philip. He stood up, patted himself down and pulled his buzzing mobile out.

'Hello?'

He had pressed speaker by accident and the glass behind him amplified snippets of the voice on the other end. It was a woman's voice, flat-toned and urgent: 'Sir Philip Ardmore? Chester Terrace. Come at once . . . Two dead . . . We have the place surrounded.'

Philip froze. 'Bixby?' His face glazed over and he stared blindly into the middle distance.

'Get here right now,' demanded the voice. 'We cannot have another Lucan.'

Philip caught sight of himself in the mirrored glass and his hand startled open in surprise. The phone dropped, spinning through the air until the corner met the concrete and the glass face shattered to opal. The phone spun on its edge, tottering like a hero cop shot through the heart, until it fell onto its back, dead.

Philip stared down at it, open mouthed.

Claudia stood up. 'What?'

His eyes were vacant and wide, his breathing shallow.

'Who was that? Philip? Sit down.'

Eyes unfocused, Philip reached for the bench to sit but then remembered suddenly he had to leave and jerked away, missing the paving stone, his ankle buckling and righting itself as she caught his arm.

Claudia tried to pull him back to the bench, 'Come – sit down for a minute.'

He mumbled something about driving.

'You're not driving anywhere alone,' she said, wishing someone had done this for her when they called about James. 'Not in that beast of a car. And you've been drinking. I'll come. I'll drive.'

2

A deep velveteen dark ebbed through the trees in Regent's Park, rare enough in central London to make night itself feel expensive. They were sitting in Philip's Aston Martin DB9, parked on double yellow lines on the Outer Circle, looking across a private garden to Chester Terrace, a long white façade of very grand townhouses, each worth tens of millions. The tedium of the white frontage was broken up with runs of Corinthian columns and pediments but the houses behind were uniform, all tall, impassive, haughty.

Except for one.

Flashing blue siren lights washed across the face of number 10. On the first floor a knocked-over lamp shone straight out of the window, slicing into the dark like a blitz-era searchlight. Uniformed police officers stood guard at the front door with their thumbs hooked into the armholes of their hi-viz stab vests, watching the road, on high alert behind crime-scene tape strung across the steps.

The street in front of the house was one way, single lane, but police cars and incident vans had driven into it from both sides. Several vehicles had doors left wide open where the occupants had run into the house.

Claudia recognised the armed response vehicle. An active shooter must have been suspected but officers guarding the door meant the scene had been cleared. The biggest scene-of-crime van was there. Multiple bodies.

Something very bad had happened.

The house itself looked cherished. It had window boxes of pink and purple cyclamen hanging messily over the sills and curtains open on windows dressed with ornaments on the ledge inside, a classic move to foreground the gaze of passersby and stop them peering into the occupied rooms. This house was loved and lived in. It stood out because so many of its neighbours were sterile, metal bars over dark windows and corporate curtains. A lot of London property sat dark: the city was the new Casablanca, a non-place where dark money could hide and fester in the warm.

In the car beside her Philip's breathing was fast and shallow. Soft yellow and pink lights from the dashboard uplit them both.

She was waiting for him to ask her to drive up to the house. He'd barked at her to stop here, just for a moment, please, he couldn't quite stand to go there yet. This was why they were parked on double yellow lines watching the house across a dark private garden, a fenced-off strip of lawn with big rhododendron bushes that blocked the view from the public road. Still, a smattering of passersby had gathered to gawp. A man out walking his dog and a cyclist chatted amiably, silhouetted by the bright lights from the house. Further along a figure was standing on an upturned plastic crate, watching the house through a long-lens camera.

Back in the car Philip's hands were clamped tight between his knees. He was tense, sitting like a small boy waiting to be told bad news about home. She had never seen him look vulnerable. She felt oddly at home in the middle of this unfolding catastrophe. Her heart rate had slowed, her blood pressure dropped. It was as if she was built for calamity now.

Philip leaned forward to look past her and she read the movement as a sign he was thawing.

'Shall we go on up now?'

'A little longer?'

'Sure.'

'Sorry, Claudia, you need to get back for the boys.'

'It's fine, Philip, my sister is there.'

'Gina's still here?'

'Still, yeah.' She touched his forearm and felt him bristle. It was too intimate. She withdrew her hand. 'Are you worried about being photographed?'

'No, I'm just trying to catch my breath. The people who live there. Friends.'

She thought suddenly it might be L.B. 'Close friends?'

'One is a school friend. Since we were seven. At school. They want me to identify the bodies.'

'Isn't there someone else who could do that?'

'Yes, but it's better if it's me.'

Identification was always a priority. No one wanted the wrong family notified of a horrific event.

She understood now why they were waiting in the dark, why he had dropped his phone and was too shaken to drive. They saw scarring sights all the time at work, bloody images and haunting details, but they all developed techniques for dealing with that: covering a victim's face, looking only at the injury instead of the whole person, avoiding biographical details. These things all helped them do their jobs dispassionately. Identifying the remains of someone they had known in life was a very different thing and Claudia knew how bad it was. She'd identified James's body and wished she hadn't.

'Who else could do it?'

'The other person is very young. Too young.'

'How young?'

'Twenty-one but not mentally robust.' Philip rubbed his eyes, 'It's complicated. He's volatile.'

He was in shock, liable to make bad decisions. She thought getting him to talk might be useful.

'When did you last see this friend?'

'Couple of months ago. I bought him a guard dog for the house. A Rhodesian ridgeback. Poor thing must be dead.'

'It could have run away?' she said hopefully but she couldn't see the dog unit van or an RSPCA truck.

'Ridgebacks don't run away.'

'Why did he need a guard dog?'

'He was afraid of his son,' Philip gave his knees a sickly smile. 'Of William. He's an unhappy mix of troubled and spoiled. Only twenty-one but a gossip page regular. You may have read about him. Viscount William Stewart?'

She had heard of him. He had a lot of money and friends and provocative opinions. He and his friends seemed to be at every party and opening in London. They were mythically confident. She envied them until she remembered that she was old but even when young she had never liked parties, or staying out late, or talking to people very much.

She looked up to the house and recalled the image of a tall glamorous young man with long hair in a sweat-soaked T-shirt, pap-snapped coming out of a club. The sheen of sweat was still on his face, steam rising from his shoulders.

'I thought he was a jolly party boy.'

'There's a dark side to all of that.'

'A violent side?'

'Jonty was scared enough to get a very big dog. He was worried.' Philip slumped forward as if he was going to be sick between his knees. He looked suddenly very old and his voice dropped to a whisper. 'Father and son are on bad terms. William's in and out of rehab. They're expensive. Promise after promise, but he always uses again.'

'Addicts aren't lying when they promise to clean up and fail. With the best will in the world rehab doesn't always work.'

He smiled at his hands, 'Jonty is used to throwing money at his problems. Thirty thousand a week, some of them.'

'For him. A lot of them charge on a sliding scale though.' Claudia watched the cyclist swing a leg over his bike and cast off along the pavement towards the photographer standing on tiptoe, holding his camera above his head and snapping furiously at the figures moving in the first-floor window. 'How did the press get here so quickly?'

'Police scanner. They'll be salivating at this. The paparazzi will be hoping for pictures of William cuffed and sobbing.'

'They aren't allowed to use pictures like that, surely?'

'Well, it wouldn't be an invasion of privacy because William has actively courted the press, giving interviews and doing photo shoots. And there was the law suit. He sued his father in open court, *utterly verboten*. People like that keep everything private, if you know what I mean . . .' He meant people like him, not like her.

She brushed over the slight. 'He sued his father for sending him to rehab?'

'No, it's a mess: William was left a hefty trust fund by his mother, lump sum deliverable when he came of age. With his lifestyle and drug use, Jonty worried he'd kill himself with it so he petitioned to get the age bar changed to thirty. Then Jonty and Francesca got engaged and William decided that Jonty was planning to start a second family to swindle him out of the money. He grew increasingly combative, giving interviews about corruption and off-shore companies and Luxembourg banks and all sorts of wild nonsense. Of course the media love it: a drug-addled upper-class twit, heir to an earldom and half of Scotland, staggering around and slandering his elders. Nothing makes them happier.' He sat up and looked past her to the house, 'I knew something might happen. I went to see William a few weeks ago but he wouldn't listen to me, he wouldn't listen to anyone. When I got that call, as soon as she said Chester Terrace, I knew I should have done more.'

'Who's "she"? Who called?'

'Maura Langston, head of the Met. I'm keeping you back—' He looked at the house and steeled himself. 'Let's drive up.'

'Okay, but I'm in no great rush to get home.'

'You sure?'

'Positive.'

Claudia pulled the car out into the quiet road. The engine was almost silent. The seats were so comfortable and the steering so light that she had the sensation of sliding along the road in a bed. It felt for a moment like a nightmare she had after James died, a dream of driving fast, lying back and nodding off.

The wide road was empty as she took a right turn off it and up a slight incline, the surface of the road suddenly as smooth as marzipan. Every house bordering it was eerily white and still and silent, all of the windows dark and empty. The few cars parked on the street were small Ferraris and Porches, little nippy run-arounds, all clean and waxed. It was like driving through an AI-generated film of a street with all the grubby, unexpected details of real life airbrushed out.

Philip pointed her right again, down through a high arch straddling the street to a narrow road cluttered with cop cars.

Claudia took the turn, slowing under the narrow arch. As they emerged from the other side faces appeared from behind the vehicles, frowning cops tracking their approach. One spoke into the mic on his shoulder, reporting their arrival.

She slowed to a stop behind the SoC van. 'Now, do you think you want to go alone or do—'

But Philip had already opened his door and stepped out.

'Keep your hands up!' she shouted after him. 'Philip! Hands up! Firearms Unit!'

Philip raised his hands, up and clear, walking fast, but heading towards the taped-off steps instead of checking in with the cops by the vans as he should have.

Claudia scrambled out after him. He was so intent on getting there that he barely noticed her trotting at his heels.

A red-faced policeman in black jeans and matching T-shirt stepped out from the side of a van and sauntered into Philip's path, watching him approach, standing with his legs wide and planted, ready to tackle him to the ground. He shouted at Philip to stop.

But Philip side-stepped him, barely sparing him a glance, and was immediately blocked by a square-shouldered woman in uniform.

Angry Cop did not like the attempt to evade him. He stepped in front of Philip and slammed a fat hand into his solar plexus, knocking him into a backwards stagger, 'STOP or I'll arrest you. What's your name?'

Philip regained his footing, reared up to his full height and looked down his nose at the officer.

'I am Sir Philip Ardmore, President of the Royal College of Forensic Scientists. I'm here at the request of CI Maura Langston.' The cop's eyes widened. 'Go and get her for me. DO IT NOW.'

The cop looked from Philip to Claudia, glanced back at the two-hundred-grand sports car and its wide, sneering grill.

He dropped back a step, turned away, and went off to get his boss's boss's boss, ducking under the incident tape to the steps. He stopped next to the officers at the front door and muttered to them. They all looked back at Philip and Claudia. One of them spoke into his comms mic.

But Philip was suddenly moving again, hands still up, lurching a long-legged stride towards the tape and through it like a half-crazed marathon winner, dragging the tape behind him until it snapped as cops appeared from the cover of the vans and flew at him. Claudia had never seen him out of control.

She ran after him, taking the first step up to the door and then the second, grabbing at his arm, telling him no, 'Philip! Don't! No!'

They were on the steps, cops above them closing in formation and more below coming to grab them. This was when the front door of the house cracked open and a slit of cold white light razored into the dark street.

Everyone froze at the bloody sight inside.

3

The walls were white, the stairs were white, the floor was black and white. Everything was neat and clean and white. It made the blood sing extra loud.

Ketchup-red arterial blood was smeared up white walls, pooled on the floor, ground into the pale runner carpet on the staircase straight ahead. This wasn't spray but hectic throw-off. Someone drenched in blood had run wildly out of a doorway on the right and bolted up the stairs. The blood wasn't theirs. No one losing that volume of blood could have made it so far. It was someone else's blood.

After only a few steps on the stairs the cast-off blood thinned and smeared.

Claudia looked at the bloody footprints on the pale runner. Fleeing or following?

She narrowed her eyes. Only one set of footprints: they were chasing someone.

The image was so arresting that it took a moment for Claudia to drag her eyes to the person stepping out of the front door.

A dumpy woman dressed in a double white paper SoC suit, hood up over her hair and a clear face-shield held on by a spongy strap around her forehead. The plastic misted with her breath making her face vague. It cleared as she breathed in and then misted again.

The woman stood very still, waiting until the door was closed behind her before looking up. She nodded at Philip. He nodded back.

Claudia recognised her from the news. This was Maura Langston, newly appointed head of the Metropolitan Police.

Langston pushed her visor up, gasping a lungful of fresh air. Everyone hated these visors, they forced you to smell your own breath for hours at a time, but it was an important precaution because the DNA testing was so sensitive now that anyone could contaminate a scene just by walking through it.

Maura slid off the paper hood and smoothed back her brown hair, taking her hand off just as a breeze from the park blew it up at the back, lifting it high around her head, a small animal puffing herself up bigger as a defence mechanism.

'I wasn't expecting you,' she said to Philip. 'You hung up on me.'

Philip muttered a sorry and explained that he'd dropped the phone.

'Well, I wish you had called back because William Stewart is now on his way over here. This is DI Nick Heely, the officer in charge.' She pointed at Angry Cop. Heely bared his teeth. Philip nodded a chilly hello.

'And DI Aisha Gupta.'

The square-shouldered woman nodded at them.

The mood on the steps had changed with Maura's arrival. Now the cops stood to attention and tried to look busy, nervous because Claudia and Philip had walked through the tape and they'd been charged with stopping that very thing happening. Langston acknowledged it.

'It's fine, officers. Stand down. I called Sir Philip and requested his attendance at this scene. Just write up the perimeter breach in the Crime Scene Log.'

Maura spoke as if she was conducting a training exercise. It was odd and officious but then Claudia noticed a bodycam clipped onto her suit. Maura was performing for a future audience.

It was a standard-issue bodycam, small, black and yellow with a blinking red eye in the centre to show that it was recording.

Claudia watched a lot of footage from those cameras and was used to being the viewer. Now she was the one being filmed at an unflattering angle and in a harsh light. She saw herself in the future, watching the film of herself, wondering if she was a liar and was suddenly painfully self-conscious, standing stiff, holding her stomach in. It felt as if she'd unwittingly stepped out onto a stage during a play.

Maura Langston peeled the paper suits from her shoulders, tutting theatrically at the clumsy bodycam as if she'd found a spider on her lapel. She unclipped the camera and turned it off, left the suit hanging around her middle. She shouldn't have taken her suit off at all;

handling PPE was bad practice. Claudia thought she'd done it as an excuse to turn the camera off. Police officers weren't obliged to keep their bodycams running, no one wanted footage of them eating lunch or going to the toilet, but they might be asked to explain if they turned it off at a crucial moment. Langston had something to say to Philip, something she didn't want anyone else to hear.

She nodded him down to the pavement, 'See you for a minute?'

They stepped through the rip in the incident tape. 'Replace that,' said Maura as she led Philip and Claudia into the shadow side of a van, out of ear and camera shot. Philip looked anxiously back at the house.

'Bixby?'

'In the dining room, shot in the head.' Maura pointed back at the front hall. 'That's what all the blood is from. The dog. One shot fired.'

He was puzzled, 'Only one shot?'

'Yes, the couple are dead upstairs. Knife wounds. Someone's walked in on a dinner, shot the dog, chased them upstairs and got them there. We haven't found the knife but there's a leg of lamb on the table and nothing to carve it with. Probably the weapon.'

'If they got all the way into the dining room Bixby must have known them.' Philip looked up at the door. 'How long ago?'

'No more than forty minutes.' Maura looked at her feet, reverting to a comforting recitation of facts. 'Neighbours rang as soon as they heard the shot. Call is logged at seven fifty-two so it started at seven fifty or so. Seem to have left across the roof.'

'So they knew the house?'

'Looks that way. Bloody mess in there. I need an ID on them and I need it quickly.'

Philip whispered, 'I don't want William seeing his pa like that.'

'Philip,' warned Maura quietly, 'he may already have seen his father like that.'

There was a short pause, a missed beat. They were both afraid that William Stewart had killed his father.

Philip didn't say anything so Claudia did, 'Why bring a gun and use a knife?'

'We don't know,' said Langston. 'Shotgun was antique, discarded next to the dog. Could have jammed. Or two or more perpetrators. One shooting, one chasing. They may have wanted to use a knife. It's . . .' she looked up at the beam of light coming from the front room, 'very personal.' That meant vicious, that meant bad. 'We're still documenting. Haven't examined anything much so far but we need definite names to move this on. I'll show you some images—'

Claudia stepped in front of him, 'Could I look at the photographs first? To crop them for Philip so that they're not too messy?'

Maura looked at Claudia as if she'd just noticed her. 'Sorry, who actually are you?'

Claudia introduced herself.

'Oh, ForSci? The Blood Spatter Probability Scale.' Maura warmed a fraction. 'Of course. And James Atkins . . .'

'His widow, yes.'

'Oh, yes, well, I'm sorry for . . . I didn't recognise you out of context. I'm so sorry about James.'

'Yes, thank you.'

Philip raised a wry eyebrow and Claudia smirked as Maura gestured back up to the house.

'Anyway,' she said, 'William's on the way here. I'll interview him right away, we have to, for the optics, because of Lord Lucan.'

Claudia didn't know what she was talking about.

'Lucan was a lord,' explained Philip. 'He murdered a woman in the seventies and then disappeared. The press were convinced that he was allowed to escape because he was titled. William is a viscount, he'll inherit an earldom, so what Maura's saying is that he needs to be investigated meticulously so that there's no doubt about her even-handedness.'

'Well, if he does turn up you'll know if he was involved,' said Claudia. 'Judging from the state of the hall he'll be covered in blood if he did it.'

'Okay.' Maura leaned in, whispering to Philip. 'The press are here. We don't want prejudicial images circulating of William covered in blood, being cuffed and bundled into a van. Can you take him in your car?'

'No,' he didn't hesitate, 'not if he's covered in blood.'

'We'll suit him up. We'll put sheets down.'

'Maura, if he did this dreadful thing I may find myself rather upset with him. I don't want to *give him a lift* somewhere, do you see? And the upholstery is white, it's a very expensive car.'

'What if he's clean?'

Exasperated, Philip conceded, 'If he's clean I'll drive him. If he's innocent we'll take him, yes, but Claudia is driving so you'd have to ask her.'

Maura did: 'Is that okay?'

Claudia shrugged.

'Right,' Maura said flatly. 'If he's clean, after you get him in your car, back out that way,' she pointed to the arch, 'and we'll drive the van fast out of the other end and the press'll chase us to get photos through the window.'

'Look,' Philip whispered, 'why even let him come here? Can't you call him and tell him to go straight to the station?'

Nick Heely had approached them as they were talking and interrupted, 'We tried. He said he was coming, hung up and now he's not answering.'

Philip tried the number but the phone went straight to voicemail. William had either turned it off or run out of charge.

'Okay,' said Maura, 'he might not even come. We'll give him ten minutes and then we'll go looking. Anyway: move on. Let's get these poor people ID'd. Sir Philip, you look quite shaken. Go and sit down in the van and we'll bring the SoC camera to you.'

Heely led Philip off to the van and Claudia went to get the camera from the Scene of Crime manager.

He was standing by his van.

George Farrell was five foot two and thin, his face dominated by a magnificent Persian nose. Bizarrely, no one on the Met had given him a derogatory nose-based nickname and the Met loved a nickname. It said a lot about how respected he was. He was a burnt-out secondary school teacher who had retrained as a scene of crime manager. He often said that he liked SoC management because it was less harrowing than teaching.

'Oi oi,' he said. 'Thought that was you. What you doing here?'

'George, how are you?'

'Yeah, kid, working. You?'

'Same.'

'You will replace every bit of this,' said George sternly, holding a bag of PPE out to her. 'Or I'll hunt you down and throw you in a pond.'

She threw her hands up, a damsel in distress, 'Help! Help! Not a pond!'

'Yes,' said George sternly. 'A slightly smelly pond.'

She dropped the bit, 'Well, your threats are to no avail. I don't need kit, I'm not collecting samples, I'm here for an ID. I just need the iPad with the scene pictures.'

'An iPad? This is the Met,' said George, his accent a lovely Essex drawl with rolling vowels. 'It's a Pie-Pad or High-Pad, some rip-off brand that cost five times as much but doesn't work as well.'

He handed it over. He was right. The camera was rubberised and chunky with a contact screen the size of a paperback book. She laughed, 'Why do they always buy weird off-brand shit like this?'

George grinned, 'Magic bean tech, innit? The sales people are young but managers are old and can't admit they don't know what they're talking about. The sales people take the piss. They could sell them colanders and say they're breathable cycle helmets.'

'Well,' she said, 'the financial year is still young.'

He showed her how to turn the strange camera on and opened the image file for her. The pictures were crisp and horrific. The dominant colour was red.

Her eyes fluttered over the images. Door locks, window locks, all intact. A dinner table with two settings. A huge ginger dog with no head, a fan of blood and bone on a wall. Red footprints next to a ruler, trainers, size seven or eight. Cast-off blood spray on the walls and floor and ceiling. The person was running so the footprints were only partial but she would be able to recreate the scene quite well through her probability scale.

Claudia scrolled down to the body pictures.

A chubby man in his fifties, lying on his back, stab marks, all the same size and trajectory, vertical, inch-long and bloody, clustered around his heart and neck. She cropped the image to frame the man's face so that Philip didn't have to see the injuries. His cheeks were speckled with blood and his eyes half open. It was bad but not as raw as the full image.

Claudia went back to the contact sheet.

Mercifully, the dead woman was face down, the pool of blood around her head so deep that her thick black hair was floating medusa-like around her head. This was harder to frame because she was splayed face-down on the floor. Her wounds weren't visible and Claudia could tell it was the neck. A dark red venal bloody arc was running down the wall. She was younger than the man, slim and dark skinned with well-turned calves, wearing a purple wrap dress that accentuated her slim waist. Claudia cropped the frame around the full-length figure so that the blood spill was minimised.

'Overpowered them both? Would they have to be quite strong?'

'Nah,' George looked over her shoulder. 'Not strong, just very angry with a sharp knife.'

'They have different injury patterns.'

'Yeah. He was further into the room so I'd guess they wanted to get past her to get to him. He's the target. She's an obstacle.'

They looked at the edge of the wound on her neck, so deep it was visible from behind, a clean, single cut. The knife had been very sharp.

'Did you see the post mortem injuries to his groin?'

Claudia flinched, 'Yowch. Really?'

George nodded, 'Bloodless stabs, bunch of them. Post mortem.'

Genital mutilation usually meant a sexual grudge or disfunction. It made a depressing scene even worse.

'Oh my God, George,' Claudia slid back to the shadows. 'I am begging you on my life to light a cigarette.'

George took his baccy tin out of his pocket, lifted one out and lit it and slipped it into her hand.

Claudia took a deep draw, eyes shut, and held the breath in, felt the nicotine seep deep into her until her fingers tingled and the small hairs on the back of her neck stood up. She blew the smoke out high, making wide fat rings, and offered it back to George, 'Thank you. You're a hero. I must owe you a pouch and a half by now. I'll pay you back, I swear.'

George nodded back to Philip, 'He still doesn't know you smoke?'

'Yeah, he knows but I'm denying it.'

George took the cigarette from her. 'A personal ID. Poor Sir Phil. Could it have been his mental wife, Mary, that did it?'

'No. Why d'you say that?'

'Mary's trouble, I know that. Got done for drink driving, asked me to take her piss sample and DNA for the sake of discretion. I've never seen anyone that drunk. She could hardly blink. Tried to fight a chair.'

She tittered, 'That's a shame.'

'Nah, it wasn't funny. She was driving a big fuck-off car. Lucky not to have mowed into a crowd.'

'Anyway, how do you know it's him and not me doing the personal ID.'

'Well, love,' he looked back at the posh townhouse. 'At a guess I'd say you're scum-zone all day, just like me.'

She laughed at that but was aware that she was just desperate to laugh at something. As if he knew how sad she felt George added, 'Yeah, anyway, Ardmore acts so posh Camilla thinks he's putting it on.'

She giggled. Humour at crime scenes was an essential tool in their emotional arsenal. Claudia couldn't watch cop shows any more because no one was fat and everyone was serious.

'Anyway,' said George, 'before you fuck off with that camera you need to fill out the crime scene log.'

She took the clipboard and signed for the camera as Maura came over looking for new latex gloves and fresh shoe covers.

George told Maura that no, she'd get them when she was going back in and not before and, by the way, you'll need to take that suit off because it's completely contaminated now. He'd told her this before, hadn't he? Yeah? Didn't she remember budgets? She should be setting an example. He'd have that contaminated suit to bag, please.

Maura listened sullenly. She wriggled out of the suit and handed it over before checking Claudia had the camera open at the right file.

They went over to the minivan where Philip was sitting.

Claudia clambered up and sat next to him in the dark. Maura got in and faced them, holding her bodycam in two hands like a baby bird she was nursing, turning it on and training it on Philip as Claudia showed him the image of the dead man's face. He winced. She looked away, giving him a moment.

Finally he said, 'Yes. That's Jonathon Stewart.'

Maura spoke into her bodycam. 'How do you know?'

'Earlobe, the one visible there? Got ripped when he was twelve. You can see the scar.'

'Thank you very much, Sir Philip Ardmore. I'm sure that was difficult. And what about the other person?'

Claudia opened the edited picture of the woman. He was calmer at this image.

'Francesca Emmanuel, his fiancée,' said Philip, glancing at the bodycam. 'I can tell it's her from her skin tone and her hair. I also recognise the ruby engagement ring Jonty bought her and that little scar on the back of her hand.'

'Which scar?' asked Maura, standing up to see the screen.

'The little scar on her left thumb,' he pointed to a white mark on the back of the woman's left hand. 'She cut herself last year on a broken glass. Deep cut. Took a long time to heal.'

'Well, thank you, Sir Philip Ardmore,' said Maura formally, for the benefit of some imagined future audience, 'for doing those identifications.' She turned her bodycam off. 'Sorry for saying your name over and over, it's just for the footage.'

Maura took the SoC camera from Claudia, turned it off and handed it to Mark Heely standing outside just as bright white headlights sliced through the back window of the van.

Outside a cop's mic crackled. He leaned in, 'Ma'am? Think that's William Stewart.'

They clambered out of the minivan, into the street, and watched him arrive.

4

The bright white headlights were eye-level and blinding. Everyone flinched as the car rolled slowly through the arch at the end of the road. The massive SUV was a novelty hen-night hire, white, with dark windows and purple lights glowing under the high chassis, the sort with sticky floors and upholstery that smelled of vanilla vape and vinegary wine.

It slowed to a stop twenty feet behind the Aston Martin, too far back to make use of any cover from the press that the vans might afford. The headlights dipped and they saw a small man dressed in a chauffeur's uniform leaning forward over the wheel, grinning open-mouthed until he realised that the street was full of police officers and vans.

His smile evaporated.

An officer was sent down to speak to him, check the passenger in the back and order the chauffeur to pull up closer to the house to avoid the press. The driver drew up carefully and got out, jogged around to the nearside and opened the passenger door, standing back.

Nothing happened.

The driver looked inside, spoke, nodded, then lifted a foot to climb in but stopped, got back out and resumed his position at the door.

Two thin arms emerged from the dark like a corpse reaching out from the tomb. Hands clutched either side of the door frame as an ethereally slim man slithered out to the pavement, bum bumping on the rubber runner, his face hidden behind cheap white plastic shutter shades. He was very intoxicated but noticeably blood-free. His hair was shoulder length and grubby. He hadn't showered.

William Stewart didn't do it.

He stood at the side of the car, knees buckling, steadying himself with a hand on the car as he turned to face the house. Maura and Philip were waiting for him at the stairs like dowdy parents angry at a missed curfew.

William was six foot four, thin as a string, sharp jawed with hollow cheeks scarred with acne past and present. Black joggers hung from his hips, one ankle cuff at half mast, clinging tightly to a calf over new neon yellow trainers. An ancient cricket jumper drooped from his bony shoulders, washed out, the knit laddered at the side. It had a very distinctive blue trim on the neck denoting it as part of the sports uniform for the prestigious Fairchurch School. It was an old, a hand-me-down from someone who had been there in the 1950s or '60s. James had been to Fairchurch. He hated it, had followed the prosecution of two old masters for historic sexual offences, crowing smugly, but just recently had turned around completely and began demanding that they send their boys there. He made the boys sit the exam and took them all for a tour of the school. They were looking in at a classroom and James pointed out some boys wearing antique blazers and ties. It was a statement, he told her, to show everyone that they were not first generation, that they really belonged.

William had nothing on under his jumper but that may have been because he had a fresh tattoo on his pecs, a detailed black image Claudia couldn't quite make out. He had been scratching it: the skin around it was scabbed and scored fiery red but beneath the tattoo she could see parallel white scars. Good tattoo artists wouldn't work over scars unless they had been healed for at least a year. William Stewart might be a drug-addled mess but he was a reformed self-harmer, he was recovering from a compulsion that was very hard to overcome. She was impressed by that.

William attempted a step away from the car and found himself unexpectedly steady. Surprised and pleased, he tried another step and another, walking self-consciously, lifting his feet high like a puppet. As he headed towards Philip, the SUV driver took his chance to get away from the police: he jumped back into the car and reversed quickly out of the road.

Philip waved William over, trying to draw him into the blind spot but William was wary of him and stopped ten feet away, at the edge of the safe zone. He stayed there, swaying from the pelvis as if dancing to some inaudible, end-of-the-night slow song. He attempted a smile. A tiny white crystal on the tip of his nose caught the light and sparkled.

Philip spoke quietly. 'Could you take the sunglasses off, please?'

William swayed slightly, 'No thanks.'

Philip looked at Maura for back up but she was scowling at William, 'Are you drunk?'

'I'm fine.' His smile widened over dry teeth, ''S going on anyway?'

Maura frowned, 'Didn't the officer who called tell you what has happened?'

'Oh.' William reached up to the sunglasses and yanked them off. 'I was with a friend all night.'

'Pardon me?'

'I have an alibi.'

'An alibi for what?'

'I've been asleep . . .' He shook his head. He knew he was getting something wrong. For a moment his expression toggled chaotically between delight and terror but then, hands at his sides, William was keening and crying real tears.

Maura shrugged over at Nick Heely, unsure what to do. Heely took control. He gestured at a uniformed officer and they stepped forward and laid a hand on William's upper back, guiding him closer to Claudia and the dark side of the van. Philip closed in on him, purring that he was sorry, so sorry, let's get you out of here, let's get into my car and go and have a cup of tea and sort this all out, how about that? He introduced Claudia, said she would drive and had her unlock the car. The Aston Martin blinked awake as Philip reached for his arm but William whipped his arm away.

'You,' he shouted back to Maura, tears dripping from his chin, 'don't you need me to look at them?'

'Philip has already done the identification,' said Maura, stepping closer and completing the phalanx around William. 'I'm terribly sorry but we know it's them.'

He shook his head. 'I've come all the way down here for absolutely no reason?'

'We didn't know Philip was coming.'

'Well, I had to find a car service to get me here. That fucking car was, like, a *joke* car? It's the wrong service. How can you *tell* before they turn up? They listed the number and I didn't know and I thought it was a *proper* service but it's, like, for stag parties or something?'

William was animated now that he had a complaint. Claudia saw this with her own boys, silent for days until they were crossed and then articulate beyond all expectation.

'And that *fucking* driver,' he continued, 'was coked off his tits, sorry to say that to, like . . . you people.'

He meant cops. The police didn't care about that, not these cops, they were attending a double murder. If they bothered about drivers on a buzz they'd have to arrest half of London.

Philip went to put an arm around William's shoulders but the skinny boy swung at him, a vague swipe in the wrong direction that Philip ducked easily. William was instantly penitent and covered his eyes and cried with a wide yawling mouth.

Philip leaned in kindly. William must be overwrought, he said, it would be strange if he wasn't. William agreed that he was, his voice small and high, moved by his own plight. Philip asked him what he wanted to do and William shrugged. Perhaps, Philip suggested, a little break? A retreat might be a good idea, a breather to regroup, how about a chat with Maura? He was trying to be kind to the boy but that struck Claudia as a misleading description of a police interview for a double murder. Still, William gave a tiny grateful nod and preparations began for getting him into Philip's car.

Maura flicked a finger to Nick Heely to pat him down but Heely was a DCI. His days of searching suspects for sharps were long gone and Maura should have known that. Heely pursed his lips bitterly and nodded over to Gupta, a stocky female officer, to do it for him.

The uniformed officer approached. Stewart spread his legs and raised his arms, placidly accustomed to being patted down. The officer was thorough but, strangely, no one read Stewart his rights. He should have been cautioned. Claudia watched the search and looked at Heely but he was looking at Langston. Gupta stood back and nodded at him, 'Sir.'

'Clear,' he told Langston.

'Get him in the car,' said Langston.

But Heely said no, wait, they needed to bag his hands first and Langston nodded as if that was her idea.

Still no caution. Claudia thought this was weird.

George came over with another forensic officer in a white paper suit. Moving in concert, they flanked William as George explained that they were going to put bags over his hands to keep them sterile and then, when they got to the station, they'd test them for gunpowder and blood. Was he okay with that?

William looked to Philip for guidance and he nodded and said it was the best way for the police to eliminate him quickly. William wasn't sure. He held his right hand out tentatively and looked at Philip again and Philip said honestly, it was the fastest way to move this on.

With practised grace, George ripped open a padded envelope. The forensic officer reached his gloved hands in and pulled out a white breathable mitten with a big white 'R' stamped on it which he fitted carefully around the tips of William's long fingers, pulled it up over his hand and tied it with a drawstring at the wrist. The street light caught a mountain range of white ridges along William's arm, old slash scars, well healed and from a long time ago.

George ripped open a second envelope and repeated the process with the left hand, pulling the drawstring tight.

As they did this Claudia noticed that William's fingernails were grubby, like her boys' when they came home from school. There was no blood in his cuticles and the nails hadn't been cleaned recently.

Claudia thought about her own boys in this situation. She would never let them have their hands swabbed because that test threw up a lot of false positives, and she would never let them attend a police interview without a lawyer. She wondered if she should say something but it didn't seem her place. She looked at William, unsure whether to be terrified of him or for him.

Big paper mittens fitted, William held his hands up to show Philip and barked a baffled laugh. He looked ambushed, suddenly just an affable drunk in a sea of hostile people. Except for Philip. He was warm and avuncular and patted William's shoulder, mirroring his laugh.

'Let's go and get this sorted out,' he said.

At the car Philip helped William through the passenger door to the narrow back seat as Claudia got into the driver's side. She was turned away to grab her seatbelt when the passenger door shut. She looked back, expecting to find Philip sitting next to her, but he wasn't.

He was outside. He stood for a moment with a hand clamped over his mouth, too upset to get into the car then loped off, crossing in front of the bonnet and walking away. Philip was leaving her in his car, with a drunk man suspected of a brutal double murder, a man who was twice her height and happened to be sitting right behind her soft, exposed neck.

Panicked, she reached for the door handle to scramble out, but then she saw William's face in the rearview mirror.

Young and lost and frightened, he stared up at the bright house, sitting very still, his paper-bagged hands held high, a big R for right and L for left printed on them.

The neck of his washed-out jumper yawned wide and she saw the tattoo: a line drawing of a giant knot with a small sword sticking out of it like a novelty cocktail stick. The hilt ran along his breast bone. It must have hurt like hell when they did it.

She complimented the work and asked him who the artist was, just to be nice. William told her the studio name and implied that he'd bribed the artist to jump the year-long waiting list. He'd only had it done yesterday.

'Is that supposed to be the Gordian knot?'

He nodded, interested that she recognised the allusion. 'Alexander the Great, yeah?'

'Why did you choose that?'

'To represent my family.'

She didn't get it. 'How?'

'You know . . .'

'No, I don't. The story I heard is there's an elaborately knotted rope, and whoever can undo it will be King. Then Alexander the Great swans into town but instead of fiddling around trying to undo it he just slices straight through it with his sword and becomes King. That Gordian knot?'

'Yeah,' said William, chopping his mittened hand in the dark, eyes gleaming. 'The Gordian knot is my family. Unresolvable except – swoosh!'

She sat very still. He didn't know who she was and that statement made him sound incredibly guilty. If he said that to the wrong person he could end up in a lot of trouble. He was frighteningly vulnerable. She caught sight of her own reflection in the window, eyes wide with alarm, looking like a startled pigeon.

'William, son, don't say that to anyone else and cover up that tattoo. You should have been cautioned before you got into this car – I don't know why they didn't do that.'

He looked at her. 'What?'

'You should have been read your rights. They're going to ask you if you did those murders. That's why your hands are bagged.'

'Murders?' He was shocked. 'I mean, yeah, I fucking hate my pa but I'd never shoot him. I'm in over my head, aren't I?'

She turned to look at him, his face an inch from hers. Her boys did that, the airlock confidence, just before they got out of the car at the school gates: I'm being expelled, I didn't pass, I took that money from your purse.

'This is a really perilous situation, William. Be careful what you say, okay? And get a lawyer before they interview you.'

Suddenly the door opened, sucking the moist warmth out of the car. Philip climbed in, pulling on his belt calmly.

Claudia looked at him, expecting some acknowledgement that he'd abandoned her but he just nodded back to the road. She started the engine and reversed carefully.

At the other end of the road a cop van rumbled loudly to life, siren wailing as the van careened in reverse, spun a turn at the end of the road and raced off towards the city. Out on the Outer Circle a single headlight raced after it, a motorbike with two passengers, following at speed.

Claudia was furious with Philip for leaving her alone in the car but counselled herself that he was her boss, he was in shock, he was doing his best in a difficult situation. She backed out through the arch and took a left towards the road, putting her feelings aside, being a good girl, until Philip said they were taking William to Paddington Green.

'Langston can talk to you there, William, it'll be better.'

That wasn't true. Anywhere was better than Paddington Green. She checked the mirror, catching sight of William. He had no idea what Paddington Green was. He should have been cautioned. He was utterly guileless. But her boss and the head of the Met were there, they all seemed to know each other and she had already warned him to get a lawyer. She didn't know what else she could do.

She drew up to the main road and indicated left, quelling the gnawing in her gut, and then, just because she didn't want to make a fuss, she drove William Stewart straight into the trap that would ruin his life.

5

Paddington Green police station had all the charm and sparkle of a bankrupt new town. Built in the early 1970s to house IRA suspects, the inside was a warren of reinforced cells and corridors. What had once been a clever interplay of solid and void on the concrete façade now looked like knocked-out teeth and yellow light seeped from the windows through peeling and chipped silver backing.

The station was about to be shut down. Claudia couldn't believe it was still open.

They drove past a windswept forecourt of uneven slabs branded with chewing gum and a row of bollard sentries blocking the stairs up to a main entrance cowering under a concrete canopy.

'Isn't that the door?' William craned up to look at the grim concrete tower scowling across the Marylebone flyover at shiny new office blocks. 'Should we go in?'

'We'll go in around the back,' said Philip, 'so that we can dodge any press hanging around. You know how they love you.'

Philip was telling soft lies again: they took people in through the back to stop them running away. Paddington Green was a compound.

They drove along the road, beside a wall relief made gothic by a thick layer of black street dust as Philip told Claudia to slow down and take this left and then another into a narrow car park beside the building, now left again.

She pulled up to a gated arch in the building. The keypad was up high, designed for a van driver to reach. She had to back up a couple of times to get close enough to press the intercom and told it that she was here with William Stewart and Sir Philip Ardmore. The metal gate groaned open and they drew up into the hollow middle of the building. The circular car park was empty.

Colour seemed to drain from the world in here, where the air was thick and petrol-smelling. The hum of their quiet engine buzzed back from the steel walls. Small, mean windows looked down at them like an audience turning against an act. This was the green zone, where teenage IRA suspects had been bundled in and out of doors with blindfolds on, not knowing which country they were in or if they would ever see their mothers again.

Maura Langston and Nick Heely were standing at an open door, waiting. Heely caught Claudia's eye and tipped his chin in a short-handed 'thanks', as if they were working together. He opened the door behind him wide to invite William in.

'Well, here we are!' said Philip lightly, as if they'd driven William to a funfair.

Claudia parked next to Heely and glanced at the rear view mirror. The full gravity of what was happening had dawned on William. Fuck, his eyes were saying, Fuck! What the actual fuck?

Philip got out and bent down, pressing the button to glide his seat forward and let William out, then stood up straight beside the car. Claudia and William were alone for a moment.

She whispered a reminder, 'Get a lawyer.'

Philip slapped the roof, 'Come along, out you get.'

Claudia and William looked at each other. She nodded softly, asking if he'd heard her and he nodded that he had as he shuffled across the seat and climbed out.

Claudia got out too and watched William walking meekly over to Maura and Heely. They directed him inside, followed him in and shut the door very firmly behind them.

Philip looked at Claudia across the roof of the car. 'Did William say anything to you when you were alone?'

'Bollocks to that. What the hell's going on?' she said. 'Why did you leave me alone with him?'

'I'm sorry, I got overwhelmed.'

'And look, Philip, this isn't right. He's drunk and young and he hasn't been cautioned. He needs a lawyer.'

Philip toed the broken tarmac floor, 'You sound like James.' He pressed the button for his seat to return to its position, watching as it did. 'I've known William since he was born, he's not quite the naïve fool he presents, but I know what you mean . . .'

He didn't know. She meant that Philip should go in with him, explain what was happening, tell William to shut up until his lawyer got there. She meant that William was over-confident, as many young men are, and anyone half smart and sober could make him admit to anything.

Philip's seat had finished its journey. He turned to slide in hip first.

It was the thought of James that made it impossible for her to leave, 'Nah, I'm staying,' she said and stepped away from the car.

Philip froze, 'Where? Here?'

'Until he can call a lawyer, I'll sit with him and explain what's going on.'

Philip sighed, 'Claudia, you don't know William, but you're absolutely right. You shame me.' He shut his door. 'I'll stay—'

A sudden set of headlights careened through the open gates, sliding across the circular walls, blinding them for a moment before resolving. A small red Ferrari screeched to a halt in the centre of the circle, the noise reverberating off the walls as the handbrake crunched on.

The door opened, a cumbersome figure effected a graceless dismount and stood up.

'Hello, fuckers.'

Charlie Taunton's booming tenor bounced high off the walls. He grinned, the black void of his missing front tooth visible even in this dreary light.

Thrilled, Claudia slapped the top of the Aston Martin. She meant to walk over but broke into a delighted jog. She hugged him and Charlie chortled, awkward as a gruff great uncle finding himself unexpectedly adored by children. He smelled of brandy and lemony cologne.

'Lawdy, Miss Claudie!' He gave her a little squeeze and pushed her off. 'Haven't see you for donkey's.'

When he spoke the brandy smell drowned out the lemon. He shouldn't have been driving but Charlie was always doing things he shouldn't. He was a rogue of just the sort that Claudia loved: funny, kind, generous, with a value system he stuck to rigidly. His principles were not hers, they fought often, but they were his. He believed in kindness and mischief almost as much as he disagreed with smoking bans and paying taxes.

They had known each other for a long time, from back when James was a trainee criminal lawyer. Charlie gave James his first few jobs.

'Charlie, I thought you were hiding in Haiti or something?'

'And yet here I am,' he announced with a flourish, 'being pleasing in Paddington.'

He looked over at Philip and dropped his voice.

'What's *that one* doing here?' The curious acoustics of the cylindrical building meant that Philip heard every word and answered for himself.

'What are *you* doing here, Taunton?'

Charlie shouted over to him, 'The boy has taken me on.'

Philip hesitated, 'William?'

'Yes. I'm his lawyer.'

Claudia didn't understand, 'Since when?'

'Since when, what?'

'When did he take you on as his lawyer?'

'This evening.'

'At what point this evening?'

'Earlier . . .' he turned away and covered his mouth. 'Yet the question remains: the fuck is Philip Ardmore doing here?'

'*Sir* Philip?'

'Accepted a knighthood, did he? Took a dog biscuit. Well, I knew him when he was a simple mortal.'

'We brought William in here.' She dropped her voice to a hiss. 'He hasn't been cautioned.'

'Really? Who asked you to bring him in?'

'Maura Langston. Why?'

He nodded. A professional giver-of-opinions, Charlie tended to be parsimonious with them in non-billable contexts. 'Bagged his hands up, did they?'

'Yes.'

He cupped his hand over his mouth again, 'I was actually holed up in the Caymans but my little *malentendu* with HMRC has been sorted out now, and then my cow of a mother died and I had to come back and make sure she wasn't faking it.' He dropped his hand from his mouth. 'Sorry I missed James's shindig.'

'I doubt he noticed.'

Charlie liked that. 'Well, I'm sorry anyway. I went out to look at the site of his crash. Odd spot to be driving so fast . . .'

She didn't want to think about James's death tonight. 'William's in there with Maura Langston.'

'Langston? Poor old thing. A sacrificial goat if ever there was one.'

'Are you coming, Claudia?' called Philip.

Charlie shouted back, 'Mr Ardmore, how are you?' His voice was thick with contempt.

'I'm absolutely incredible, Charles,' hissed Philip. 'How are you?'

'Astonishing,' boomed Charlie, his voice echoing around the circle. 'Dined at Kettner's, golfed in the Guildhall all the morning, I simply cannot wait for the sun to rise on another triumphant day.' He nodded at Claudia, 'I'd better move my very beautiful car.'

It was a struggle to get back in.

The Ferrari was old, not yet vintage, just old. It looked like a sports car young men used to have posters of in their bedrooms, the sort a hard-scrabble up-and-comer would promise themselves when they made it. He started the engine as Claudia walked back to Philip.

'Don't you two get on?'

'Charlie Taunton is a money grubber of the worst kind. He can spot the hole in someone's pocket from two miles away.'

'He was good to James, you know, when he started.'

In the empty car park, Charlie's car tried to nudge into the space Philip was standing in. They had a stand off until Philip caved and moved.

Complaints against Charlie were not unusual, but it seemed more like Philip had done something to offend Charlie. Still, blame-shifting was part of being a good lawyer, and Charlie was a very good lawyer.

He opened his door and wriggled free of the bucket seat, stepping out so that he was standing face to face with Philip. They didn't bear comparison. Philip was nearly sixty but fit, slim and stately, Charlie portly and balding, his thinning hair scraped back across his pate in graphite scratches.

'So, Ardmore,' Charlie swung his car keys in a circle around his forefinger as if warming up a throwing star. 'Got something to say?'

'No.'

'Well,' Charlie flashed a dazzling grin at Claudia and she, conditioned to please, reciprocated. He looked at Philip. 'You'd better fuck off into the night then.'

At the door Charlie pressed the buzzer and gave his name. A crackly voice told him he couldn't park there and Charlie said yes, he could, Maura Langston told him to. He turned back to Claudia and winked and her traitorous smile gave a cadaveric spasm.

The steel door zapped open and Nick Heely looked out. He looked at Charlie, he looked at the Ferrari.

'This your car?'

Charlie shook his head.

'Who's car is it?'

'You tell me,' Charlie walked towards him, chest bumping him into the building. The door slammed behind them. Only the echo remained, a metallic slap they could feel in their chests long after they could no longer hear it.

Philip couldn't look at her. He said he was sober enough to drive now and would drop her home, taking his toy back to punish her for loving Charlie.

They got in.

'Charlie has a way of drawing you in, you know?' she said, reaching for the seatbelt. 'He was very good to James. He and my sister, Gina, are having a messy on-off love affair.'

Philip's eyebrows rose as he reversed out of the space, 'On-off?'

'Well, he went into hiding because of a tax dispute and she's often too baked to turn up.'

' "Baked"?'

She sighed long and hard. 'It's a complicated relationship, put it that way.'

'Well,' said Philip quietly, 'I wouldn't recommend Charles Taunton to anyone as a romantic proposition. You know his wife killed herself?'

Claudia held a lot back from Philip. He didn't know that she suspected James had killed himself. Before the accident he'd been disappearing for days. They fought about money and all that he was spending researching the fraud case he was defending. She knew he'd had suicidal thoughts when he was young, it haunted her, and James seemed manically happy before he died but wouldn't tell her why. Philip implying that Charlie was in some way to blame for Kiki's suicide hurt her deeply.

She looked out of the side window, eyes trailing tail lights, and talked herself out of saying anything: Philip didn't know about James's mental state before the accident. Tonight had been awful for him. He was her boss.

It was late. London was deserted. Colourful homeless tents were up under the shiny shop canopies on Oxford Street. Shadows wandered aimlessly in Hyde Park. No one talked about the homeless, she'd noticed, including herself. The affluent of London just went about their business as if someone else should be sorting that out.

She lived in Lambeth but Philip was taking a roundabout route there, cutting through Belgravia, home to embassies and fluttering flags. Regal old trees swayed in the gardens. This was a lovely area, blue plaque country. She knew those grand façades hid heartache and troubles, just as many as council houses or bedsits did, she knew that people were the same whatever their housing arrangement. But if people in Belgravia hated each other at least they could sleep in separate rooms or drive away in a nice car. They didn't have to lie in the dark, back to back, crying silently the way she and James used to.

She reminded herself not to mention Charlie Taunton to Gina. They were messy together and Gina ended up in rehab the last time Charlie disappeared.

'Look, I'm so sorry about Charlie.' She meant her own behaviour around Charlie, how easily she got swept along with his bonhomie.

Philip sucked his teeth, 'He was a few years below Jonty and me at Fairchurch, you know.'

'I didn't know that.'

'Hm. A pipsqueak. He was a scholarship boy. He's chippy and he's always been chippy. Uses the old bon vivant act to disarm people.'

He had a point. If Charlie Taunton asked her to hold his coat while he robbed a bank she'd consider it.

'Anyway,' she said, 'the Royal College is officially open. I hope your night wasn't totally hellish.'

'Not entirely. You were there,' he said sweetly. 'We can celebrate another time. An anniversary or something. Poor old Jonty. Poor Francesca. Poor, stupid William. Who knows what he'll do now, with all that money.'

He slowed down as they drove through a nice area near Victoria Station. It was one of those unlikely pockets in central London, mini hamlets with a flower shop, chichi boutiques, an off-licence or deli and, often as not, a pub. These were clean, rich villages but villages nonetheless. The residents were often away or at work all day. The real locals were the staff. This neighbourhood had a hat shop, a pharmacy and a bakery with wooden chairs and tables chained outside for the night. The streets were clean and quiet. She thought Philip was slowing down to look for something in the car until he pulled into a side street and parked.

It was a narrow road with two high Victorian street lights shedding a soft grainy light across a row of Georgian townhouses.

'Look, there,' Philip pointed to a tall dark house. 'That's the clinical director's accommodation. That's where you'd be living.'

Number six was four storeys tall with a brick frontage, small rooms and no front garden. It would have cost a hundred times her annual salary because it was in London and in this part of London.

'The whole house?'

'Yes. Five bedrooms. No garden, though.'

Claudia looked at it again and snorted, 'Are you kidding?'

'What about?'

She looked back up at the windows. She would have sold a kidney for her boys to live there. 'I'm taking the job, Philip. I'd already decided anyway.'

He nodded, over and over, as if consoling himself that something good had come out of tonight after all. 'Good, I'm pleased,' he said and nodded again and said again that he was pleased but blushed at how much he meant it.

Claudia said seriously, 'Well, there's no need to gush.'

They laughed, a welcome release after an awful night.

A sudden loud chime from the dashboard made Philip jump. A text notification appeared on the car command screen. It was from Maura Langston.

'Read out text,' Philip told the car.

An automated female voice filled the cabin, intonation all wrong, words spaced evenly out, draining the meaning from them:

William has solid alibi.

Time stamped footage in our possession from Cheyne Walk.

Thought you would like to know A.S.A.P.

Good night Langston.'

Claudia watched a sheet of rock slide from Philip's face as he wilted forward, resting his forehead on the steering wheel. She was shocked at the rawness of him. William Stewart was very obviously innocent: he had no blood on him, his demeanour was calm and people who committed double murders were rarely annoyed at a car booking less than an hour later but Philip seemed relieved nonetheless and covered his face as he cried.

She waited quietly, patting his back once or twice. Philip took a linen handkerchief from his pocket to wipe his face but it was dry when he took it away and tucked it in his pocket again.

'Wow,' she said, 'they got that CCTV processed very quickly.'

'He was staying with my ex-wife over in Cheyne Walk. She must have sent it in voluntarily.'

'Thank God for her, then.'

He nodded, mortified at his loss of composure and then pulled the car out. He drove her all the way home in an exhausted silence.

She was glad when they finally pulled up, happy to get back to the modest estate with its long balconies and multicoloured doors.

She felt she should say something to reassure him before she bolted out of the car so she patted the arm rest, 'We all get upset sometimes.'

He shut his eyes, nodding a silent thank you.

Claudia got out and watched him drive off before turning away. She walked towards the flat and felt the tension in her shoulders and neck.

Long shift.

The lights were orange here, warmer. A dog barked in the distance. Green bottle glass lay smashed on the path. She stepped around it and walked up to her block, still acting able and grown up, keeping her face straight as she glanced up to the windows of their flat on the third floor. The curtains were open. A flickering blue light from the telly licked the back of the living room window and a red light throbbed in Bernie's bedroom. He was still up and still gaming at one in the morning on a week night. Her tired heart sank.

She walked into the lobby, nodded at the camera out of habit and took the back stairs.

She stopped on the first landing, a place she always stopped. It smelled of piss and creeping damp. Cigarette ends and beer cans and a scattering of disposable vapes littered the floor, smashed under heel and kicked around.

She listened to be sure she was alone, heard no one and turned to face the damp plaster wall. Quite gently she banged her forehead off it, over and over, a rhythmic bap bap bap. She had been batting off memories of James all night. Now they flooded her.

His hand, fingers opening as he reached across her for something.

Sun-bleached hairs on the nape of his neck.

The velvet tone of a groan as he woke up and rolled onto his side.

Even when he stopped loving her, she still loved James. She adored him. She ached for the sight of him. But he was gone.

Lost. Gone from the world forever. No one else would ever see these things. No one in the history of the world would ever see those miracle moments or witness the softness of his voice at night, the smell of his pillow in the morning, the way he always smiled at cats.

She was sobbing, struggling to breathe, chest heaving.

She couldn't let the boys see this. Her grief was so powerful that to witness it would rent the fabric of their world. They would never feel safe again if they saw how big and ragged and fierce her pain was, so she scheduled grief for when she was alone and in these moments the world was no more than a giant, aching vacuum of lost wonders.

She stayed there for ten minutes, silently howling at the wall. Then she dried her eyes, thinking about Philip's dry hankie, his inability to cry, and checked her face on the camera on her phone. She always looked great after these grief moments.

Then she carefully cleared her throat and went on up to the flat.

6

Gina was slumped low on the settee, legs over the arm, drinking a can of fizzy caffeine and watching a true crime documentary about the Yorkshire Ripper. She pointed at a still of Peter Sutcliffe on the screen.

'That guy's a cunt,' she remarked succinctly.

'I believe that is the clinical consensus.' Claudia stayed in the doorway and slumped against the frame, watching a rostrum shot glide across a black and white photo of Sutcliffe looking happy and dressed for his wedding.

'You're late tonight. Good party?'

Claudia didn't know where to start. The delicious scent of stale cigarettes lingered in the living room.

'Oh Gina!' she said loudly so that the boys could hear it. 'Please don't smoke indoors.'

Gina sat up and said loudly that she hadn't been smoking indoors and flashed Claudia a guilty smile as she lay back on the sofa.

She was taller than Claudia, with a peroxide pixie cut and a boyish figure that looked good in everything, even the basketball vest and three-quarter cut-offs she had on tonight. The flat they were renting was always too hot because the neighbours two floors down were growing weed in a cupboard. They pretended not to know because it was a nice family, smelled lovely and everyone in the block benefitted from the heat. It was old and the insulation was terrible.

Gina was tattooed all the way up her arms and legs and neck, with ear plugs that she tugged at incessantly. She spoke like a low-level Glasgow drug dealer though she had graduated with a BA in Fine Art and worked as an art therapist for a few years before her drug taking got out of hand and her life fell apart. Claudia wore navy-blue suits most of the time with low heels and tights. She loved money and status, Gina lived hand to mouth and couldn't understand Claudia's craving for security.

They were very different because they hadn't grown up together. Their mother died of a fast-acting cancer when they were both in their early teens and each was sent to a different family, Gina up north to a cousin in a hippy community that focused on crystals and Jesus, Claudia to their elderly Auntie Ray in Northumberland. Auntie Ray had no truck with religion or emotions. She made dusters out of old underpants.

Gina became an artist, Claudia a scientist. Whenever they met each was baffled by the other, by their differences. Gina would try to take Claudia out clubbing. Claudia took Gina to museums and the theatre. Gina's drinking and use of what she called 'secondary substances' escalated until she needed rehab. Claudia got married and had two babies. They had nothing much in common apart from how much they liked each other.

They had been reaching out to each other less and less, always failing to connect and sad about it, until James died. Then Gina checked herself out of rehab and came to look after the boys. Claudia treasured living with someone who knew who she used to be, the girl James met at university, someone she could speak to in her own accent, someone to smoke with and swear at. Gina was less keen on the arrangement. She complained that Claudia treated her like a housewife, that her life was being subsumed, and it was, but she had saved Claudia's life and given the boys stability they badly needed.

Claudia looked for the cigarettes, 'How come you're still up?'

'Can't sleep.'

'You're necking full-fat Red Bull. It's all sugar and caffeine.'

Gina gave her a look of sincere annoyance and told her to fuck off.

'You fuck off,' said Claudia fondly.

'No, you fuck off.' Gina snuggled into the sofa and smiled as the blue light from the telly tumbled around the messy room.

The big room was still full of boxes Claudia had yet to unpack. They were stacked against the back wall, full of James's papers and books, a stereo system and LPs that he had lovingly carried from student halls to shared flats and every house they ever lived in.

Claudia couldn't face unpacking his stuff. She was paralysed mid-step.

'I got offered a massive promotion tonight.'

'Another one? Well la de fucking dah.'

'This one comes with a free house in Belgravia.' Claudia nodded to Gina's phone in her hand, 'Gerald Road. Street view it.'

Gina unlocked her phone to look. 'What number?'

'Six. Boys still up?'

'Dunno.'

Claudia blinked and saw the bloody hallway in Chester Terrace: cast-off spray and footprints, red on white. She slapped the door frame to bring herself back to the present.

'I'll check on them.'

Out in the corridor she heard the growling bass of the upstairs neighbours' computer game rumbling through the ceiling. She should ask them to put some magazines under their woofer. The sounds of life in the building were comforting at night. They had moved here after James died, broke; his expected vast future earnings had never paid off and his family money had dwindled. He refused to do anything to mitigate his tax liability and invested in hopeless local social enterprise projects. If her new job came off, if she didn't have to pay rent in London, she might have actual disposable income.

Walking up to Bernie's door, she stayed near the wall, trying to creep along the laminate flooring and catch him out but one plank gave off a high squeal and she heard Bernie scuttle across his room, snap his light off and jump into bed.

She hurried to his door, opened it a fraction and called into the room in a furious whisper, 'You sneaky wee bastard!'

He stuffed the duvet into his mouth and stifled a panicked giggle.

Claudia opened the door wide and looked in.

He was in bed, the covers pulled up to his tightly shut eyes. The room was a mess, clothes strewn on the floor, dirty plates and empty cans and mugs perched on the edge of the desk. His computer screen was still glowing, the pixels cooling slowly. He must have been gaming for hours. Bernie was not moderate and his eating had become chaotic since his dad died. He was putting on weight and she didn't know what to do about that or even if it was right to try.

She slipped in and sat on the edge of his bed. 'You okay?'

'Wha'?' Bernie rolled his head, acting confused, pretending to wake up.

She back-handed him gently on the leg. 'It's after one in the morning.'

He sat up and rubbed his face. 'Where have you been?'

She said she'd been at a work party and he should be asleep. 'You'll be tired at school tomorrow.'

'I'll be all right.' They looked at each other in the dark. He wouldn't be all right. They both knew a lack of sleep was part of why his moods were so volatile.

'Been thinking about your dad all night,' she said. 'He was everywhere I looked tonight.'

'Yeah?'

She was desperate to keep talking about James with the boys and to keep them talking about him. 'I met an old pal of his.'

'Who?'

'Someone he used to work with.'

'Who? What's his name?'

And now she couldn't avoid saying the name without drawing his attention to it.

'Charlie Taunton,' she said, and only then did it occur to her that she could have said another name. But maybe Bernie wouldn't remember who he was.

'That fat old dude with one front tooth?'

Oh, God, she wished she hadn't said it. 'Hm, funny man.'

'Oh yeah, he worked for Dad or something?'

'Dad worked for him.'

'And he came to visit us in that cottage in St Ives that summer, he came with Gina and he smelled weird.'

'Yeah. That smell is brandy. Or whisky. Whichever is available.'

'And he was driving.'

'I know.'

Bernie looked hurt, 'You shouldn't drink and drive . . .' He was thinking about James's death.

'Dad wasn't drunk, Bernie. Your dad didn't drink and drive.'

He nodded but she wasn't sure he believed her. She stood up. She couldn't talk about this tonight, it was too sore.

'Gina was taking pills back then. She used to talk really slow.'

'Yeah,' she said. 'She's clean now though.' She glanced back at the screen, 'I can see she's keeping you on a tight rein.'

'She's strict sometimes.'

'She's not your nanny, Bernie, she's your auntie. She doesn't get paid to keep you in line.'

'You should pay her a bit, she does all the house stuff and she never has any money.'

Claudia didn't trust Gina with money, not yet. 'Well, she's just helping me out. Don't take advantage of her, okay? Be respectful.'

Bernie scooted down in his bed and pulled the covers up. She looked back at him from the door. 'Shall I sing you to sleep?'

He gave a great dirty laugh. Claudia's singing voice would wake the dead.

'G'night, my wee monkey man.'

'Night, Mum.'

She shut the door behind her.

Sam's door was across the landing, shut tight. She could guess what he'd been doing all night on his own. Wary of walking in on him, she listened at the door. Sam was never any trouble. He was clever, good looking, sporty but not too sporty, liked by all. He was her golden boy, her comfort child, a consolation for those moments with Bernie when she wondered if she was doing everything wrong.

She listened carefully. When she was sure she could hear steady breathing she opened the door quietly and looked in.

The room was worryingly neat, his bag packed, school uniform folded on a chair, ready for the morning. She hoped he hadn't ended an evening of masturbating with a shame-spiral of cleaning. That didn't seem like a good pattern at all.

Witnessing her sons coming to their sexual peak often made her wonder at the design flaw in puberty: a low point of self-control coupled with a sudden raging libido. It was like nature giving a bazooka to a baby.

Sam was asleep. His alarm clock blinked red onto the ceiling. Sam had Claudia's wavy hair and he wore it long; it was draped over the pillow like a Disney princess waiting for someone to come and kiss him alive.

She blew a kiss into the dark and went to shut the door.

'Night, Mum,' whispered Sam.

She looked back in, hopeful, but his eyes were shut.

'I missed you awful much tonight,' she said and waited, hopeful of a response. A sleepy smile twitched his cheek. 'See you in the morning, Sam.'

She shut the door and went back down to the living room.

Gina had left her a can of lager on the table. Peter Sutcliffe was on trial now. Claudia sat in her armchair and sipped. It was cheap and strong and caught the back of her throat on the way down.

'See the Gerald Road house?'

'It's fucking amazing!'

'I know. A lot more room. Five bedrooms. You could have a studio. Will you think about staying with us? I like this, so far. I was worried you might use again but you're all right aren't you?'

'I'm good, yeah.' Gina kept her eyes on the telly. 'So what happened tonight? How come you're so late?'

'A call came in for a double murder.'

Gina sat up. 'Shit off!'

'Mm hm. We'd to take a suspect in to the police station with his hands forensically bagged. Went in Philip's fancy car.'

'No fucking way,' Gina used the remote to turn the telly down a little. 'Who'd you take in?'

'The dead man's kid. He didn't do it, though. He's got an alibi and he was clean. His dad and stepmum were murdered – stabbed in their fancy house up in Regent's Park. Guard dog had its head shot off.'

'At the door?'

'No, dog was shot in the dining room. The man had a lot wounds, clusters of stab wounds, you know?'

'Yes,' said Gina, who watched too much CSI, 'that's called

"overkill". That means it's personal. And the dog must have known them. Did it bark?'

'Don't think so. The neighbours called when they heard the shot so maybe not.'

'They knew them.'

'Well,' said Claudia, 'get this for personal – shoots the dog, drops the gun, chases them upstairs, kills the fiancée with a knife to get to the old geezer, kills him and *then*, post mortem, stabs him in his meat and two veg over and over.'

Gina reeled back, a half-smile on her face, 'Uh! Jesus! What is wrong with people? Yep. Revenge. He's raped someone, that guy, or been unfaithful.'

'Reckon?'

'I know it. *Fact*.'

'Thank you, Detective Crazy.' Claudia saluted her. 'Why oh why are the Met wasting money on investigations when you're just sitting around, shitting out half baked opinions and smoking all day.'

'I know,' said Gina sadly, 'it's so wasteful. Why are the cops looking at the son?'

'The kid's troubled, self-harming, drug use. Turned up pissed and coked but it's not him. He'd no blood on him.' Claudia had to say it before Bernie mentioned it: 'The kid's lawyer is Charlie Taunton.'

Gina sat up, 'Charlie's back?'

'Yeah.'

'Fuck!' Gina's eyes widened and, suddenly self-conscious, she sat up and stroked her stomach. There was nothing there, she was slim and always had been. It was a bit of a nicotine-fuelled accident but she was very proud of being thin. Staying thin was her one concrete achievement in life.

Claudia liked Charlie very much but didn't understand anyone being attracted to him, 'He's not good for you, Gina. He's still drinking and he's much too old for you.'

'He's only twenty years older than me, he's early fifties or something.'

Claudia was genuinely shocked. 'Oh my God, early fifties?'

Gina laughed, 'I know. Looks well fucked, dun'he? It's the drink. It really shows with age.'

'Bloody hell. And he's still only got one front tooth.'

'Well, he has got a falser, for formal occasions. He still fat?'

'He's even fatter.'

'Hmm,' Gina smiled lasciviously, 'I'm a fan of the chunkier gent, as you know.'

'Stay away from Charlie, his drinking, it's not good for your sobriety.'

'Yeah, you're probably right . . .'

Gina's distant smile reminded Claudia of the aftermath of Gina and Charlie. They had a series of nights together, holed up at the Savoy. Gina was briefly detained in the manager's office on suspicion of being a sex worker. The objection was not, Charlie declared over a dinner with James, that they thought Gina was a sex worker but that they thought she was a rough-trade sex worker. Gina took it as a compliment.

Claudia sipped her beer and the building settled around them, radiators creaked, the fridge buzzed, from downstairs they could hear the echoed yelps of teens and the responsorial psalm of other people shouting at them to shut up.

'That house in Gerald Road?' said Gina. 'Lord Lucan lived near there.'

'They mentioned him tonight.'

'Cunt.'

'That's what they said. Nice house though, isn't it?'

'Gorgeous.'

They sat back and watched the true crime doc until Sutcliffe lost an eye in a prison fight and then Gina turned it off.

'I know that one anyway,' she said as if it was a classic song. 'Don't even know why I'm watching it.'

They sat in the dark and, because it was dark, Claudia mimed two fingers to her mouth, asking for a cigarette. Gina's shoulders jumped with delight as she got up and opened the window, shut the living room door, took out her cigarettes and gave Claudia one.

They sat in the dark together, being naughty, watching blue smoke swim above their heads as Claudia sketched vignettes of her night: William's SUV, his forensic mittens, the headless dog and how much she missed James tonight. Gina half listened, nodding, sometimes sleepily, sometimes interested as Claudia told her about Lord Lucan and said they wanted to make a big public display of even-handed policing because the dead man's son was a viscount. Gina asked what a viscount was and Claudia didn't know either so they googled it: it was the title given to the heir of a lord or earl until they inherited the title.

'You might run into the poor wee earl at your meetings one day.'

'I'm not really going to meetings any more,' sighed Gina. 'I haven't been for a while.'

'Feeling all right, though?'

'I'll be all right.' She said she was ready for bed now and groaned as she got up.

She passed Claudia and brushed her hand over her hair and stood behind her to say, 'Sitting there in the dark chatting, with car head-lights outside rolling over the ceiling and the house making sleepy creaks, it's like when we were wee, eh?'

It was.

Then Gina went to bed, leaving Claudia in the armchair, strad-dling midnight worlds in Lambeth and their shared Rutherglen bedroom back home, before their lives ended. She remembered static sparks from nylon sheets, dogs calling to each other across back gardens and their mum drunkenly screaming at some man she'd brought home from the Chapmans' pub in the kitchen downstairs.

She slept there, under a smoky sky, on the cusp of worlds.

The fire exit doors opened out into the courtyard and everyone turned to look. Philip and Claudia stepped out to a smog of soft smiles and admiring nods from people gathered around tall space heaters, sipping drinks. The party had been waiting for them and here they were, Mop and Bucket, looking marvellous, winning dogs at a show.

This was their victory lap.

But Claudia was about to ruin everything for everyone.

She checked her facial expression, forced her shoulders down as she smiled back at the crowd.

Everyone that mattered in the world of contemporary forensic science was here: the court staff and lab managers, judges and lawyers, even secretarial and admin people. In amongst them were important strangers, journalists and others half recognisable from podcast thumbnails or by-line photos in annual reports of the companies they CEOd, all mini-celebs in this small world, bringing the glam, a garnish on the gathering.

They all looked marvellously orderly and tidy. Splinters of light crackled from expensive spectacles, jewellery, glasses of champagne. Everyone had nice teeth – but not too nice. Everyone had a sensible haircut. Not a single tattoo was visible. No one had misunderstood the dress code or dyed their hair the wrong colour. The lack of variation was a little bit creepy. They looked like an AI image of successful professionals at a party.

Claudia yearned for the chaos of Gina, tattooed and bra-less, but Gina wouldn't talk to her any more and Claudia couldn't blame her. She had cut all ties and Claudia was glad in a way. It meant that at least Gina would be shielded from the bomb she was about to set off.

The glass corridors were ablaze, flooding the courtyard with cold white light that ricocheted back and forth: headache as architecture.

Larry Beecham KC floated over to their side and kissed her on both cheeks. Larry always wore clothes that were too tight for him. She was never sure if it was a style thing or if he thought he was thinner than he was.

'Drink? They're literally giving them away.' His tongue rasped across the roof of his mouth. His antidepressants gave him dry-mouth and he shouldn't drink on his medication. She hoped he had a good night. If she got to the stage tonight he'd be one of her casualties.

'I'm all right, thanks, Larry.'

'See you've had a couple of drinks already, Larry,' Philip said archly.

'Well, I tried Dry January last year and it was hell.' He gave a pained smile as if he'd stepped on a nail, 'So I'm doing Ginuary this year.' He nodded at Claudia, 'You should probably stay off the sauce until after your speech.'

'Well, you know us Scots,' said Claudia, code-switching her accent back to Glasgow. 'A wee drink might make the evening go with a bang.'

Everyone snickered uncomfortably, worried about being offensive about Scottish people, ambivalent because Claudia was a Scot and it was she who had made the joke.

Rob, her assistant, was holding court across the courtyard, telling an adoring audience an anecdote about his international sports career. Rob was affable and fun. His rugby days had furnished him with a font of stories about bad behaviour and drunken team antics, honed from a secondary career as an after-dinner speaker. He needed the money. He had five children and a stay-at-home wife. He caught her eye as he reached the punchline of his story and winked over to her. The people listening duly whooped with laughter when he arrived at the end. He was always the best companion at any party.

Claudia's neck was very tense, even her scalp felt tired. She would love a drink but they could use it to discredit her afterwards. She had to treat tonight like a court appearance.

'Anyway, congratulations, Larry,' she said.

'Thank you so much,' drawled Larry. 'Very happy.'

Philip shook his hand. 'Delightful news. Are you having an engagement party?'

'No,' Larry waved his hand over to Amelia Dibden who was all the way across the courtyard, inside the sliding glass doors. Amelia saw him but didn't wave back. 'Her Majesty said she can't be arsed.'

They watched the crowd in front of them part as if a tiny snowplough was trundling towards them. Maura Langston arrived.

'Hello?' she smiled, desperation in her eyes.

'Good evening, Maura,' said Philip, cold and formal.

Maura smiled anxiously but everyone pretended not to notice.

'Okey dokey,' said Larry, slipping away into the crowd to get away from her. 'Well, jolly good luck, everyone. See you all at the coin toss.'

Maura tried to fill the moment with some dull chat, 'Nice evening for a—'

'Oh shit,' Philip tensed up. 'Evan Evans.'

Sir Evan Evans looked more rosy-cheeked than usual, a white goggle stamp around his eyes from skiing. He was twenty feet away, telling an unwilling listener a very long, loud story.

'Move, move!' Philip tugged Claudia's sleeve, turning his head so that he didn't catch Evan's eye.

Evans was one of the very few people Philip didn't like. They had been at school together and these old school grudges never seemed to go away. They were presented as if they were geographical features, a river to be forged, a cliff to be climbed.

Philip and Claudia shuffled to safety along the path and Maura stayed close behind. Maura was in need of allies. She had been forced to resign just a month ago after a damning public inquiry into her handling of the evidence gathering against William Stewart. It would blow over for everyone but her. She had no power and no one wanted to know her now and they felt free to admit that she was unnervingly odd and a bore but Maura hadn't accepted her social death. She kept appearing at things like an unwelcome ghost.

This was Claudia's fate. Soon no one would admit to knowing her either. They'd turn away when she tried to speak to them.

Claudia didn't want that. She wasn't martyr material. She could leak the information to a journalist and stay anonymous as the facts dripped out. But James deserved better. Charlie deserved better. They had risked everything for the truth and anyway, she was too fucking angry for caution.

Large glass doors had been pushed open at the far side of the courtyard so that the party could flow in and out of the building. Something inside caught Claudia's eye. A woman in an unflattering maroon tube dress, high necked and sleeveless. The face was obscured by a smear of light on glass but a plastic Alice band winked at her.

'What the fuck is Kirsty Parry doing here?'

Philip looked up, shocked. 'She's not here . . . oh my God, she is . . .' He turned away. 'Who invited her? She must be someone's plus one. Shall I ask her to leave?'

Claudia felt sick, 'No, don't make a scene.'

'I'm so sorry. How unnerving.'

It really was. Claudia stood under a broiling patio heater, needing the loo, armpits prickling with sweat, the shush of her racing heart loud in her ears.

Kirsty Parry had conducted a campaign to discredit Claudia in the courts, in academic journals, at parties, in front of everyone they knew. She should not have been invited here. Because of her behaviour she had been frozen out, had to give up on forensic reporting and had gone broke before moving away to France. Someone had gone to a lot of trouble to get her here this evening.

This was more than awkward. Whoever invited her had done it to wrong-foot Claudia and she had no idea who did it or why.

Worse, she didn't know what else they would do to stop her speaking tonight. It was ominous.

7

Philip and Claudia were in the back seat of a sleek black Daimler, waiting in a long queue of cars snaking up through Fitzrovia. The cars edged slowly forward, bumper to bumper.

It was difficult for Claudia to come because so much was happening. The removal company had been booked for weeks and were coming today to move all their stuff to Gerald Road. Gina said she didn't mind doing it all herself: Claudia should go to Jonty's memorial and report back. She was convinced that the murderer would be there.

Gina had a lot of theories. Watch Philip, she said, he must suspect someone. She thought it was a man, a young man, wildly in love with Francesca who was heartbroken at her engagement. Or an older woman who was wildly in love with Jonty and heartbroken at his engagement. Maybe it was a dog breeder who was wildly in love with Bixby. William Stewart had been released on bail, a bit of signalling from Maura Langston that the Met were being very thorough, or, said Gina, maybe everyone knew that William Stewart was in love with Francesca and killed them both in a fit of jealous rage but they didn't have the evidence yet. Claudia pointed out that he'd been filmed in Chelsea at the time of the murders, his aunt Mary Dibden had handed in the CCTV on the night, plus he had no blood on him. Well, Gina said, he could have paid someone else to do it for him. Mary Dibden could be lying. And actually secretly be his mum. Or a man. Or a ghost.

Claudia laughed at her but she knew that somebody coming today probably knew more than they were telling. They were a secretive bunch.

'So, Philip, is this service in lieu of a funeral?'

'They can't release the bodies yet,' he sighed. 'William could have waited, that would have been the proper thing to do, but this is part of his campaign to accede to his father's earldom. He'll get it eventually but he's "in remainder" while he's still out on bail. They're jittery about titles since Jimmy Savile. They should never have given him a knighthood. Thatcher pushed for it. In her defence she didn't know he was a rapist.'

'She probably just thought that's what all working-class people were like.'

He looked hurt, as if mentioning social class was somehow an attack on him, but he shook it off. 'When William is exonerated they'll pass him the earldom but they'll want to drag it out to signal that they have reservations.'

'Will his drug-taking go against him?'

'Surprisingly, not really. It never has before, not with hereditaries. Perhaps it should. His chumminess with the press will be more prejudicial than his drug abuse.'

William was giving interviews about his arrest, calling it a witch hunt, still bad-mouthing Francesca and his father for trying to swindle him out of his trust fund. Even if he was right it wasn't a great way to talk about people who'd been horribly murdered. He was drawing a lot of attention to himself, none of it favourable.

The Daimler edged forward, turning right into Margaret Street. They could see the line of cars ahead of them and people disembarking further along. Philip sat forward in his seat, 'Oh God, what is the hold-up here?'

'Could we get out here and walk?' asked Claudia.

'I'd rather wait. The press are out . . .'

She could see photographers assembled across the road from the church being managed by two uniformed police officers.

Their car edged slowly up until they drew parallel with All Souls Church.

Set back from the street, it was a sweet, fat little church with polychrome brickwork that looked like a stripy jumper. Between the pavement and the church a low wall and shallow yard with benches and pot plants. Mourners milled around in there, greeting one another with sombre delight, checking out clothes and companions, keeping their backs to the photographers.

Their car nudged the last few feet forward, the driver stopped and Philip stepped out onto the pavement, holding the door for Claudia. They needn't have been concerned about the press across the road, no one was interested in them. The photographers dropped their heavy cameras, taking the moment to check their settings or squinting at the cars behind.

Passing through a small arch, they joined the gathering in the fore-court while, at the doors, a vicar in a white surplice welcomed people inside, shaking hands, cupping elbows, his head tilted sympatheti-cally.

There were two distinct groups at the service: Francesca's people were young and dressed in elegant Euro formal: dark blue and black with single colour flashes: a pastel scarf or white pearls. Jonty's were older and wearing a British iteration of mourning dress that looked like a school uniform, neither fitting nor flattering anyone. Black suits and three-quarter-length coats and the sort of functional black handbags that everyone has but nobody loves.

One face was turned straight at her, eyes wide, face open. Kirsty Parry nodded hello to Claudia, surprised to see her there, holding her eye for slightly too long, as if she had been thinking a lot about her since the last time they met. Claudia nodded hello and broke eye con-tact, hoped that Kirsty wasn't going to ask her to give her a reference for a job. Claudia was important in the field, a good get, and it would be awkward to turn her down, especially here.

There were other faces in the crowd that Claudia recognised from the news or the arts, politicians, newsreaders, important members of the judiciary. They all knew each other, the spiderwebs of soft power briefly laid bare by Jonty's terrible death.

She shadowed Philip as he wove his way through the crowd, nod-ding and shaking hands, enquiring kindly after a failing parent, remarking that yes, it was a sad day but thank heavens for dry wea-ther at least. He was heading straight over to a beautiful woman in her sixties with dark hair slicked back in a chic chignon, a chunky gold necklace on her slim, bronzed neck.

'Elena,' Philip took both her hands and kissed her cheeks so tenderly that Claudia felt a flair of misplaced possessiveness.

She wondered fleetingly if this was L.B. until she saw that the
woman was crying and had been crying for days. It was Francesca's
mother. That didn't preclude her from being L.B. but Philip's open
warmth made Claudia think her an unlikely secret lover.

'The things he says about her.' Elena looked over at the entrance.
William Stewart was next to the welcoming vicar and also shaking
hands with people as they filed in.

He had made a real effort with his appearance. His long hair was
clean and pulled back and he wore a sombre suit, a clean white shirt
and black tie. But as he reached over to shake someone's hand Claudia
saw that the suit didn't quite fit him: the sleeves were too short, there
was too much material on the front panels, it was made for a fatter
man. His gold watch strap hung loose on his wrist like a woman's
bracelet.

Philip noticed it too and swivelled away, hissing, 'That's Jonty's
watch. Jonty's suit.'

Claudia didn't think that was such a crime, 'Maybe he can't afford
a suit.'

Disinhibited, he tutted at her, 'One doesn't need money for a suit,
one needs *credit*.'

Philip had never spoken to her disdainfully before and it sent a
shock through her. She wondered, deep down, if he always felt she
was beneath him.

But Philip corrected his expression immediately and mumbled an
apology. She said, 'No, no,' and rubbed his arm, while thinking
about punching his face. But his childhood friend had died. Evan
Evans and half his school friends would be here. His ex-wife might
be here. It wasn't always about her.

Elena panted and turned away, 'I cannot . . . I will not shake hands
with that boy.' She stepped away to the the street.

Keen to get away from Philip, Claudia took her arm. 'Come on,
come with me.'

She led Elena to the far side of the church door, body-blocking so
they could skirt behind someone shaking William's hand, chatted

banally as she did about the boys and schools and Fairchurch and how hard it was to get places for them in the same house because Bernie had been expelled from a couple of prep schools for being too rambunctious.

They got through the door and stepped down into the church. Relieved, they stood and looked, standing close and holding hands like lost girls. It was a pretty church with an altar panelled in beaten gold and a tiny turret pulpit of multi-coloured marble. Coloured light from stained-glass windows dappled the mosaic floor.

'Thank you so much for helping me.' Elena squeezed her hand. 'That was very kind.'

Claudia looked around. 'Is Mary Dibden here? I've never met her.'

Elena motioned over to a very pretty woman, small and neat, wearing a black silk suit and a chic veil over short blonde hair. Her skin was suntanned and a little withered. She wasn't resisting aging so much as styling it out.

'It is costing her a huge amount of money to be here,' smirked Elena who seemed to resent her. 'Her tax liability only allows her to be here for sixty days a year and she had used them all up.'

'She was already in London when it happened though, wasn't she?'

'Oh no. She was in Monaco. I know because we flew in together that night.'

Claudia nodded, tucking that morsel away for Gina later. Mary Dibden didn't give the police the alibi CCTV. Someone else at Cheyne Walk had wanted him free.

'I like the sound of your son Bernard.'

Claudia squeezed her hand, abruptly aware of how painful it must be for Elena to hear about other people's children, even if it was about them being an ungovernable little shit.

Elena squeezed back and left Claudia, making her way up to the front pew to her friends and family.

The two mourning factions sat segregated as if at a wedding: Francesca's family and young friends on the nearest side, Jonty's on the other, shedding coats and flicking through Orders of Service. She saw Rob's head sitting higher than the other heads, over at the far side next to Larry Beecham. Sir Evan Evans saw Claudia and raised a hand, mouthing a surprised little 'Hello!', waving her over to sit with him. He had been laser-focused on her since James's service and it was becoming obvious that she was avoiding him. She pretended to misunderstand and helloed back and then looked away quickly. She'd been stuck with him before. He was kind but tedious. She looked around for Philip and found him talking to Mary Dibden.

For the first time that day Philip looked openly sad, his eyebrows tented as he spoke to Mary. She kept her chin down and her eyes up, adoring and passive, nodding as he spoke. Then she reached out and cupped his forearm and they both looked sadly at the point of contact. It seemed to have enormous meaning.

Philip broke away and she melted into the crowd, resurfacing next to Sir Evan Evans who made space for her.

Philip looked for Claudia, penitent eyes inviting her to sit next to him on Jonty's side. She walked over.

'Claud, I'm terribly sorry for being sharp with you. There's such a lot going on. That was very kind, what you did for Elena just now.'

Claudia looked over at the small chic woman next to Sir Evan Evans.

He rolled his eyes. 'My ex-wife, Mary. *Soon* to be ex-wife. She came back from Monaco just for this. Lives there for tax reasons. First time I've seen her sober in five years.'

'I thought she was L.B.'

'Oh, that's finished, my dear,' he smiled awkwardly. 'Anyway, you're very sure L.B. was female.'

She was surprised at that, and then surprised again that she'd never wondered about that, given his sartorial fastidiousness. Then she worried she was being a bigot.

As commanded by Gina, she watched his gaze skim the room, washing over the faces on Jonty's side, but she didn't see any clues. It was a memorial service, she reminded herself, and Philip didn't necessarily suspect anyone.

She parked the thought and saw Sir Evan Evans gesticulating wildly as he monologued at Mary who was nodding next to him. Maura stood in the aisle talking intently to a controversial right wing cabinet minister.

'Should she be seen with him?' whispered Claudia. 'I thought the Met had to be politically neutral.'

Philip hummed, 'Policing is politics. Good policing makes it look neutral.'

They were in the last pew on Jonty's side of the church. Philip stood close, his arm flush with hers. She was next to the aisle and didn't much want to be, she didn't know these people, but men Philip's age and older were shoving in at the other end, eager to sit together in a clump. The morning coats, the weirdly similar bonhomie, the texture of their irresistible social charm, were all the same. They went to the same school, she realised. They weren't charming because they were special, it was just the house style.

She picked up the Order of Service and looked at the photograph on the front. Jonty and Francesca, arms linked, squinted under a foreign sun. Francesca looked puffy-eyed and the earl smiled miserably, his yellowed British teeth on full parade. The age difference between them was a little grotesque. It was an unkind choice of image. Anyone who wished them well would have slipped that photograph to the bottom of a pile.

Inside, the text was sparse: A welcome.

A hymn.

A eulogy for Jonathon Harold Aloysius Stewart by Lord William Stewart, Earl of Strathearn.

Closing hymn.

'*Earl*?' Philip tutted and dropped his onto the seat behind him. 'Stupid.'

The stream of people coming through the doors was thinning out. William was at the front talking to a slim young woman, watching those arriving over her head. The woman stood arrow-straight as though a thread ran from her crown to the ceiling, a dancer's stance. Her silver blonde hair hung loose down her back, cut so straight across that it looked guillotined.

'Is that William's girlfriend?'

'God, I hope not,' muttered Philip. 'She's his cousin. There's been so much intermarriage in that family they're a pinch on the bum away from a Hapsburg jaw. She's Mary's daughter actually.'

Claudia was surprised, 'You have a stepdaughter?'

'Only on paper. Amelia was at university by the time Mary and I married.'

The church filled up around them and soon the pews were full. People without seats gathered at the back and sides as a pipe organ huffed to life somewhere above them, ineffectual notes that warned them that the service was about to start. A last-minute kerfuffle broke out as men gave up seats to women and youngsters gave way to their elders.

The vicar, a man of very high colour, welcomed everyone on this sad occasion to celebrate the life of Jonathon Harold Aloysius Stewart and, of course, his dear fiancée, lovely Francesca Emmanuel. His voice was nasal. He paused for breath mid-sentence, sucking all narrative pace from what he was saying, dropping his voice at random moments.

He nodded to the organist and led the congregation in a hymn 'from school'. Claudia had never heard it before but the men on their side of the room knew every word and sang with gusto.

The hymn went on for a very long time.

It was seven verses long.

When it ground to an end the vicar reiterated his welcome and William Stewart stepped up to the pulpit, taking a grubby sheet of paper from his pocket. He unfolded it, flattening it on the lectern with the edge of his fist.

He began with a factual breakdown of his father's life: Jonathon Harold Aloysius Stewart was born here, went to school there, studied this at Balliol. He worked for the mining industry in South Africa but came back to set up a company. He could have been reciting his father's CV. Jonathon met Daphne and they were married for twelve years.

Then William zoned out, staring into the middle distance.

The audience shifted uncomfortably in their seats.

William jolted back, reanimated, and carried on.

'They were on a yacht and, as we all know, Daphne went over the side and drowned. So that was sad. I was ten and I wasn't invited on that holiday because the yacht belonged to Tommy Barchester, over there,' he pointed at a small man sitting with his teenage son. The boy had a bad cold sore on his top lip, 'Does your father still dislike children, Lawrence?'

Thomas Barchester was crying hard, ashamed about it and suppressing his sobs so hard it made his head bob. Lawrence, a gangly man-boy, glared at William as if he'd like to wrestle him. William met Lawrence's loathing, reciprocating.

'You were at Jonty's parties in the South of France, weren't you, Lawrence? When you were a kid. Remember. Did you enjoy *those*?'

Mention of Jonty's parties sent a ripple of consternation through their side of the church. Men looked shifty, covered their faces, glancing at one another and looking away immediately. It was obvious that there had been sexual misbehaviour at the parties, strippers and possibly sex workers. All of those discomfited by the reference to them were male.

'Shall we talk about those?'

A man near the front began coughing loudly and the congregation looked accusingly at the vicar. William gave them a sadistic smile, 'Perhaps not here.'

Claudia saw Elena sitting straight, hands in her lap, listening impassively.

William was only warming to his subject though, and his subject was grievances. He detailed his father's offences: Christmases missed, trust funds thwarted, Luxembourg bank accounts and allowances stopped, slights and asides that were obviously moments of exasperation with a difficult son – 'And he told me, right in front of everyone, to go and wait in the car.'

The speech was distasteful. William Stewart was a petty, bitter man.

Sensing he had lost the sympathy of his audience, William turned to the vicar, waved his sheet of paper and shouted in a cracked voice: 'A bad man and a worse father.'

For a moment it looked as if he was denouncing the vicar, who looked so guilty he may well have been a bad man and a worse father.

William was finished. He shoved his paper into his pocket and stomped down from the pulpit, walked over to his cousin Amelia and fell heavily into his seat.

No one quite knew what was going to happen now.

Tommy Barchester keened quietly and Lawrence glared theatrically at the back of William's head.

Someone coughed.

The organist hit a vague questioning chord, as if to remind the vicar that they were still there and a hymn might help?

But then a sharp step rang out from the middle aisle and Elena Emmanuel walked up to the pulpit.

Silence fell as she turned to face the congregation, a single index card in her hand. She took a breath, looked out at them and spoke.

Her daughter, Francesca Maria Veronica Emmanuel, came from a loving home. She was a beloved pupil at school in Dorset where she made life-long friends, and many of those girls were here today. Francesca then attended finishing school in Lausanne and, after a gap year volunteering at an orphanage in Uganda, she came here, to London, and attended Central Saint Martin's. It was while she was there, helping a friend at her degree show party, that she met Jonty Stewart. Elena cleared her throat and looked accusingly around the church.

'Francesca was my only child,' she said. 'We all know who did this. He is standing right here. What have you people done? Nothing. You have all the power in the world but you do nothing.' She looked at William Stewart. *'He is standing right here.'*

The church fell still. Her hand trembled as she reached for the handrail to step down from the pulpit. She walked down the central aisle, head high, swept to the back of the church. The door slammed shut behind her.

The room held its breath.

The organ huffed, another old school favourite began and Philip muttered, 'What a fucking shambles.'

8

Claudia waited until she was in the lift to her office before phoning Gina. There was no answer.

The ForSci offices were just off the Euston Road, on the fourth floor of a characterless glass and steel high rise. Claudia's office was not pretty or old or grand, it was a large square space of plaster partition walls with a long window looking out at other office windows.

She loved this room. Within these walls she knew what she was doing and what she was about to do, who she was and what it all meant. She found it hard to leave sometimes. The rest of her life was chaotic but in here all was facts and reason.

Her desk was so big and square that she could have the books and forms and notes for the different cases she was working on all sides. She had only to move her chair around to get to the next thing.

The shelved back wall was full of expensive textbooks, box files of technical papers and unpublished theses that she could use as citations in her work. One entire shelf was taken up by the *New England Medico-Forensic Journal*, its lovely pale blue spine with a red band providing a clear, solid design accent to the otherwise bland room. Claudia read each issue cover to cover. She'd had several articles published in it, and it bolstered her ego to see who else was in the table of contents each month. It was a social round-up of the winners in her area as much as a way of keeping up with the science.

Her phone pinged. A text from Gina.

Murderer confess?

She texted back no, but she had mean-spirited gossip to share about sex parties in the South of France. It would wait if she was too busy.

Gina sent her a chef's kiss. She must be busy with the removal men.

Claudia opened her computer to a Scene of Crime image.

A dead woman in a nasty flat. It was a smoke house: drinks cans with windows cut out of the sides lay on the table and floor. Wipe marks and the remains of dried powder were visible on the coffee table.

Everything in the room was tobacco stained from the walls to the curtains to the carpet except for a clean and white North Face beanie hat, folded and placed carefully over the arm of a chair.

The dead woman lay on her back in the foreground of the photograph, slack in a puddle of dark red. All the blood came from a single source: a deep horizontal cut through her chest into her heart. Blood covered her hands and forearms like evening gloves. She had held her chest as her heart beat its last, pumping the life out of her. She had lifted her gory hands to look at them as she fell and the red freckled her face. Claudia could trace these movements from the cast-off spray. Even without running it through the BSPS reconstruction she could see both hands coming to her chest, pressing the wound, coming away covered in blood. Semicircles of cast-off were detectable on the wall next to her at waist height, while she was still upright. Then a messy, chaotic fall and hands by her sides, blood pooling under her chest and arms and head.

The woman was young and slim, her thin brown hair was stuck to the blood on her face, her bare arms scattershot with tattoos. She had lost so much blood that her skin underneath looked silvered, her open eyes were shrunk back in the sockets, hands slack at her sides, palms up, dried blood pooled in them.

The suspect, Roland Garret, was twenty-three, six foot one, had a profound learning difficulty and a five-year-old sexual offence conviction. He confessed to this woman's murder under questioning but claimed he'd strangled her. He admitted it was his hat. He'd been wearing it for months. He was on CCTV all over the estate wearing it.

The prosecution had a streamlined forensic report with DNA results that put him in the flat and identified him as the murderer at 99 per cent probability. Claudia's commission was from his defence team. She was to counter those findings.

She ran the points of evidence through the Blood Spatter

Probability Scale. This analysed all the information from the scene, drawing a line through each blood spatter mark to trace the direction and volume of travel to recreate the event.

With enough marks mapped carefully they could easily recreate the actions that caused the bleed.

During her doctorate Claudia had experimented with graphic recreations, animating the findings to create a visual of events, but in the real world of criminal trials it was felt that watching a cartoon of one side's version of events would sway juries so she had rolled it back to produce a simple probability number. According to the BSPS, there was a 17 per cent likelihood that Roland Garret inflicted the fatal wound. He was not left-handed and was too tall to have stabbed the woman at that angle. The arterial gush was so powerful that there was no possibility of him escaping the scene without blood markers on him. It was very different to the original report. She didn't understand why Roland had been charged until she saw the mistake: topical DNA. The original CPS forensic report hadn't made any allowances for it.

The 99 per cent would have been correct if the DNA was as concentrated throughout the scene as it was inside the North Face hat. A tiny sample had been taken from inside the beanie, replicated and amplified for a clear reading but the specific locale of it was obscured by the multifactored probability scale. It made it look as if Roland had been shedding DNA all over the scene instead of just wearing a hat that came to be at the scene of a crime.

Topical DNA was an issue they were seeing more and more because testing was increasingly sensitive. They could take a low copy result and amplify it to a large sample. Crime scene examiners had to wear two full paper suits, three sets of gloves and face masks so that they didn't muddy results with their own DNA.

Poor Roland had been set up. Someone had planted his hat there. The Crown Prosecution Service shouldn't have charged him but he'd confessed because of this shoddy forensic report.

Claudia looked up the author and was astonished to see that it was Dr Kirsty Parry, BSc (Hons), DPhil Oxon, working for Hamilton Analytics. Just a month ago Kirsty had been hustling for work at parties but now here she was, commanding reports and misreading tests. The presentation of the findings was terrible too: some percentages, some decimal points, some ratios. It was bamboozling and shabby.

She wrote her refutation. Parry's conclusions were wrong, she said. She was sorry to be so blunt but there just wasn't enough room in the comment box to soften what she meant. But, honestly, there was something personal in there too. She didn't enjoy being challenged by Parry and didn't like how fast she had appeared on the scene. It took Claudia fifteen years to establish herself. Kirsty Parry only declared an interest a month ago. She wouldn't admit it but she felt threatened by her.

She emailed the rebuttal to Rob in the office next door for him to proofread and submit to the lawyers with an invoice. She was shutting down the case file and photographs when an email pinged into her inbox.

It was another commission for a report, this time on the forensic evidence in Chester Terrace against William Stewart. It was quite shocking.

There were two types of report: a broad one that might give the police new lines of investigation to pursue and a narrow one that explored the strength of the forensic case against a named individual. It was a precursor to bringing charges. This was a request for the evidence against William Stewart. They were going to charge him even though he had a solid alibi.

She sat back and took a breath. It had been barely an hour since Elena Emmanuel accused him at the memorial service. This was the worst kind of knee-jerk policing.

She shouted for Rob and heard the thump of something big smacking into the door. The door opened and there sat Rob, a massive man in a massive chair with a massive grin. 'Boss?'

'Enjoying that incredibly expensive ergonomic chair?'

As an ex-rugby international, Rob had the broken nose and spinal injuries to show for it. He had played for England and was quite famous, adding a little glamour to their world, and brought all the playfulness and determination from that experience to this.

To show off his chair, he pushed off from the door frame, wheeling an expert circle that stopped dead centre in the doorway, hands out. 'Answer your question?'

'Succinct to the brink of rendering a nod loquacious,' she said and became serious. 'Rob, did we bid for the Chester Terrace case?'

'Of course. We bid for everything.'

'I think this should have gone to Hamilton. Can you check it's meant for us and it's not a mistake?'

Rob said sure and wheeled his way out of the door frame back to his desk. After a moment he wheeled back into frame. 'Yeah, you're the named recipient. They want us to handle everything: DNA, blood spatter and anything else they need. It's marked priority and they know we meet deadlines. Hamilton don't. They're crap.'

She nodded solemnly, 'They really, really are crap. That's just science.'

Rob nodded sadly, 'Can't deny science.'

'It's what we're all about here, isn't it?'

Rob gave her a finger-gun salute and slid out of view.

Maybe Maura Langston had panicked and overlooked the potential conflicts of interest. Or maybe what she had actually overlooked was Charlie Taunton on defence.

Taunton was good. If he didn't accept Claudia's report he could make an issue of her being there that night, her knowing Philip. There would be photos of them attending the memorial service together. Charlie would show no mercy. He'd dent her professional reputation without a backward glance.

All expert witnesses had humiliating experiences in court and Claudia was no exception. She'd learned the hard way that she had to over-prepare, memorise back-up statistics. She even used the classic trick of drinking a pint of water before she got up on the stand. That way she'd need the toilet and keep her answers short. The ramble is where they got you.

But her court days were over and this was potentially far more damaging. If Charlie disputed her neutrality the reputational damage to ForSci Ltd could be serious. Commissions would dry up. The whole business could go under.

She couldn't just refuse the report though. They had a cab rank system to stop forensic firms knocking back the less profitable work. She'd have to make a case for passing on it and, as the newly appointed clinical director, she had to notify the accreditation service of any potential conflicts of interest.

She opened a new email and began to list the points of contacts she'd had with the accused, in the car, at the service, Philip knowing Jonty, but the more she tried to clarify the problem the less clear it seemed. She didn't have to be right though, she just had to report potential conflicts and let them decide.

She sent it off and shut her office door before texting Philip. Could he call her when he got a moment?

He returned her call immediately. He was at a board meeting, they were on a break so she'd have to make it quick.

'I'm sorry to have to tell you this but we've been asked for a forensic report on William Stewart.'

He was quite shocked, 'They're not looking for anyone else? Are you sure it's not an interim progress report?'

'No. Has something happened that I don't know about?'

'Not that I've heard. I think I would have heard.'

'Is it odd that we've been commissioned to do it?'

'Do you think it is?'

'Yeah. I've written to the Accreditation Service to notify them of a potential conflict.'

'Okay. I see, I see. Best be safe if you're worried. I don't see the conflict though. Is your concern actually that Charlie Taunton is on defence? Because that's not a conflict, that's a fear of Charlie.'

'It did cross my mind but there's also you being at school with Jonty.'

He hummed, 'Several of the other firms' shareholders knew him. Andrew Hamilton was at school with him, actually, and that's a closer relationship than mine because I'm out of forensic services now. You've notified the accreditation service. Let them decide. Anyway, Hamilton tend to take too long. They'd end up subcontracting the DNA testing through your labs anyway so the conflict remains. This is more upfront. Check with Langston but don't write it down, ask her in person. Don't leave a big dirty trail for Taunton to make a meal of.'

'Hmm.' She still wasn't sure. 'You're still sure he's innocent, aren't you?'

'I know he is but I can see why they've done this. They want to show the press and public just how weak the case against him is, get his alibi out in the open.'

'So they can move on to investigating someone else?'

'Of course.'

She left a pause but if he had any suspicions he wasn't sharing them with her. He told her to go and ask Langston. She was giving a lunch-time talk at the Wellcome Library today. Better ask her face to face.

'There aren't any evidentiary surprises in there, are there?' he asked.

'I don't know. I haven't opened the attachments yet.'

'There'd be no harm in having a look. Incidentally, thank you so much for coming with me today. Greatly appreciated.'

He hung up without saying goodbye.

Claudia sat back in her chair and looked at her computer.

She scrolled down to the attachments, steeling herself. She had seen the worst of it already. She'd seen the bodies. There was no real reason to feel afraid.

She clicked and the .zip file flowered open on the screen.

9

It contained detailed lab test results, requesting more and ordering reports giving details of samples taken and locations.

William Stewart had no blood on his hands when tested at Paddington Green on the night of the murders. He had no blood on him anywhere. His DNA was found on the gun under the table but nowhere else in the house. It was a topical shed, just like Roland Garret's hat.

Of more interest was the fact that partials of Mary Dibden's DNA had been found all over the house, on the stairs and under Jonty's body. They were only partials, not fragments. The points of confluence were minor, amounting to no more than a three per cent match. She was on file because of her drink driving charge but the match wasn't strong enough to make her a suspect. It wasn't terribly useful. They'd need a clearer sample and swabs to compare it to. Half of upper-class London would probably be a partial match.

Included in the file were two .mov files and an unusually small word document, title: 'CCTV'. She opened it. It was a receipt for approximately forty hours of CCTV from the streets around Chester Terrace, covering a twelve-hour time frame around the murders. William Stewart had not been identified in any of the footage. It was great for his case.

If he hadn't gone in and come out he couldn't have done it.

Claudia clicked on the big video file. It was the walk-through of the crime scene.

Beginning on the street outside the front door, looking over the as-yet unbroken police tape. The front door lock was shown up close: it was intact and unscratched. No sign of a forced entry. They wouldn't be interested in the lock if the back door or a window had been smashed in. The attacker had been invited in or had their own key. They were known to the couple.

The film was silent. They'd all heard of defence lawyers playing walk-throughs in court and turning the volume up to broadcast crass comments made by cops and SoC in the background. These were flippant, throw-away comments, dumb things they said to each other to fend off PTSD. Bad jokes or puns sounded very different in a quiet court room with the victims' families hugging and weeping in the gallery.

This crime scene videographer knew what they were doing.

They were in the hall. It was black and white, quite narrow. On a glass console table were a stack of letters next to an orange leather coin tray, a bunch of house keys and two Mercedes car fobs. This was not a burglary.

Above the console hung a large bevelled mirror, the slim edges showing a partial reflection of the dead dog in the room across the hall, an oblique hint at the horror behind.

The camera turned slowly for a long wide-shot of the hall and the curved stairwell. Scarlet blood was smeared on the floor and walls and stairs, frenzied, as if a person drenched in blood had bolted upstairs. Then the lens turned into the dining room.

A chair on its back blocked the doorway.

Inside, the room was bright and colour-filled, pale pink walls crammed with paintings, new and old, colourful and bright. A foxed Venetian mirror reflected the light over the table. A long table filled the room and, at the nearest end, sat two dinner settings of heavy silver cutlery and empty plates, one with a pink serviette unfurled and plopped messily on the table as if the person sitting there had excused themselves for just a moment.

The uneaten meal was a green salad and a small joint of lamb, cooked very rare, sitting in a puddle of blood on the serving dish with a wooden-handled carving fork next to it. No knife. The bloody meat plate was scattered with quartered lemons, the yellow flesh pink now, tainted by the puddle of blood.

The camera panned down to the big dead dog.

It was huge, ginger haired with long muscled legs. Alive, it must have stood four feet high but now it was crumpled in the corner like a drunk asleep at a bus stop, except that the dog's head was gone.

Blood and black bits of matter were sprayed up to the white cornicing. It had been shot under the chin before it fell. Shards of white bone were stuck high up into the plaster wall. The blood was so deep on the floor that it had spread and soaked into the white fringes of the rug under the table.

The camera turned slowly to the table and lowered down to look underneath. In the shadow on the floor the camera focused on two small dark circles. The muzzle of a shotgun. The image focused in closer. An old shotgun, the steel pitted, well-kept and oiled. Whoever threw it there must have bent down and held it by the warm barrel. It had been planted there like Roland Garret's hat.

The camera panned out, mapping the footsteps in the dog's blood as they backed out of the room and around the fallen chair. They were about Sam's shoe size, a seven or eight, maybe even nine.

From experience, she could recreate the events: a couple sitting down to eat. An unexpected intrusion, someone coming in with a key or a knock at the door. Maybe one of the couple put their serviette down and stood up, to greet the person who had come in or to answer the door.

However they gained entry, the trio assembled in the dining room. The mood could have been hostile or benign. What the hell are you doing here or great to see you.

But then the gun is raised.

The second person at the table stands up quickly, alarmed maybe. Their chair falls back, crashing loud. The dog, sensing threat, snarls. They all look at the shotgun.

Bang. Close range. Bloody mess up the wall. Brutal.

Seven fifty-ish. The neighbours ring the police.

The gun is placed under the table. Quite far under the table. It hadn't jammed, according to the report, and there was another round in it. It didn't belong to the house either, it was an antique. The assailant had brought it and then bent down to put it under there.

The videographer turned and followed the trail out of the dining room to the hall and up the stairs, walking at the side of the stairs, keeping to the sterile path George would have identified.

The assailant moving fast, chasing, blood flying from them and hitting the wall in perfect elongated cast-off trails, the marks fewer and thinner as they turned on the stairs and went up to the first floor.

The bloody footprints were erratic, hard to anticipate, seemed to splay outward, running, missing some stairs, toes pressed hard into the edges on others.

At the first floor landing a large archway opened into a yellow room running the length of the house. The camera panned around.

Floor-length windows at the front and back, trees and greenery visible in both. At the front a big red velvet couch sat proud of three big windows, blue police lights washing the underside of the leafy trees in the gardens outside.

The room was hung with more art, gold frames jostled with hangings and carvings. Glass shelves on either side of a big marble fireplace displayed silver ornaments and coloured-glass gewgaws. The furniture in the room looked valuable: bright armchairs and footstools and expensive cushions, a big desk, a glass coffee table stacked with art books.

As the pan shot came to the back of the room it slowed. They were approaching the bodies. The videographer stepped back onto the landing to capture the footsteps into the room from the top of the stairs. They were less clear here, most of the blood had been shaken off; trainers, size seven or eight, running through the door.

Francesca Emmanuel was just to the left of the entrance, face down, arms flat by her sides, one hand still clutching a pink serviette that matched the one left on the table. The linen had soaked up the blood pooled under her and it glinted, still wet and dark and heavy. It was rare to see that. Crime scene videos were usually made long after the blood had dried.

The wall next to her was marked with bright arterial gush, a spray of blood so heavy that it hit at shoulder height and trailed down to the skirting board. Spray, a space, another spray, another space, falling vertiginously lower and lower, a musical annotation of the notes of her heart as she emptied and fell. Francesca had gone down so fast that she didn't have time to reflexively raise her hands to protect her face or even take an evading step. The heels of her bare feet were clean.

She had been ahead of them as they chased her and grabbed her and slit her throat from behind. Francesca was dead before she hit the ground.

The lens moved over to the back of the room, to a reading nook with an armchair and footstool.

Poor Jonty Stewart was slumped against an armchair. He was a big man, wide and portly, his vertically striped blue evening shirt too long, tucked in at one side to camouflage a heavy belly. He wore deck shoes with no socks, a flurry of thread veins on his water-swollen ankles made him look heartbreakingly exposed. His injuries were terrible to look at.

He had been stabbed in the chest and neck and cheeks and jaw many times, parallel incisions shaped like a tear drop, all made by the same weapon from the same angle. Blood was washed down his shirt front. But there were other injuries, bloodless rips around his groin. These injuries were post mortem. There was barely any blood at all.

The gruesome house tour continued up one floor to tidy bedrooms, more art and books, too much furniture. Full wardrobes, ornaments and throws and photos on the wall of Jonty and friends, a curated museum of his rich and plentiful life. In the maid's room, through the ensuite bathroom under the roof, a small door opened up to the roof. It sat open to the night.

The carpet in front of the door was clean with just the imprint of a heel pressed into the fibres. This was how the murderer got out of the building without being seen. Chester Terrace had a continuous roof. Once they were out there they could have hidden or run north or south. They had escaped unseen.

Claudia fed the video into her Blood Spatter Probability Scale. With the old tools every drip and drop at a scene needed to be measured and fed into the computer. Claudia's scale made that unnecessary. Within seven to fourteen minutes it could show a recreation of the events with a figure of the approximate height and build of the perpetrator, including any physiological idiosyncrasies. It was pretty useful.

This scene ran quickly: she watched the recreation and saw just what she expected. A tall figure arriving in the dining room door, moving into the room, raising the shot gun, the angle the dog was shot at, the gun being discarded and the flight upstairs. Then the two murders.

She noticed something odd: the figure was tall but the feet were small. According to the data set they were only about a size seven or eight, unusual. It bothered her.

The figures in her programme were designed to be gender neutral and without facial expression, it was a recreation, not an animation, but sometimes the blank face and the cold beat-by-beat movement made it especially horrible. This was one of those: bang, run run run, stab stab stab. Step back. Step forward. Genital stab, genital stab, genital stab.

She watched to the end, as the figure stepped back from Jonty, turned and walked out of the room. All the trace evidence lost them at the door to the roof. They probably laid out some sort of plastic covering and shed their bloody clothes. But where did they go afterwards? The police arrived shortly after the gunshot was heard. Even if the murderer went along the roof and down a fire escape they could have been caught. Nothing suspicious had come up in the door to doors but many of the houses were empty. They might have hidden in one of them for days.

She shut the file and did some breathing exercises, reminding herself that bad things happened only rarely, seeking comfort in the passive tense. She corrected herself: bad things were *done* rarely. Someone had done this to these people and she was witnessing it so that they didn't get the chance to do it again.

She opened the smaller .mov file. It was a fish-eye doorbell camera, low-res, grainy, taken at night from a low angle, time-stamped and dated at the top: seven fifty-four p.m. on the night of the murders.

Dark was falling in an urban street, the road at the end of the path was partly hidden by a tall box hedge. Amelia Dibden walked up the path, wearing a high-necked, mutton-sleeved dress. Her approach triggered the porch light as William Stewart trailed behind her. He was wearing his cricket jumper, neon trainers and the washed-out black joggers.

Amelia was tipsy but William was eye-rollingly wasted. He rolled his shoulders back as he inhaled. Even breathing looked effortful.

Amelia reached into her shoulder bag for her keys, rummaging until she found them, smirking to herself as she leaned across the lens and opened the door. Warm orange light from the hall flooded the frame and she stepped inside.

For just a moment William Stewart stood alone on the step, swaying, blinking, his cricket jumper sagging at the neck, showing his new Gordian knot tattoo. Something shifted behind him. Through the break in the hedge, on the street outside, a very small man walked past. The man was dressed like a tiny gentleman in grey slacks and a dark suit jacket but only four feet tall, swamped by a massive backpack. He looked creepy.

In the bright foreground, William stumbled forward into the hall and out of shot. The light was swallowed up as the door was shut.

Claudia sat back and sighed with relief. It wasn't him and this proved it. Someone had tried to set him up but they didn't know about the door cam.

William was innocent.

Even if the accreditation service found no conflict of interest and Claudia had to do the report, there was no danger of Charlie Taunton tearing her work apart in court. This and the absence of CCTV sightings of him in the streets nearby. Camden was awash with cameras, like most of London, and it was impossible to imagine that he'd avoided being filmed.

This is what Maura wanted to make public. She was smarter than she seemed.

Claudia was relieved. She treated herself to another watch of the stumbling couple staggering up the path, fitting the key, the odd little man scurrying past the break in the hedge and William Stewart tottering on the empty step.

Claudia picked up her phone to call Gina and ask how the move went. The phone rang out and the film began to replay.

William behind Amelia. His tattoo was fresh, still pink on the edges. No scabbing. Not yet.

Claudia dropped her phone from her ear. She hung up and watched the film again. No scabbing. When she met William at Chester Terrace that night his tattoo was scabbed.

She watched it again.

It wasn't a small man in the background. It was a boy in a school blazer with a satchel on his back, a boy hurrying to school. It wasn't getting dark. It was getting light because the film was not of seven in the evening. It was seven in the morning. The time stamp on the doorcam film was wrong.

William Stewart didn't have an alibi.

She was hurrying across Euston Road to the Wellcome Institute and rang again.

'Gina?'

'Why'd you hang up on me? We're outside the house.' Her voice sounded strange but the road in front of Claudia was choked with cars and buses and she was straining to hear.

'Sorry, I'd spotted something on a work thing. You okay?'

'And the men are emptying the van, know what I mean? Nearly done, getting there, and they've got the beds in already and that and the clothes, most of the clothes and just, a bit more, know what I mean? Like back of the van, inside the van. I'm looking at it. The stuff. Inside. Know?'

Claudia stopped walking. She recognised that speedy, stumbling speech pattern. Gina had taken something.

'Oh, you sound excited.' It wasn't the day for a massive argument.

'How?' snapped Gina.

'How what?'

'In what way, know what I mean? Like, how do I sound excite – I mean, excited?'

Claudia stopped at the roadside and watched a bus hurtling towards her, wondering where the fuck Gina got hold of anything. She was moving house for god's sake. 'Gina – have you had a lot of coffee or something?'

'Couple of double espressos, yeah!' Gina shrieked a manic half-laugh Claudia had heard many times before. 'Why's it so noisy there, are you at an airport?'

Claudia looked across Euston Road to the Wellcome Institute, 'Why would I be at an airport?'

'I don't know, know what I mean?'

'Okay. Um, so, I was just checking in on how the move's going.'

'Good, good. Where d'you want James's boxes to go? Not taking up half the living room again? They've brought the couch in already. Everything looks tiny in this house, y'know? Like fucking minuscule.'

'Attic for the boxes, maybe?'

'*Minuscule.*'

'Okay, so, I'll be back about four and the boys should get in after me, okay?'

'Yup. Yup, yup, yup.'

'Bye.' She hung up. Fuck. They'd been here before. It would not end well.

Claudia had wanted to tell her about meeting Mary Dibden, about Philip Ardmore implying he'd been in love with a man, all the drama of the memorial service. Where did she get drugs from? She didn't have money.

But then Claudia remembered that she'd tipped the removal men a fifty quid on her way out this morning and they were very grateful. They might have reciprocated the courtesy by offering Gina a bump.

Cursing herself, she crossed the road and climbed the steps into the warm lobby of the Wellcome Institute. She only had minutes to spare before Maura's talk began and hurriedly jogged up the marble steps to the Reading Room, walking through the door just as everyone took their seats.

The room was two storeys high, Art Deco, with a sweeping staircase running up to a balcony. The stern bones of the room were softened with domesticating decor: the bookshelves had been removed and a large red rug had been set in the middle of the floor, scattered with yellow beanbags. A portable lectern was set up at the bottom of the stairs and a few rows of office chairs were around it in a semicircle.

Maura Langston stood at the side of the room checking through her notes as an organiser coaxed the audience to fill up the front rows. It was a small audience, less than twenty people, made up of junior police officers and admin staff, all conscripts here, trying to please the boss. They were packed tight into a small area but Claudia didn't see anyone from Hamilton there, no lawyers or lab managers. Her heart sank further as she realised that this wasn't a real event, it was content generation for Maura Langston's résumé. The audience were just props, being crammed near the front of the room to make it look busy in the photos.

Two journalists sitting at the front already looked bored. One was poised with a notepad, the other held a voice recorder. When the organiser offered them a transcript of Maura's speech they grabbed it, gathered up their jackets and bags and left in a hurry.

Claudia couldn't leave until she spoke to Maura but she could sit at the back and avoid being in the photographs of The Great Maura Langston giving an address at the Wellcome Institute.

She pulled a yellow beanbag up behind the last row and slid down into the cloudy seat as Maura began to read her talk word for word from the sheet, beginning with a broad-strokes history of forensic services in England and Wales, keeping her eyes down as if she couldn't be bothered with the cheap razzamatazz of looking at people or modulating her voice.

She read for thirty minutes, detailing the privatisation of forensic services, going over ground everyone here knew well.

Before this new system a lot of court time was lost to prosecution and defence lawyers pitting expensive expert witnesses against each other, courts weren't nimble enough to adopt developments in science and the government's forensic service had been running at a terrible loss. Something had to change. She went on at some length about human rights and why privatisation was so good for them. It didn't make a lot of sense.

The speech was tedious and cobbled together. Claudia recognised a couple of lines that had been copied and pasted from the published government report on the issue. The talk seemed to have been written by someone else and Maura wasn't familiar enough with the source materials to recognise that they'd been plagiarised.

Claudia zoned out. She thought about Gina's last stint in rehab, how thin she was when she was admitted. She'd thought Gina was going to die last time. They said she was lucky her heart was unaffected.

She sighed at that memory, setting off an avalanche in the beanbag beneath her that shifted her right buttock and left her pelvis tilted at a tricky angle. She sat forward carefully to change position, difficult in the low chair, and saw a pair of legs resting on a chair at the very far end of the row.

They were Charlie Taunton's legs.

Maura summarised with a series of pro words: bigger, better, more, thank you for your attention. Then she opened the floor to questions.

Toady hands shot up, ready with questions that Maura had prepared answers for, but, at the very end of the row, Charlie Taunton's hand rose with drunken languor. Maura saw him and looked away.

She picked a friendly person to ask her about the storage of the historic exhibits held by the old Forensic Science Service. Oh, great question, yes, she said, everything had been saved and stored in a new archive.

Charlie's hand rose again.

Again, Maura picked someone else. Yes, also a great question, thanks for asking, yes indeed, there were many regulatory provisions.

She answered another couple of dull questions by reiterating that this was the best possible system. Finally, when she couldn't reasonably ignore him any more, she called on Charlie.

He stood up to ask his question, turning to address the audience like a jury, his plush voice reverberating around the lovely room.

'Is it not the case that, under the push for privatisation – an absolute value in the choppy waters of life, no doubt – this system concentrates power in the hands of just a few, effectively reversing the burden of proof from the prosecution to the defence?'

Maura mumbled no, not really.

Charlie tried again. 'If not *reverse* the burden of proof, is it fair to say that the new system changes the *site* of decision-making from the court room to the office of the expert witness?'

No, said Maura, the juries decide.

'How can the jury decide,' said Charlie, engaging the audience's attention more than Maura Langston and she was their boss, 'when they're not even asked? The whole system is designed to remove scientific questions from the purview of the courts.'

Maura said that wasn't necessarily a bad thing. Juries were not always able to comprehend very technical questions and many of these questions concerned extremely complex scientific issues. The audience snickered here about how dumb juries were.

'Lawyers are not always able. They're just as likely not to understand complex science. I myself am a practitioner of law and honestly, many of my compatriots are idiots. Middle class but idiots nonetheless. So: no one understands except the expert witnesses and they're not in court and unlikely to ever admit they're wrong, are they?' Charlie turned to the audience. 'Which supports my point, viz: What checks? Whither balances?'

The audience looked uncomfortable as Charlie sat back down. Claudia thought he was making a good point. It was a shame that no one was listening.

Maura said that Sir Philip Ardmore's Ethics Committee would be considering these very matters but they had run out of time today. People had to get back to work. Thank you for coming.

The audience began gathering their belongings like a class dismissed for lunch but the organiser signalled for a round of applause. They duly clapped. Maura suffered it, her thin mouth twitching in a semblance of a smile.

The room broke up and Maura, avoiding Charlie, hurried over to Claudia by the door. Charlie watched them as he slowly pulled on his overcoat.

'Thank you for coming,' said Maura, keeping her back to him.

'Very interesting,' lied Claudia.

'Your office is very close by, or did you come from home?' She was launching into the Londoners' fall-back conversation: how you got here and how the hell you were going to get home, but Claudia wasn't here for small talk.

'Maura, I need to ask you: we were sent an order for a streamline forensic report on William Stewart for Chester Terrace. I wanted to check that you think it's all right, conflict wise, given Philip's—'

'I do. I suggested it go to you specifically. We need this done quickly by an irreproachable firm. Hamilton are using experts with, let's say, questionable qualifications. They're trying to undercut your prices.'

Claudia nodded. 'I had a look at the evidence and noticed, from the BSPS reconstruction, that the attacker left via the roof. Did you test for traces there?'

'Of course we did. It was completely clean.'

'And the door to door? The neighbours saw nothing . . .?'

'Most of the houses were empty. The people who were resident are all accounted for and no fire escapes or drainage pipes were out of place or soiled.'

'I see.' Charlie was coming towards them so she spoke quickly. 'Also, I'd recommend sending the doorcam footage for digital analysis.'

'The alibi footage? It's not disputed.'

'It should be. I think the time stamp is twelve hours out. It was seven a.m., not p.m.'

They looked at each other and she could see the implication dawning on Langston. 'William doesn't have an alibi?'

'Well, he doesn't have *that* alibi.'

Maura paled. If William didn't have an alibi but she'd let him out on bail the press could accuse her of bias.

'I see,' she said, head bobbing anxiously, 'I'll tell Heely to request a digital report on it.'

The footage had misled the investigation and the CPS might have to charge whoever submitted it as film of the night with attempting to pervert the course of justice. If that was Philip Ashmore's ex-wife it would be a scandal. If it was William it would be damning. Either way it was a mess.

'How marvellous!' This was Charlie, arms out, one-toothed and smelling of Scotch. 'Ms Langston, may I say that you command the attention of the room like a latter-day Cicero.'

'Thank you, Charles.' Maura gave him a sickly smile.

'One might almost think you were their boss.'

Maura's smile faltered. 'Thanks for coming. Very supportive.'

'I love you deeply. To demonstrate the depth of my regard I'm tempted to say something inappropriate but I have been advised by my professional body not to do that any more.' He grinned at Claudia and she grinned back, beguiled again into the role of sidekick, 'Claudia, my dear, I hear from your delightful sister that you are delivered of a lovely new house?'

'Have you spoken to her today?'

'No.'

She couldn't discuss Gina's drug using in front of the Met Police Commissioner so she explained to Maura, 'He's seeing my sister. It's like watching two full bin lorries smash into each other at high speed.'

Charlie looked sheepish, 'I adore the lady.'

The room around them had half emptied. Some of the attendees hung around pointlessly so that Maura Langston would notice that they had come but they didn't approach her.

'Coming out, Claud?' asked Charlie.

She said yes and followed him through the open door. As she stepped out onto the landing she heard Maura whisper behind her, 'Thank you for telling me. Thank you.'

Maura Langston was very badly shaken.

II

Downstairs, through the heavy brass doors, Charlie led her back onto Euston Road. He seemed suddenly very sober.

'Are you really drinking, Charlie? You always smell of spirits but your drunkenness seems variable. Are you dabbing whisky behind your ears to seem less of a sharky threat?'

'How dare you accuse me of sobriety. I'm a notorious lush.'

They grinned at each other. Claudia took her cigarettes out and offered him one. He demurred and watched her light up.

'There you go,' he cooed. 'Suck all the bad feelings down.'

She laughed and coughed and laughed again. That was exactly what she was doing.

Charlie watched her smoke. 'They're worse for you than drink. I heard about Jonty's sentimental goodbye. Heard that the German mother demanded an invasion of Poland.'

Claudia was irritated by that. 'She's Spanish and her daughter was murdered.'

Charlie conceded, 'I know, you're right. I'm being a shit.'

She said she'd expected to see him there, singing school songs with the others, but Charlie said he couldn't face it. They all hated him and he just couldn't face it. He checked his watch. 'Anyway the cops were doing a search of the house William was staying in that night. Get it out of the way while the Dibdens were at the church. I wanted to be there.'

'Did they find anything?'

He hummed and frowned. 'They found knives in the kitchen, *highly* suspicious.'

He was making light of it but they really shouldn't be discussing this at all or anything about the forensic report.

She imagined the tall person with too-small feet, faceless, genderless, stepping out onto the roof that night, shedding their skin onto a plastic sheet and folding it up and walking away into the dark. The attack had been so vicious and sustained, so brutal, she couldn't comprehend resentment deep enough to make someone do that.

'Who hated them enough to do that to them?'

Charlie shook his head, 'I don't know about her but Jonty was a nasty bastard. A lot of people hated him.'

'William hated him.'

'A lot of people did.'

'What happened in the parties in the South of France?'

Charlie looked at her askance. 'That's ancient history. How do you know about that?'

'William mentioned it in his eulogy.'

Charlie laughed and she told him about Tommy Barchester and his cold-sored son and he laughed more.

'Sex parties or something, a lot of drinking and coke, I suspect. Ugly stockbrokers thinking they invented French kissing and the blow job.'

She told him she was worried that Gina was using. He said, no, Gina was clean, wasn't she? She was abstaining. But Claudia told him about the phone conversation and he said oh, yes, that did sound as if Gina had used something but she was having a busy day and, you know, not his thing, but didn't lots of people have a little bump on busy days? His mother's milkman used to deliver at night and his pupils were often so dilated he could probably see in the dark.

'She's an addict, Charlie. It's different for them. It's not functional. I've seen her abuse nicotine chewing gum. She was using so much she cracked two teeth. She was buying out-of-date multipacks cheap from a dodgy chemist in Baillieston.'

He found that funny but actually it wasn't that funny.

Reluctant to part but with nothing much to say, they walked aimlessly down towards King's Cross. The pavement was busy with pedestrians, students from UCL and commuters heading to and from Euston Station. They were buffeted along, separated and blocked on the corner, diverted by cyclists and scooter users, so they left the busy road and turned down a side street, walking on until they came to a leafy square.

It was quiet and calm. The lawn was neat and child free. A smattering of dog walkers watched their charges carefully. A tall man in a nice suit sat on a distant bench looking miserable.

They headed for a bench in a quiet corner and Claudia sat down and lit another cigarette.

Charlie stayed on his feet and looked down at her steadily. She knew now he was totally sober. 'Claud, what do you know about James's last case?'

Her stomach tightened. She had been trying so hard not to think about him and Charlie was just casually throwing his name out there. 'Not much.'

'You don't remember him talking about it or where he was doing his prep or anything?'

'No.' She drew hard on the cigarette. It was hard enough that James had died. She didn't much want to admit that she had lost him long before that. She shrugged, 'Loss foreshortens the memory a little.'

'True.' Charlie looked across the park, watching a Border terrier snuffle at a bin. As if aware it was being observed, the dog stopped and looked back at him. Charlie smiled. 'I love those dogs. They look so indignant.'

'James was secretive about that case. Secretive about most things towards the end. Lots of pressure. We were pretty broke because he was building his practice.' Her voice had changed, the tone was higher and quieter, as if it was coming from somewhere deep inside. 'But still he resented me having a job.'

'No, Claud, he resented you having *that* job. He loved you desperately.'

'I don't think he did.' She started crying, her chin convulsing despite her best efforts. Charlie sat down and wrapped his arms around her. He held her tight until she gathered herself.

She apologised and took out another cigarette. Charlie lit it for her. She breathed the smoke deep into her lungs and exhaled and apologised again for crying.

'Thank you for saying that,' he whispered into her hair. 'Emotions are disgusting.'

She couldn't even smile. 'He didn't love me any more, Charlie. He was angry with me before he died. No one else saw it but me. He despised me. I think he killed himself.'

He was shocked, 'James? No, he didn't. He wouldn't. You musn't think that. Why would you say that?'

She blurted out all the horrors that woke her up at night and intruded on her day: because James had died in an accident that didn't look like an accident. Because he'd been unhappy, moody and erratic. He had this obsession with safety, making them safe, keeping the boys safe. He was desperate to get them into Fairchurch even though he'd been miserable there, even though two masters had been done for sexually abusing boys there.

'Well, that abuse was historic,' said Charlie. 'They were arrested and sentenced, those two masters. The safeguarding is manic there because of that, so he might be right, they would be very careful now. They have to keep the boys safe because diplomats and kings and oligarchs send their kids there.'

That wasn't the point, she said, even if Sam and Bernie would be safe, it was such a sudden change in his thinking that even the boys, who hung on his every word, thought James sounded crazy, paranoid. Who thinks their kids are in danger? They were nobodies. So that's why she thought he'd killed himself because does that sound sane? Does that sound well?

'No,' Charlie said. 'He sounds bonkers. But why would he think the boys weren't safe? Was it the case he was working on? Did he talk to you about it?'

'The RS Trusts fraud case? Not really. Most he said was he'd discovered that they were owned by a Jersey company.'

'Viscount Court Associates,' nodded Charlie.

'Yes! And *they* were owned by a Cayman Island company called Tontine. A string of companies owning a string of companies in different jurisdictions. I've forgotten the names. He was going through all the discovery documents while this was happening.'

'*While it was happening.* Maybe it's what was making him crazy and paranoid.'

'Why would it?'

'I don't know. Maybe he linked the string of companies to some-one who didn't want to be discovered, someone who'd threaten him or you or the boys to keep their name a secret? What did he find?'

'He didn't say.'

'But he was worried about the boys' safety so there was some element of peril there. And he didn't like you working for ForSci Ltd?'

'He said they were exploiting my professional reputation. I said, I mean, that's employment, that's what businesses do, they employ you because of your good reputation and then they exploit it and pay you . . .' Her ramble spluttered to a stop. 'That was an uncharacteristically inelegant segue, Charlie. Are you saying James thought ForSci was owned by RS Trusts?'

Charlie shrugged softly. 'Maybe Viscount Court Associates or Tontine? They own a hell of a lot of things for a post office box. Does Philip Ardmore still own your company?'

'No. He sold it. He'd been in negotiations since long before James died.'

'Who did he sell it to?'

'I don't know. A conglomerate of companies, I think. Could that be why James hated me working there? Is that why he killed himself?'

'He didn't—' Charlie shook his head, annoyed. 'Look, when Kiki took the pills, it wasn't her first time. She'd tried before we got married, before we met. She attempted several times when she was with me and, looking back, there were signs that I missed. Was James unusually calm or euphoric before his accident?'

'No. Just grumpy.'

'Did he hint at some intention? Did he sort out his papers or leave instructions? Did he prepare in any way?'

'No.' She drew heavily on her cigarette and it scratched her throat all the way down. 'He hadn't even kept up his life insurance. That's why we lost the house.'

'Well, something was going on with him. Did he say *anything* about Viscount Court Associates?'

'Nah.' Charlie could try to comfort her but she was so shocked at herself for articulating her fear that she was only half listening. 'And he didn't leave a note. They don't always, though, do they?'

'No, but there are often signs. You know, even if he did it on impulse, it wasn't about you. It was about him.'

'That's almost worse.' She dropped her cigarette and stamped it out with the tip of her toe, 'How could he leave our boys? I don't get it. What a prick.'

'You don't know for sure he did it.'

'I kind of do. He was a prick.' She bent down and picked up the cigarette butt to put it in the bin. She felt lighter having said it to someone and looked up at Charlie. He wasn't actually that old, she saw suddenly. His affected old-time manners made him seem like a creature from another age but he wasn't really old.

'How did you end up at Fairchurch? Family tradition?'

'No. I was a brainy grammar school boy who got a scholarship. The school was full of idiot heirs so they needed clever boys like me to bring up their exam results, make them look like a good educational establishment. The other boys knew that I was working for them. They were not gracious employers.'

'Were you there with Jonty Stewart?'

'He was quite a bit older than me. He fitted in well.'

'You saw the SoC video. Saw that he was stabbed in the groin post mortem.'

Charlie's face paled. 'If I'd have been there I'd have stabbed him myself.'

He hadn't meant to say that, she could tell. 'Did Jonty sexually assault you?'

'No. Other boys. He was nasty. Still ashamed of saying nothing at the time. I got terribly fat there, trying to grow armour around myself. It wasn't just Jonty though, that was the culture. General sexual humiliation, scared little boys being grabbed or groped in public, stealing clothes during showers and after games, that sort of thing. Then there were the masters . . . it wasn't about sex, we knew that, when you're that age everything seems to be about sex but you know, later, that it was really just about fear and power.'

She was afraid to ask about Philip Ardmore but did.

'No,' said Charlie, 'No. Ardmore was bookish, kept to himself. Bit of a science nerd, as I remember.' He looked at the unhappy man in the suit across the park and waved. The man waved back, confused.

'Could Jonty have sexually abused William?'

'Honestly, I'd be surprised. It denotes a degree of interest in William that Jonty rarely evinced. Could have been something like that in the villa in Cannes, or a visitor could have done something. Jonty seems like one of the less unsavoury men he grew up around.' Charlie picked up another stray cigarette butt and put it in the bin. 'These are poisonous to dogs.'

It was getting cold. She stood up and lifted her bag. 'You're convinced William's innocent, aren't you?'

'Yes, I am, but like a lot of us furious imbibers, he's quite likely to get the blame for this and much else in life besides. Because,' he smiled kindly, placing a hand on her back, 'people who never get cunted lack humility and that makes them inclined to be complete and utter bastards.'

He led her gently back to the street.

Kirsty Parry stepped into the space left by the open doors and looked out to the courtyard. She was searching for someone. Claudia braced herself, backing away from open ground until she was standing directly under a patio heater, in a blast of heat so fierce it felt her hair might burst into flames.

'Are you hiding from Kirsty?' asked Philip. 'Is it too awkward?'

'No, no,' said Claudia, straightening up, acting unconcerned, feeling her ears burning. 'She's as entitled to be here as anyone else.'

He smiled at the party, 'Tonight feels significant, doesn't it? Like the end of an era or the start of one.'

He was right. It did. He sipped his drink and looked across the gathering, 'I was thinking about Charlie Taunton today, how sad it was.'

Claudia was startled at the mention of his name, 'Sad?'

'Sad what some people will do for money.'

His eyes lingered on her. The statement felt like a provocation, as if he was trying to nudge her into agreeing.

'You think Charlie was defending William for money?'

'Well, I think he was dragging it out to milk William. He was terribly clever at school, you know, a little chubby boy. Quite a brilliant mind.'

'So I believe.' She wanted to get away and lock herself in the loo, to be alone and catch her breath.

But Kirsty Parry was blocking her path, standing square in the opening between the sliding glass doors, staring at someone longingly. Claudia followed her eyeline to a man on the other side of the yard. Kirsty stepped out through the doors and made her way towards him.

Claudia excused herself, heading to the door, keeping her eyes on Kirsty, and saw the man turn. It was Andrew Hamilton and his oddly lush hairline. Andrew was not pleased to see Kirsty there and tried to slip away behind someone but Kirsty helloed him over their head. Hamilton hadn't invited her here.

Inside, Claudia slipped left, heading for the bathrooms, when a hand caught her arm.

'Claudia? Claudia!' It was Amelia Dibden. 'Listen to this one, have you heard it? It's too funny . . .'

Amelia had matured in the last year. Her hair was cut short now. She still dressed in exquisite clothes and tonight wore a red Vivienne Westwood suit and pink stilettoes with moulded tiger toes. She was telling Maura Langston a joke and Maura was already laughing because Amelia was rich and Maura was unctuous. A number of social hopefuls were hovering around, vacant smiles, keen to be seen with this extraordinary woman.

Claudia clutched her document folder tight to her chest and forced herself to breathe.

'So.' Amelia could hardly tell the story for laughing, 'A man is test driving a Rolls Royce and the salesman says, he says, *this* button is for the air conditioning, *this* button warms your seat, *this* button warms the door handles. And the man says, but where's the button for the windscreen wipers? There are no buttons for windscreen wipers. And the salesman says no, but if you press this button:' She leaned forward and mimed slamming the heel of her hand onto a big button, 'This button stops the rain!'

Amelia laughed. Maura roared and did a little stagger, as if she was not only enjoying the joke but found it so funny that she could barely stand up. Amelia appreciated her reaction and laughed at that as well.

Claudia made a laughing sound with her mouth, but she was too angry to carry it off and Amelia noticed. 'Oh, you've heard it?'

'Think so,' said Claudia, dropping her gaze and sliding off into the bathroom.

She hated Amelia Dibden more than anyone alive. She had fantasised about murdering the pretty, slender young woman in many different ways. Strangling, stabbing, but drowning was the method that really held her attention. She fucking hated that joke as well because it wasn't a joke. It was a story about power and wealth and exceptionalism and privilege.

She locked herself in a cubicle, sat on the loo and breathed. She was not going to murder anyone. That would be silly. She had a better plan. Her speech was a daisy cutter bomb. She took it out and looked at it. She'd be cut down too and that was fine.

The stakes were high for telling the truth but she knew that was no accident. The mines had been laid to keep her in line. She was deeply invested in upholding the status quo. They all were.

She looked at her handwritten speech. She'd bought a new ink pen with a calligraphic nib to write the speech and her careful penmanship, neatly spaced into black ink lines, looked like a document from another age.

She stacked the papers on the leather folder, flushed the toilet for cover and unlocked the cubicle, stepping out. The room was empty.

The sink was black marble with down lights under the mirrors. She checked her reflection. She looked fucking terrified. She didn't know why someone hadn't stopped her already because even her hair looked frightened, it was knotted and sticking up at one side.

She put the papers down and ran a tap, wetting her hair and curling it behind her ears. She stepped back.

Better.

She could hear the party outside, voices rising and falling, as she washed her hands, careful as Pontius Pilate.

Soap slipped under her wedding ring. She moved it up her finger to the first knuckle and washed the soap off before sliding the ring back. She was holding her hands up to the hand dryer, watching the rope of veins on the backs of her hands melt away, her hands regressing back to before, before the kids and James. Claudia had always liked her hands, the miracle of them, the engineering of the veins, the complex pully system of tendons. Warmth floated up her sleeves and dried her damp underarms. It felt so nice that she didn't hear the door opening behind her.

The dryer finished its timed run.

'What the hell is this?'

She turned. Maura Langston was standing by the sink, leafing through the pages. 'Why is this handwritten?'

Claudia lunged across and picked it up, pressing the papers to her chest, 'Philip asked – I'm to give – that.'

Maura frowned, 'Why didn't you use a computer? For security? What is this?'

'To help me remember. I remember better if I write it out by hand.'

Maura wasn't buying it. She looked at the papers, 'What's the title about?'

'Nothing.' She brushed past Maura to the door, threw it open and stepped back out into the party. 'Nothing is happening.'

She slipped out of the door and ducked through clumps of party-goers, putting distance between herself and Maura.

Stupid. What a stupid thing to say. With just minutes to go. What an idiot she was.

As she tried to slip out to the open courtyard Larry Beecham grabbed her elbow and swung her gently back around to meet someone.

'Claudia, this is Kitty St Helen. Kitty's in television. She's the head of the True Crime Documentary Network. She's been dying to meet you for ages.'

Claudia had been blanking Kitty's emails for months.

Kitty's handshake was intense. 'I'd so, so love to meet for lunch. We're keen to work on something with you. Not just William Stewart, I have a few ideas already—'

Behind Kitty's shoulder Claudia saw Maura coming out of the bathroom, scanning faces in the busy lobby, looking for her.

'I have to get miked up,' she said and slipped away around a corner to a back corridor at the side of the auditorium.

She looked at the papers in her hand to see what Maura saw.

It was the title page of the speech. It read: '*Chester Terrace: The Case Against Maura Langston.*'

A shadow fell on the page. She looked up.

Kirsty Parry was standing in front of her, too close, blocking her escape back to the party.

'Claudia Atkins,' sneered Kirsty. 'Didn't bloody well think you'd ever see me again, did you?'

12

Claudia followed Sam into the bathroom at four a.m. and held his long hair back as he threw up, waiting with him in the fug of eye-watering smell, got him back into bed and brought him a glass of cold water. She pulled his covers up, tucked his feet in and waited, watching, until he fell asleep. Back in the bathroom she found an old Sponge Bob strip thermometer in the cabinet and held it to his fore-head. His temperature was high but not terrifying. She crawled back to bed, praying that it was the twenty-four-hour virus doing the rounds at school, that he'd be well enough in the morning to be left alone because she was due in court for Roland Garret's trial.

She was falling back asleep when she heard Gina come in, the front door slam open, the unsteady steps on the creaky wooden stairs.

Claudia hadn't seen Gina for a week but she stayed in bed. She was doing her utmost to avoid her. Gina was really ill again, skinny, scabby, frantic moods, but Claudia didn't have it in her to stage another intervention. She was adjusting to James not being there, to James choosing not to be there, and felt as if she had enough to deal with. She didn't have the bandwidth for Gina's infinite needs.

It was just after six when she woke again to the sound of Sam gal-loping across the hall for another round. After she got him back into bed she decided to stay up. She'd rather be too tired for court than too late.

Sam heard her grinding coffee beans and came down, dragging his duvet, carrying his laptop, colonising the sofa in the living room. He dozed off and on until she brought him a mug of tea. He took it and sipped and let her stroke his hair. He had been distant recently, a little hostile, just normal teenage pushing-off, but it upset her and she enjoyed the truce.

'Heard Gina coming in,' he said, his voice hoarse from the hard night.

'At least she knows where we are.'

'She needs help, Mum. Her face is all banged up.'

'It's her choice, Sam. I've been here before. If I try to order her around she'll leave and we may never see her again.'

'She's stealing from you.'

'Don't. Just don't.'

She sat with him until he fell asleep again.

Back in the kitchen, she reread her report on Garret, trying to memorise the numbers. She checked her emails.

A lab report had just arrived, testing on a large knife from the Dibdens' house. It was found under a wardrobe in the guest room William Stewart had been staying in at the time of the murders. It was a match for the kitchen knives in Chester Terrace.

Blood was found on the blade with DNA, a mixture of Jonty Stewart and Francesca Emmanuel. No fingerprints were identified on the handle. It had been wiped.

That seemed strange to her, that someone would leave blood on the blade of a murder weapon but take the trouble to clean the handle. The whole case looked like a heavy-handed set up.

But they'd have to charge William Stewart now.

She scrolled through, looking for any mention of Mary Dibden's DNA being found. No one had requested a match. The knife was found in her house, her partial DNA was all over the crime scene but no one had pursued that because the report was about William Stewart. They weren't examining evidence against anyone else.

Claudia looked at the crime scene pictures again then sat back and looked out of the window. She felt something draining from her. It chipped away at her, witnessing all this carnage, but that was the tiredness too. She'd only had five hours.

She forwarded the test results to the CPS, knowing they would pass them on to Charlie. She trusted him to pick up on the anomaly and to ask why Mary Dibden's DNA hadn't been tested for.

It was almost seven thirty, time to get Bernie up for school.

She woke him and took a shower. Then, dressed and dried, she went up to Gina's floor.

They had been living in Gerald Road for just over two months and the top floor had become Gina's own. The ceiling was low but the skylight windows made it bright and welcoming. Gina's bedroom and bathroom were on one side of the stairs and, through the other door across the landing was a long box room that Gina had set up as a painting studio she never used.

Claudia knocked lightly on the bedroom door and opened it. Gina wasn't in there. Her unmade bed hadn't been slept in. The discarded clothes on the floor were where they'd been the day before.

Spurred by faint hope, she opened the door to the studio/box room.

It was a dusty room. She had bought an easel for Gina but it sat vacant, as redundant as a question to an empty room. A roll of canvas remained in the plastic sheath it had arrived in, lying along the wall like a dead body, grey dust settled over the top. Beyond them, James's document boxes were stacked up, one on top of the other against the far wall; they were always there but today some of the lids were off and papers lay scattered on the floor.

Claudia walked over and touched the loose papers. No dust. Gina had been going through them this morning. Claudia sank to her knees. She hoped to God that Gina hadn't been looking for James's clients' bank details. She knew they weren't in there but it would mean she was escalating.

At first Gina had been gone for an odd evening, then a night, then two. Claudia didn't know where she went but things were going missing from the house. Claudia had started taking her jewellery to work with her. But they were all pretending nothing had changed and Claudia was too tired to confront her. She had enough to deal with. Gina was a third teenager in the house, not another adult.

She trudged back downstairs to find Bernie coming out of his room dressed and ready for school. Her mood lifted at the sight of him.

He wasn't feeling sick he said, but he was hoping to catch the bug later today because he had a French test tomorrow. He'd be licking door handles all day. Said he was feeling lucky.

They went down to the front hall, Bernie pulling his blazer on as

Claudia hung in at the living room to look at Sam, slumped on the sofa, tangled in a duvet, with a spew bowl on the floor next to him. 'Hey Sam, Bernie's jealous.'

Sam didn't look up, 'You don't want this. It really hurts.'

Bernie opened the front door, 'Fuck off, you germy bastard.'

Claudia play-slapped the back of his head. 'Stop swearing so much, ya wee shitter,' she said but he turned, hand over where she had cuffed him, giving her a sad-puppy look that almost caused her physical pain.

'Oh, Bernie, I'm sorry.'

He looked shocked. 'I'm joking, Mum.'

'Yeah.' She was embarrassed at her over-reaction. 'No, so am I. I'm joking too. Have a good day. Don't catch whatever he's got.'

He turned and took the steps down to the street and she knew he'd forgotten her the minute she shut the door. She was oversensitive and misreading cues because she hadn't slept enough. She'd have to watch out for that when she got up in court.

She went into the living room. 'Are you sure I can leave you alone today?'

Sam's cheeks were pink but he wasn't sweating any more. He said he'd be fine.

He was wearing a T-shirt and pyjama shorts. The brand-new black hairs on his long legs were so new and defined they looked as if they had been drawn on with a marker pen. Puberty came late and suddenly for Sam and, because he'd been one of the smaller boys for so long, he still had a sweetness to him.

His fine face was as thin as his father's but his hair was long and blond. James would never have let Sam grow his hair so long. The school made him tie it back and tuck it into his collar.

The institution policed secondary sexual characteristics with a fervour that was Torquemadian. The building was listed, a glorious Victorian gothic masterpiece looking onto the Thames. Recently a governors' letter emphasised that it had to remain single sex because the cost of fitting girls' toilets, or even gender-neutral ones, would be prohibitively expensive. It would cost so much they might as well burn the whole place down or shoot it into space.

The teaching was bad; the able kids did well and the children who needed help crashed and burned, but it was a feeder for better schools so it was popular and expensive. Claudia was keen for the boys to be liked by the school. She was scraping the fees together, term by term, searching for scholarship programmes in the best schools, dreaming of a bright future for the loves of her life.

So Sam tucked his hair into his collar, worked hard and got A*s in everything, while Bernie wrote bad words on the toilet walls and vaped CBD in parks at lunchtime. He was perpetually in trouble. She loved everything about his little wild self and hated that education saw the work of the next few years as changing everything about him. She envied his optimistic defiance. She was paralysed with self-pity and felt they should cherish his wild side and do something with it. The paucity of ambition appalled her.

She looked at Sam and saw sunlight reflected from the windows across the road catch his hair, making it shine buttercup yellow. At a time when a boy's nose might bulb or his skin break out in spots, Sam was very pretty.

He'd been so distant recently and drifting further away all the time. She was thirsty for clues about his life. She squinted at the screen on his laptop but couldn't read the text. He noticed and slowly twisted the screen away from her. All she could see was black text under a red banner. He could be reading a newspaper or joining a cult.

Struck by sudden pangs of loss, she stepped into the room. Sam stiffened, wary and none too happy about her coming in. She was determined to talk to him though, just a chat, a connection, something to cling to throughout the day. She crossed the room and sat down in an armchair.

'So . . . think you'll be sick again?'

'No, I just need some peace and quiet. Some sleep.'

'Good.' She patted the armrests. In the kitchen the news headlines were on the radio. A bill, a death, a crash on the M1. 'Good. I'm on in court but then I've been invited to lunch at Claridge's.'

He winced, 'On a date?'

'No, no, it's – remember that memorial service I was at? Well, the mother of the woman who died asked me to lunch in the residents' restaurant. Ver' posh.' She was mocking herself, putting on a posh voice but Sam gave a little eye roll and head shake.

'What does that mean, Sam?'

He tutted, 'Nothing.'

She had eight minutes to spare before she had to set off for court so she lingered, 'What, the little head shake, what's that?'

'Dad used to say . . .' he hesitated, 'that you bought into all that stuff. He said you're a climber.'

She stiffened. It was said unkindly, he meant it as a reproach but Sam so rarely brought James up that she didn't want to let it drop.

'Well, Dad didn't need to be a climber. He was born at the top. What did he say?'

He smiled. 'That you'd go to a Klan rally if it was at Buckingham Palace.'

'Fuck off.'

'I didn't say it! He said it!'

'That's not true, anyway,' but she knew it was. She was seduced by power and a nice venue.

'Well, don't take pictures of your food for Facebook.'

'I'm not on Facebook. How old do you think I am?'

He smiled but looked sad, 'Do you miss Dad?'

'Of course I do! How can you ask me that?'

'You don't seem to miss him. You're like a robot. You just get up and work and sleep and never feel anything.'

He had no idea how she felt. 'I actually miss him all the time. Do you?'

'Dad wanted me to go to Fairchurch.'

She didn't want to talk about this. Not now. She'd been up since six and Gina was missing and she'd just seen James's boxes. A sudden spark of anger made her reckless, 'Well, I can't afford it anyway and you're not going without Bernie.'

He didn't like this at all. 'You know, you're why Bernie swears all the time. He gets in trouble because of his bad language and it comes from you.'

'Fuck off, Sam,' she tutted. 'You're very superior for someone who's been vomiting on himself all night.'

'Mum, you're trying to hold us all together but we're all trying to get away from you.' It was said to wound and test her. 'D'you mind me saying that?'

She did but she said, 'No, it's important to be honest in a family.'

Sam slapped his laptop shut and sat up so quickly she thought he was going to be sick again. But he was suddenly angry and the viral flush on his cheeks made him look furious. 'You're lying now! You want us to be honest with each other? Admit you smoke.'

She stood up, hands up in surrender, 'Oh, look, come on, look, I'm just trying to talk to you—'

'Gina's dying. She has dealers coming up here in their cars. She runs out and pays them through the window. They're dodge as fuck and they're checking out the house.' He was right and she knew it. 'It's not safe and Bernie's only young and she's killing herself and you're too lazy to do anything about it.'

It was obviously true. 'Please don't say anything to Gina, if you see her.'

'Mum, she fell asleep walking upstairs the other day. That's how she hurt her face. Even Bernie knows what's going on.'

'Sam, she's very touchy and if you say anything, one wrong word, she might—'

'Did Dad kill himself?'

She held her breath. Sam glared at her, willing her to tell the truth.

'Dad had an accident.'

He squinted, twisting his shoulder towards her, adopting a defensive stance. 'Pretty unlikely accident.'

She could have told him that she had her doubts too but she didn't: 'Most accidents are unlikely.'

His eyes narrowed as if he was trying to shut out the sight of her. 'Mum . . .'

'I've never been secretive about that.'

'You're secretive about *everything*, Mum.'

'What am I secretive about? I'm not secretive.' She was being defensive and evasive. She wouldn't get away with that on the stand, she should be careful.

'Before his accident, Dad was angry. He made me promise I'd go to that school. He said it's the only place I'd be safe. What did that mean? Was he just crazy?'

They'd all witnessed James shouting over dinner about Claudia working too much, storming out of the house, slamming around the kitchen. It made her think of Gina. 'Gina was rummaging through Dad's boxes this morning. She was looking for something.'

'Yeah, she asked me if Dad had files labelled "Trusts" or "Viscount Trusts" or something.'

'This morning?'

'No, back in Lambeth. Before we moved. She wanted the files.'

Claudia nodded. That explained why Gina agreed to handle the house move on her own. She was looking for files and the only person interested in that was Charlie.

'Mum? What is "Viscount Trusts"?'

'It's the last case Dad was working on, a fraud case he was defending when he died. Maybe someone was looking for some old files or something . . .'

She looked up. Sam was crying quietly and his voice dropped low, 'I want to get out of here. I want to board. I don't want to be held back for Bernie's sake. I need to get out of here.'

Claudia stepped towards the door, 'You want to go?'

'I do. I want to go.' He swatted the tears from his flushed cheeks, a man wearing a boy's pyjamas. His beautiful hair slid over his face and he left the curtain there to hide behind.

She wanted to get out of here as well. She wished she'd never come in. 'Well, I can't afford it. And your dad was paranoid.'

She was exhausted. And she wanted to run away or have the freedom to fall asleep walking up the stairs. She wanted to stop thinking. She went back into the kitchen and called Charlie.

Charlie said he was glad she'd called because William Stewart had just been charged with the Chester Terrace double murder.

'You're joking?'

'No.'

'What the fuck are they doing?'

'Caving in. I wanted to ask you about the BSPS, actually. Can we meet?'

'Charlie, did you offer to pay Gina for documents from James's document files?'

'No, well, it's complicated. I asked her to look and she asked me for money. Funnily enough she called me this morning but I missed her and now she's not answering.'

'Text her. She'll call when she's finished buying whatever.'

'I will. Where are you?'

'I'm about to set off for the Old Bailey. I'm due in for Roland Garret.'

'No, you're not. Check your emails. Continuation.'

'What?'

'I'm in already and I'm looking at the call screen right now. Garret's been continued.'

She opened her email and found that she had been notified four minutes ago. She'd been up since six for no reason. 'Oh for fuck's sake.'

'Indeed. Come anyway. Meet me outside the public gallery of court seven. Interesting expert on this a.m.: Dr Kirsty Parry is up. Rumour is that she's testifying under oath that you're a liar.'

13

The continuation of Garret's case meant that her pass into the building was cancelled so she had to use the entrance to the viewing galleries.

The public entrance to this part of the Old Bailey was through Warwick Passage, off the street in an enclosed alleyway that was tiled and dimly lit in piss yellow and had an almost palpable air of despair. The queue was already long, snaking around the corner.

There was a drama unfolding in front of her and she didn't want to involve herself in a family argument in a language she didn't recognise, conducted in guttural, furious whispers. She read the noticeboard to busy herself. Posters behind vandal-proof glass ordered visitors not to punch or spit at the staff, not to bring bombs or guns into the buildings. Swords and knives had a separate poster that went into a lot of detail about what qualified as a knife and what had to be done with Sikh kirpans.

The Old Bailey courts complex was built on the site of Newgate Prison and only heard the most serious criminal cases: murder, rape and terrorist offences. The queue snaking down the lane was an uncomfortable mix of excited history nerds holding guide books and people here to witness justice being served on people they loved or absolutely hated. They were here to listen to the biggest event of their lives discussed and decided on over days or weeks or months, often in alienatingly technical language.

The large family in front of Claudia were dressed in their Sunday best, women in dresses, men in suits and ties. Today was important for this family, someone was being tried or avenged, it was hard to tell which, but they had come here together to support each other, give a good account of who they were and claw back some dignity.

Usually Claudia went through the professional entrance for court staff. That entrance opened earlier, was grand and warm, had a wide staircase up to a wood-panelled hall with high ceilings, judicial portraits and wedding-cake plasterwork.

This was not that. This entrance was dark and draughty, designed to intimidate people into behaving.

There was a huge emotional disparity between the subjects of justice and the personnel and the queue was an uncomfortable reminder of the secondary consequences of what she did for a living. Surreptitiously, she looked around for Roland Garret's family or anyone resembling the dead woman in the crime scene photos. The courts were not known for the efficacy of their notifications and people often travelled all the way into central London only to find out that they didn't need to be there.

The large family group in front of her resolved their argument. Hands were squeezed, hair was ruffled and peace broke out. Claudia thought about Sam begging to get away from her and she envied their ability to face disaster together. She'd never envied that before.

At ten to ten the door was opened. Two stern guards stood in front of a steep flight of stairs that rose into the belly of the building.

One of the guards announced to the queue that they could not bring mobile phones or bulky bags in: these had to be left outside. A print shop two blocks away had lockers that cost four pounds. Claudia knew this and had already dropped her phone off there. The Crown took no responsibility for valuables left there.

He announced this all slowly and loudly, making eye contact with everyone. When he finished several people in the queue groaned and left.

Shuffling forward in the queue, Claudia thought about Sam asking if James had killed himself. He suspected it too. It was possible that James took his life, she could admit that now. What would her world look like if it were true? She would feel sadder, more humble, diminished certainly, but not so very different. Nothing would change. She hadn't made a claim on a life insurance policy, she wouldn't have to pay money back. Sam had noticed that they weren't getting on, that James was depressed and angry and going away for days at a time without telling them where he was going. There was no point pretending all had been well before he died.

Owning the possibility made her eyes burn but it was a relief too. She took out a hankie and dabbed her damp nose, sniffing, as the queue moved slowly forward. The stairs were steep and they took them single file, all bracing themselves for what the day would hold.

At the top of the stairs the security was fierce. Most of the people in the queue had done this many times before but it was Claudia's first time to hand over her bag and empty her pockets into a plastic tray as the security guard prodded the contents of the bag with a stick, put it through the X-ray and waved her through a metal detector arch.

She collected her things on the other side and made her way up the stairs.

The walls were chipped and grey, the steps bald concrete, oddly characterless for such a grand and storied place. They could have been in a windowless municipal building anywhere.

All the way up the stairs there were harrying signs at eye level – don't sit there, be quiet, no loitering. Ushers were on guard on each floor too, ready to tell them where to sit, stand, when to move, when not to move. Legal professionals were given a little more freedom. They could come and go in the public gallery of cases but even they had to be on their absolute best behaviour: no chatting or clattering about.

Claudia took the stairs all the way up to the landing for court seven. As she pushed through the double doors a court officer hurried over and told her to get out, the court wasn't open yet, but she explained that she was looking for Charles Taunton at court seven. He softened instantly: Mr Taunton was through there. He apologised for mistaking her for a member of the public.

Around the corner, at the very far end of an empty corridor, Charlie was sitting on a ripped office chair, arms crossed over his belly, his head tipped back to rest on the wall behind him. His eyes were shut and he looked terribly content.

Claudia was struck by the absolute conviction that he was thinking about his wife, Kiki. Charlie hadn't had a happy day since she died. She knew the bond between Charlie and Gina wasn't sexual, not really, that what they had in common was depression, but that was a profound connection. If Claudia ever met anyone who understood how she felt after James she didn't think she would ever leave them.

He heard her approach and opened his eyes. 'Hi.'

'Hi Charlie,' she bent down and gave him a kiss on the cheek. 'You look tired.'

'I am tired.'

'Were you thinking about Kiki just then?'

He smiled beatifically. 'I was. Sometimes I feel she's here, you know? And if I just open my eyes she'll be standing on the other side of the room, ignoring me. I love that feeling.'

She let him sit with it for a moment and then said, 'Shall we go in?'

He pointed up at a blue light above the door, 'Wait for it. We'll be keel-hauled if we go in early and see them wigless. You think about James much?'

She shook her head.

'Too sore still?'

She nodded, glimpsing the depth of her sorrow. She couldn't face it today, 'Shouldn't you be with William Stewart if they've just charged him?'

He flapped a careless hand. 'He's being processed. I'll see him this afternoon. They found a bloody knife with a clean handle under his bed or something. Isn't that odd?'

'It's odd that they didn't look at Mary Dibden. There was a weak match to her DNA found in Chester Terrace.'

'Well, she was in Monaco at the time. That's absolutely certain.' Charlie stood up, 'Two square kilometres of frightened old rich people. More security cameras than GCHQ. They can tell you how many burps she did that week. Anyway, you know how sensitive the testing is now. It's a weak sample, could be from anyone related to her and honestly, they're all inter-related.'

'Someone related to Mary?'

'My God, you'd have to swab half of Debrett's. Her father *was* the Swinging Sixties. Any one of us could be a genetic Dibden.'

She dropped her voice. 'Why did you ask Gina about James's files? Why didn't you ask me?' Her hands were balled into fists.

Charlie grimaced fearfully and they both laughed. 'You're kind of angry. She said you hate those boxes. Believe it or not I was trying to be considerate. There are some files missing from his office, I just thought he'd left them in a box somewhere. She gave me papers before but they were no use to me. She said she'd look again.'

'Did you give her money last time?'

'It wasn't a bribe, if that's what you mean.' He blinked hard. 'She asked me for some dosh and I gave it to her happily.'

'Well, she's been rummaging through the boxes again. Must need another spontaneous gift.' But she was wrong to suggest Charlie was responsible for Gina's drug taking. However much money he'd given her, it wouldn't be enough. 'I'm sorry, Charlie, I didn't mean it like that. I'm just, she's not good. Really not good. If you want to look through James's papers come over and take them. I don't want them.'

'Great,' he rubbed his hands together, 'because I think he'd actually managed to identify the beneficial owner of Tontine.'

'What's a "beneficial owner"?'

'That's who gets the dosh. Some jurisdictions allow you to name an owner who isn't the actual beneficiary. That's very valuable to avoid accountability. A lot of shifty be-doings occur behind the veil of corporation.'

'Why wouldn't he know who they were? If he was defending the company, weren't they his client?'

'Legally, no. In reality, yes. He shouldn't have looked beyond RS Trusts but he must have seen something he didn't like and started digging. Legally RS Trusts were his client. He was investigating some pretty sinister off-shore activity, you know.'

'He was a corporate criminal lawyer, Charlie, he was always investigating sinister off-shore activities by corporations, they were his client base.'

Charlie nodded and looked away, disappointed that she wouldn't listen. She was moved that he cared so much. She took his hand and said, 'Look, Charlie, I get that it's easier to be angry than sad, it feels less passive, chasing a grudge feels more useful than just feeling loss, but we might have to accept that James was overwhelmed and had an accident.'

Charlie nodded but she noted the pity in his eyes. The blue light above the door blinked suddenly and Charlie looked at it.

'You know,' he said, 'it strikes me that companies are bad fictional characters, little golems made of capital, as if the law breathed life into money and we all go along with it and pretend they're real people. They kill and colonise and we talk about it all as if there are no people involved. What a cheap trick the law is. What an idiot consensus. So much of being an adult is resisting the urge to stand up and shout: *that is a total fucking lie.*' Smiling, he nodded sideways at the padded door to Court Seven. 'We'll get the rocket if we're late.'

'What's Parry saying?'

He opened the door for her. 'Show don't tell.'

They stepped out on to a high balcony looking over a modern room. The furnishings below were vibrant yellow pine, the upholstery in navy blue, an echo of the glories of older courts in the building which were rich oak and blue leather. Looming high behind the judge's dais was an outsized plaster medallion of the Royal Court of Arms, flanked by the Lion and the Unicorn.

They were alone in the vertiginous balcony, where the sound carried and they had the best view of the room. It must have been an uncontentious case because there was no officer stationed in the gallery to maintain order.

Below them, in the well of the court, a clerk was stationed at a table in front of the judge. Other personnel sat at their desks. The accused in the dock was young, blank faced, wearing a black tracksuit with a zip-up top. On defence were two lawyers Claudia knew well from James's practice, Abir and Tim. They were called Tweedledum and Tweedledumber by everyone for no reason other than that they were always seen together and dressed alike. They didn't look alike and neither was especially rotund. They were nice men though and took it in good humour.

The jury were a salve to the eyes in their jumble of clothes and styles and ages, some ready to take notes, some watching the action carefully.

Everyone was ordered to stand and did and then the judge came in and they all sat down, court personnel at their places, papers in front of them, eyes on computer screens. Claudia hadn't heard of the case, and didn't know her Blood Spatter Probability Scale had been used. It was so usual in cases now that she often only heard when the licensing fee came through. She looked at Charlie questioningly and he gave her a smug signal to listen.

After five minutes of lawyers mumbling to one another, passing papers and looking for prompts, a witness was announced: Dr Kirsty Parry, DPhil, Oxon, for Hamilton Analytics.

The entrance to the witness waiting room opened, and Kirsty came out in a nasty pea-green business suit, the jacket buttoned up wrong. It looked quite bizarre. Perhaps she had done it in a rush of stage fright behind the door but it looked as if she'd failed the rudimentary test of doing up three buttons. The KC who had called her turned away, rolling his eyes back so hard they could see it in the balcony. Then he caught his breath. He glared at the floor. He turned to watch Parry take the oath to tell the truth.

From there Kirsty's performance didn't go downhill so much as fall out of the back of a plane.

She was visibly nervous, something an expert witness should never be in front of a jury, her voice high and trembling. She knew there was something wrong with her jacket but didn't dare look down and sort it out. She tugged at the hem over and over and moved the sleeves around but kept her eyes forward. Startled by a stray shoulder pad creeping up by her ear, she jerked around and then pretended she hadn't. The KC who had called her asked if she was okay and she said yes but sounded puzzled and frightened. Kirsty was so cocksure in social situations but all that confidence evaporated on the stand.

Yes, she said, she had a DPhil in Organic Chemistry from Oxford and was trained in statistical analysis. No, she was not refuting the forensic report's contention that the accused's DNA was found on the victim. His DNA was present.

The KC looked at Kirsty to go on but Kirsty tugged her jacket again and looked confused.

'Which elements of this forensic report,' his voice was clipped, 'are you refuting then?'

'The Blood Spatter Probability Scale is fundamentally flawed in terms of its algorithmic equation.'

'How do you mean?'

'Well, it's just wrong. If the attacker stood on a stool and shook blood off their hands to vary the height of the trails and satellites, then the model of probability elevates from a 28 per cent base line to 67 per cent probability.'

'Are you saying it's 67 per cent?'

'No, I'm actually saying it's actually closer to 28.'

He wasn't happy with her delivery, gave her a little prompting nod of the head. She recognised that it was going badly and raised a hand to her hairband, tapping it with the tip of her middle finger as if she was trying to turn herself off and on again.

'You're saying the BSPS was wrong in this instance?'

'No,' she said. 'It's wrong in every instance. It masks obsolete variables, especially when matching occurs on several loci.'

Cringing at the unwieldy sentence, he asked her to explain what 'loci' meant.

Kirsty tugged her jacket and cleared her throat. 'Places. It's places.'

'Can't you just say "places" then?' The KC set his shoulders as if resigned to this going badly. 'Is there a way of rephrasing the probability question in laymen's terms?' He gestured to the jury.

'Well. The test brings together a lot of factors and produces a probability number but some of those factors are wrong, outdated, and it warps the final outcome.'

'Some of these factors are wrong?'

'Yes.'

'Can you be specific?'

'Well, some of them are subjective tests where two assessors looking at the same evidence might not deduce the same thing. Spatter-analysing science has moved on. Volumising drip velocity is being questioned and the estimated height calculation can be manipulated if a long-handled weapon is used. But these individual factors can't be parsed because they're included in the overall scale.'

Having lost faith in Kirsty, the KC explained her point back to Kirsty: if they visualised the BSPS as a fistful of uncooked spaghetti it would be hard to break, very strong, but if half of the strands of dried spaghetti were missing, it would be half as strong, was that what she meant?

Kirsty agreed that this was the case but it wasn't made of spaghetti.

Claudia was sitting very still. She felt suddenly very cold. Kirsty was right.

Her ego threw up defences: that work on volumising drip velocity had a very small sample size. Kirsty was an opportunist. To manipulate the height calculation the perpetrator would have to understand exactly how the test worked.

But the scientist in her knew that Kirsty was right.

It didn't matter though. The jury didn't believe her. They could hardly bear to look at her and her stupid jacket. Even the avid note-takers had put their pencils down. Knowing he was defeated, the KC who had called her shrugged at the clerk. He didn't want to ask her anything else, he said and slunk back into his seat.

The prosecution KC got up to cross-examine her. His case was essentially that the BSPS had been used for ages and what was Kirsty on about and juries were more than capable of understanding, especially this jury, who were brilliant. Perhaps the problem was that Kirsty Parry didn't understand the BSPS or had misapplied it to the evidence. How long had she worked for Hamilton Analytics?

'About three months . . .'

Wasn't her PhD actually in a study on caterpillars? Yes, she said, yes but she did understand statistics.

Was this her first time giving evidence in court? Yes, it was.

Condescension dripping from his voice, he congratulated her on her performance and thanked her for coming here today as if she was an unsuccessful contestant on a game show. She was shown out of the witness box, her steps loud and clumsy on the wooden platform.

Charlie looked at Claudia, his eyebrows raised. He nodded to the door out. They crept up the stairs and out to the corridor and Charlie shut the door softly behind them.

Claudia was so angry that she was trembling, and hissed, 'She can't say that, I could sue her.'

Charlie was disappointed in her, 'Oh God, no, don't. Don't do that. Don't even say that. It's unstylish.'

'Why do you make everything into a fucking joke?'

'It's a trauma response,' he said simply, as if everyone knew that. 'Why do you cry when you're angry?'

She wanted to tell him to fuck off but she was too upset to speak.

The court officer appeared at the end of the corridor and held a finger over his mouth. They weren't allowed to talk out there.

They tripped down the stairs, back through the security guards and metal detector, out through Warwick Passage and walked down to the Strand, stopping in the first coffee shop they found.

It was vegan and organic. The pastries looked scolding and sarcastic and they had to queue up to order drinks like children in a school canteen. While they waited in silence at the side of the counter for two oat-milk lattes Claudia thought through all the ways in which Kirsty was wrong, why it was bad of her to question the BSPS and what her real motive might be. She was wrong and Claudia's husband had died and Kirsty probably had kids who didn't cause trouble all the time or hate her and she probably had a sister who wasn't a drug addict.

But there was a fracture in her conviction. What if Kirsty Parry was right? The technology had moved on. Maybe the BSPS could be updated but Claudia admitting to any error could jeopardise all the convictions based on it. And who the hell doesn't know how to do up a three-button jacket?

They took their coffees and settled down at a table by the window. An angry rant gushed from her: Kirsty had a fucking cheek. Who the hell put her on the stand? What were Hamilton doing? Her reports were shit, unreadable, the grammar in the Roland Garret report would shock him. Charlie must tell them not to use her in future. Claudia would if he didn't. She'd make sure no one ever commissioned her for this work again.

Very calmly, Charlie listened, watching her over the rim of his cup as he sipped his coffee. It went on for some time. He put the cup down, fitting it carefully into the little dip in the saucer before saying, 'Please don't do this.'

'Don't do *what*?'

'Turn into an arsehole.' He reached across to her hand but she yanked it away and lifted her drink.

'Why would you invite me to see that?'

He hummed again. 'We both know,' he said carefully, 'that being bad on the stand doesn't mean the science is wrong. How does that evidence relate to William Stewart?'

Her voice dropped to a frightened murmur. 'If the volumising drip velocity measure is altered then the attacker at Chester Terrace could be up to a foot shorter.'

'So, perhaps not six-foot-four William, perhaps even five-four, five-five?' He attempted a smile.

She sat back, 'Charlie, my entire fucking professional reputation is on the line so you and your stupid grin can fuck right off.'

'Ah, I see, thank you, that clarifies all the technical questions I had about that.' Charlie nodded and sat back. 'We lawyers are often wrong and have to learn to deal with it. I'm sorry if you haven't yet but it's a handy skill to nurture as you get older.'

Claudia understood why she was here now. 'Are you depending on Kirsty Parry's anti-BSPS evidence to rebut the forensic report I did on William Stewart?'

'Yes. Her performance was shit there but I wanted to know what you'd say. I'm going to dispute every single item on your report and I wanted you to know why before I did it.'

It would ruin her. She did not need this. 'You'll have questions of your own to answer, Charlie. Like how did you know to turn up at Paddington Station that night? Did William phone you on his way to Chester Terrace?'

'No, William didn't call me. Heely called me. He was the officer in charge of the investigation but Langston came lumbering in and took over. She was going to interview William without a lawyer or a caution and Heely knew he'd get the blame if it came out. Which it will.'

He was right about that. They had been shabby. Maybe she wasn't the only person he was going to expose. 'Is Langston stupid?'

He tilted his head. 'When did Langston last make a mistake that was detrimental to her career? She can spot a tailcoat a mile off. She was sucking up to Philip Ardmore.'

She smiled grudgingly. 'It hasn't done her any harm.'

'They're going to crucify her. Maura's not one of them, that's why she was given the job. The Met are in a crisis and she's disposable. It's a glass cliff appointment.'

She wanted to ask if she was on a glass cliff too but was afraid of what he'd say. But Maura had made a lot of mistakes in the case, it wouldn't all be about her scale. 'Did the digital analyst come up with anything about the time zone on the doorcam?'

'It's the factory setting, they didn't bother changing it to GMT when it was set up. Amelia sent it in.'

'Why would she give him an alibi?'

'She's his cousin. They're very close. She knows he's innocent.'

'Is he?'

Charlie looked at her, disaapointed, 'Come on, Claud, you saw the mess in there.' He dropped his voice. 'Francesca was emptied like a bucket. William turns up less than an hour later and he's spotless?' He raised a shoulder and looked out of the window. 'Nothing of him at the scene, just a tiny trace of DNA on the gun barrel. What damns him is accumulation of circumstantial factors, that's what I'll have to chip away at. That and his obnoxious personality.'

'Well, it's very noble of you to defend the richest man in England in the most time-consuming way possible.'

Charlie wasn't offended. In fact he was so relaxed he seemed almost sleepy. 'William has no money.'

'What about his mother's trust fund?'

'Oh no, that's gone. It went back into Jonty's estate and he's dead now. If William's found guilty of killing his father, which is looking increasingly likely, he'll inherit nothing. Law of Forfeiture. Whoever inherits Jonty's estate gets Daphne's trust fund too. It's a hefty sum. No, I'm working for Legal Aid and I can't charge for the same case twice so, even if he gets off, it's thin soup for Charlie.'

She didn't believe him. 'Legal Aid? That's barely minimum wage. You'd make more cleaning tables in here.'

His steady gaze held hers. 'Maybe I'm not who you think I am.'

Just for a moment she glimpsed an honourable and earnest man behind the bluster, saw in big, braggy Charlie's eyes the ghost of the man he had been, or would be again.

The shrill shriek of the milk steamer drowned out their conversation for a moment.

When it died down Charlie looked deflated and old. 'He'll be found guilty. William is not a likeable young man. He's an entitled little shit actually. He never needed to be appealing, not with all that he had coming, but he's not guilty. A jury will give him life for his tattoos and his sneer.'

'Juries aren't that thick.'

'Yes they are. They're vacuity incarnate and you know it. Why do we make our clients wear suits? Why do we get their hair cut? The science stuff that you do is a justification for instinctual outcomes. It's worse now, with the streamlined forensic service. It's even less about truth, it's just bad theatre. I think someone has tried to take the element of chance out of this. I've never known a case so pat and I want to know why.'

'And who?'

'Yes. Who knows enough about this to set a forensic scene? Who knew Jonty well enough to get past that dog and into the house? Not many.' His cheek twitched. 'I'd better go and see William. Can I come over and look through James's papers?'

They agreed to meet that evening at Gerald Road.

Outside, Charlie pulled his coat closed against sudden needling rain and they parted on good terms.

Claudia turned away, fingers itchy for her phone, craving a cigarette, thinking about Gina and how much she hated Kirsty Parry. She was so preoccupied that she barely glanced back at Charlie standing on the kerb, watching her leave.

Later, and for a long time, she would wish that she had turned back, that she'd given him a hug at least. He was the last good man in England.

Rain had freshened the day. Now the light was bright and crisp and Mayfair looked like a film set. The streets were clean, red-brick buildings glittered in the sun and the windows of designer shops were freshly washed, the pavements in front of them wet and darkened.

Because William had been charged it was not quite proper for Claudia to meet Elena for lunch but, she reasoned, the poor woman had lost her daughter in tragic circumstances and the residents' dining room at Claridge's was supposed to be quite special. Elena wanted to thank Claudia for her kindness at the church and Claudia wanted to see inside. It was just lunch. No one need know that they had met. It wouldn't do any harm.

She should have been at work, trawling through everything she could find about the new studies in volumising drip velocity, or out looking for Gina or at home looking after Sam. But she couldn't face any of those things right now and she deserved a bit of time off, a little self-care, something nice for herself. And anyway, she was here now.

She stubbed her cigarette out on a bin and put a small mint in her mouth, the perfect cover for smoke-reeking clothes. Claridge's was around the corner but she stopped and took her phone out and texted Sam, moderate in tone, sounding reasonable: How's the temp?

He texted back immediately:

I'm Fine. G came to get her stuff.

What stuff?

He didn't answer so she repeated herself in caps but again, Sam didn't reply. She had to threaten to ring him before he texted back.

G took clothes & passport & easel & roll of canvas.

Gina was picking up stuff she could sell. She texted Gina directly,

Meet for a drink?

Then she stared at the screen, willing her to answer, knowing Gina wouldn't. She waited for longer than was reasonable but got nothing back.

Checking her emails, she found one from Roland Garret's lawyers. She wouldn't have to come to court for Roland Garret after all because he had pled guilty to the murder. Thank you for your work on this. Please invoice us at your convenience. It was ridiculous, Roland wasn't guilty, but his lawyers must have told him about the evidence, the DNA at the scene. They were bound to enter whichever plea he asked them to and a guilty guaranteed a one-third reduction in his sentence. She had worked on cases where guilty accused were found innocent, that was always possible, but an obviously innocent person claiming guilt was different. It hadn't happened to her before and it felt far, far worse.

She slipped the phone into her breast pocket so that she could feel it vibrate if Gina replied, straightened her shirt and walked around the corner to Claridge's.

A uniformed doorman opened the wide brass door for her, bowing deeply as she stepped into the white marble lobby. It was cool in there, bright, an antechamber to mock-deco heaven. Claudia could smell the cigarette smoke radiating from her clothes. No wonder Sam had guessed. Her denial must have sounded pathetic.

Through another set of doors she found herself in a wood-panelled restaurant where a slim maître d' greeted her politely and asked who she was here to meet. This restaurant was solely for residents of the hotel and he knew who Elena was before Claudia got to her surname. He led her to a quiet corner where the light was soft and flattering, seasonless, a timeless place to drink and linger.

Elena was walking over to greet her, smiling, a slash of red lipstick brightening her face. She was dressed in flattering white linen, her hair down around her shoulders and looked ten years younger than the last time they met. She conferred four air kisses on her, back and forth, slipped her arm through Claudia's and led her to a horseshoe booth upholstered in green and pink velvet.

Claudia had expected them to be alone but there were several other women at the table. She shouldn't be seen here. It was unprofessional of her to stay.

'Elena, I don't know if you heard that charges have been brought—'

'Sit down first,' Elena pushed her onto the banquette and sat next to her, pinning her in, as the other women shuffled around to make space.

They all looked alike. For a moment Claudia thought they were related, but then she saw, beyond the glow of the lamp in the middle of the table, that the resemblance was superficial. They were dressed the same, their hair was the same and they'd all had the same work done. Except for Amelia Dibden. She didn't need any enhancement.

Elena introduced Claudia to the women telling them that this was the angel who saved her life that day. They nodded at her. Amelia kept her hands under the table, a girl in a sea of women, and looked up through her eyelashes, holding her gaze. There was a hesitancy about her, a vague detachment as if she was unsure of herself. Claudia felt she should say something friendly.

'Amelia, I'm a great friend of your stepfather, Sir Philip Ardmore, I work at ForSci.'

Amelia blinked slowly and her mouth tightened. 'Really?'

'Well, we used to work together,' Claudia wasn't too sure why this was going down so badly. 'Before he left the company. He left to serve on the Ethics Committee. He's doing great work.'

Amelia nodded stiffly, baring her teeth in a sick smile.

'I divorced him.' This was delivered in a bitter drawl by the woman next to Amelia, her mother, Mary Dibden. Claudia hadn't noticed Mary. She was slumped in her seat, obscured behind the table light.

Amelia and Mary were so alike they looked like a before-and-after cautionary tale about the wages of sin. This was why Amelia had a slightly fraught manner. She recognised the dynamic between them: Amelia sat, half-turned to Mary, her intense attention reading every gesture of her erratic mother, guessing at her next move, trying to be ready to avert disaster. It was Claudia and Gina, the helper and the addict.

But she didn't want to think about that right now.

She joined the conversation, spewing out bland, polite fillers, how nice to meet you, Mary, I've heard so much about you, lovely restaurant, I've never been here before.

'I have,' said Mary belligerently, reaching for her glass. 'Tons.' She drained the white wine and fell back in her seat. The other women looked at their laps.

Claudia said, 'I hear you live in Monaco?'

Mary nodded but didn't bother to answer.

Amelia was ashamed by her mother's lack of grace. 'Mummy doesn't come back very often.'

'I saw you at Jonty and Francesca's memorial service.'

Again, Amelia waited a moment to allow her mother to speak but when she didn't she filled in for her, 'Jonty meant an awful lot to her.'

Claudia addressed Mary directly, 'I'm so sorry for your loss.'

Mary sneered, perhaps meaning Jonty was no loss, perhaps meaning Claudia's condolences were fuck all use to her.

'They were close . . .' Amelia smiled awkwardly, a tiny fold between her eyebrows.

'Did you visit Jonty before he died?' Claudia persisted, wondering about Mary's DNA in Chester Terrace.

'We used to summer with them in the South of France.' She flicked a finger to the waiter to refill her wine glass, 'Great days, weren't they Ami?'

Amelia, cowed but not yet broken, addressed her reply to the waiter pouring wine. 'Well, William and I were left alone a lot.'

'They ran wild in the fields,' said Mary proudly, reaching for her glass before the waiter had finished.

He narrowly avoided pouring wine all over her hand by whipping the bottle away with a theatrical twist. Claudia felt there were many such accommodations made for Mary.

Then, to move the conversation along, she said something so bland she gave a disgusted, wincing smile at herself before she reached the end of the sentence: 'The South of France is lovely.'

All of the other women agreed that, yes, the South of France was indeed, quite lovely.

'Do you know,' said Amelia seriously, 'that people who have a house abroad spend, on average, more time boasting about it at parties than actually living in said house abroad?'

Everyone laughed, glad of the change of tone. Amelia had given them that, as a gift. She was sweet and funny and Claudia hadn't expected it. She was seeing herself in the co-dependent girl and wished they were sitting closer together, but then she remembered that she shouldn't be here at all, with Elena, with a girl who had tried to give William an alibi, with a woman whose partial DNA had been found at the scene. She shouldn't be here but a thought was forming at the back of her mind as she looked at Mary and Amelia. The matches from Chester Terrace were partials not fragmentary matches to Mary's DNA. She had to get out of here.

She hissed, 'Elena, I'm so sorry, I can't stay—'

'Oh, don't mind Mary, she's always drunk.'

'No, because William was charged, my position . . .'

'. . . No. No, no.' Elena wasn't talking to her. She was speaking past her to the waitress who was holding a sheaf of leatherbound menus. 'No, thank you, no menus.' She looked at the women around the table. 'Fruits de mer and champagne, yes?'

Everyone agreed that this was ideal and the waitress left with her menus. The women settled in with pleasantries, conversation rolling around the table about people Claudia didn't know, places and parties she hadn't been to. She wasn't going to eat, she was just waiting for the right moment to leave but keen to see the fruits de mer.

'Elena, I hope you didn't order any for me, I can't stay for lunch.'

'Just wait for the toast, darling, wait.' Elena waved over a waiter carrying a large bottle of champagne. He filled everyone's glasses. 'A toast to my Francesca.'

Claudia let him fill her glass and then all the women lifted their glasses as Elena stood up. She raised her glass over the table.

'To my darling Francesca on this special day. And to friendship.'

Everyone, including Claudia, raised their glasses and repeated 'to friendship' before taking a sip. The maître d' reached over and handed

Elena back her smartphone. A picture had been taken of them together. Claudia was alarmed by that.

Elena sat down.

'Elena, because William has been charged I can't stay for lunch—'

'You know, of course, Lorna?'

Elena leaned back so that the woman next to her could reach across and shake Claudia's hand. Lorna was younger than Elena, pink-cheeked and fresh with carefully dyed blonde hair.

'Dr Claudia O'Sheil? I'm Lorna Coole.' She let go of her hand, 'I don't think we've met exactly. I'm the admissions officer for Fair-church. I've been processing your sons' applications.'

Claudia looked at Elena. She was nodding and smiling. This was why they were here. This was why Elena had invited her.

'Now, we had a look at Sam's test results and made the case for him and his brother being housed in Bowes together. Final decision today and the letters will go out but I wanted to tell you: it's good news!'

'Yay!' said Elena flatly and nodded a prompt to Claudia to say it back.

'Ah,' said Claudia, failing at the first round. She couldn't afford it and she didn't want it but this was not the place to say it so she smiled and she nodded.

A waiting team arrived with the food and, with a great flourish, set a cake stand of fish down on the table. It was three tiered, with oysters on a bed of ice on the bottom, razor fish and langoustine in the middle and fat red crab claws on the top. Seafood was low calorie and these looked like women that mattered to. Next to each of their plates they were presented with a long board of sauces in tiny pots. It took a long time, there was a lot of fish admin with crab claw crushers and fork picks. While this went on Elena chatted about who had been at the memorial service on Francesca's side. Claudia didn't know any of them. There was a Spanish tennis star she'd never heard of, very well known in Spain, Elena assured her. Also a soprano with an Italian name who Claudia pretended to recognise. She's wonderful, she said, to be amenable. Yes, nodded Elena, she really is.

The team of waiters withdrew, looking back at the table setting, gratified at their performance.

Elena held up a staying hand and spoke across the table, 'I invited you all here to celebrate Francesca, for us all to get together, as *women*.' It wasn't quite clear what she meant by that. Several of the women glanced away, their porcelain faces communicating confusion only through their shifting gaze.

Elena clarified. 'Feminism.' She smiled softly as if she had just heard the word for the first time. 'Women looking after women.'

Lorna, perplexed, nodded slowly.

That was enough. Claudia gathered her bag and coat.

'So, Elena, I'm so sorry, I can't stay. It's quite improper.'

'You English and your manners!'

'I'm not English, I'm Scottish.'

'Really?' Elena didn't know what to do with that.

'It's like calling a Portuguese person Spanish.'

Elena nodded happily as she used a tiny silver spoon to scatter chopped onion on her oyster and watched the grey muscle contract away from the touch of the vinegar, 'Why did you come then?' Elena picked up her oyster and tipped it into her mouth, chewed twice and swallowed. 'And who'll know?'

The suggestion of a shared secret set alarms off in her head. She had to get out of here. 'Excuse me.'

Elena got up to let Claudia out and then Claudia stood awkwardly at the side of the table. She didn't want to ask but she had to. 'I'm so sorry. Could you delete that photo of us all together?'

A chilly silence fell over the table. She was asking not to be pictured with them. Indignant, Elena took out her phone and deleted the photo, showing her the screen. 'Happy now?'

Lorna Coole leaned forward, 'You're leaving?'

'Yes, I'm so sorry. I do absolutely have to.'

Lorna looked disappointed.

'Thank you so much for inviting me,' Claudia addressed the table, bowing a little, very stiff and formal. 'It was lovely to meet you all.'

The other women smiled and nodded pleasantly, not terribly sure what was going on.

Elena grabbed her forearm. 'Your boys, Bernardo and Sam, they'll go to Fairchurch now?'

'You're so kind to think of us, Elena—'

'Oh, it's not me. Sir Philip asked me to get you two together for us to fix this.'

Claudia was surprised. It was reassuring though, that Ardmore ever thought it would be fine for them to meet but circumstances had changed.

'Still, I think a day school might be better. Lorna and I can talk about this another time—'

'No, the notifications go out tomorrow,' said Lorna. 'It has to be decided . . .'

'Well, let's say no.' Claudia blushed; she couldn't say anything negative about the school to Lorna's face. 'And me being here with you, Elena, it could be perceived as a bribe . . .'

Elena tried to read her face. 'Is this a problem? For you to have this from Lorna? For what?' Elena was really offended now. 'You applied to the school long before we met, didn't you?'

Claudia admitted that she had.

'You toured the school and they sat the exam,' said Lorna forlornly. 'Sam in particular did rather well.'

'Well, I think they'll just stay home. But thank you for thinking of me.' She reached over and squeezed Elena's forearm. 'And Lorna, lovely to meet you. Amelia, Mary, enjoy your lunch.'

All of the nice ladies were looking down at their plates of low-calorie food, sad that Elena's feminist get-together had been ruined.

Except for Mary Dibden. She was watching Claudia with a raised eyebrow and a smirk. She raised her glass at her and wobbled her head. 'Quite right.'

Claudia saw Amelia, the shame burning on her cheeks.

She slipped past the booth but Mary caught her wrist. She turned back. Mary pulled her down and hissed, 'Quite *fucking* right.'

She twisted her hand free and slipped out of reach, hurrying through the door and back into the bustling day.

Taxis passed in the street, people walked and shouted into phones. The city purred around her. She lit a cigarette as she walked down side streets, zigzagging away from the restaurant in case anyone came after her, looking purposeful. She turned a corner into a curving lane of mews cottages and found a bench. She was light-headed. Her chest was buzzing. Briefly she wondered if she was ill but then she realised it was her phone.

She answered it.

Sir Philip Ardmore said, 'William has been charged.'

'I heard. I'm so sorry.'

Philip wasn't calling for a catch-up, he wasn't phoning to tell her the news headlines, he was the head of the Ethics Committee. Kirsty Parry had spoken out in open court, not well, but made a very clear and cogent case against Claudia's Probability Scale, a measure Philip had championed. There was no way he wouldn't have heard what she'd said. And now Claudia had been at a lunch with the family in a high-profile case.

She was fucked.

'Philip, I've just left Elena Emmanuel. She invited me for lunch to meet Lorna Coole, I know you asked her to but when I got there Mary Dibden and her daughter were there. I'm sorry, I know it's inappropriate, I don't think she meant it to get so out of hand, but I left as soon as I could.' She didn't know what else to say.

'Ah. I see. Look, could you come to my house later? There's something rather delicate I want to talk about.'

Of course, she said. He gave her an address in Fitzrovia. He had never invited her to any of his homes. He wanted to talk to her in private.

She was so fucked.

15

She tried all afternoon to find Gina. She didn't even know which area of London she was hanging out in. She tried Lambeth and their old neighbours, starting with the family who grew grass. The lady wouldn't let her in and shook her head sleepily when she showed her a photo of Gina.

Claudia explained that Gina used to attend Narcotics Anonymous meetings near here and didn't have a car, would she know where they were held? The woman told her the name of a local church and said they met there on Monday and Thursday nights at seven. It was Friday. When she saw how hopeless and frightened Claudia was she stepped out onto the landing and gave her a cuddle.

'What was she on?'

'Mostly Benzos and Diazepam, I think.'

She shook her head, oh no, she said, a lot of the street vallies had fenty in it and you had to be careful. She didn't really know pill people, she just did grass and heroin because they were organic. Keeping it clean and old school. 'You don't really know what's in that other stuff. You'll find her, don't worry.'

They both knew she probably wouldn't.

The afternoon evaporated as London afternoons do, in a mess of underground trains and an accumulation of long walks from place to place.

She was sitting on a bench in Soho Square, drinking an unsatisfying take-out coffee when her phone rang. It was Gina.

'I've been looking for you everywhere. Are you trying to sell James's papers to Charlie?'

'What?'

Claudia could hear a man shouting in the background of Gina's call, the beep-beep and a recorded voice warning that a lorry was backing up. 'Where the fuck are you, Gina?'

'Wha' was that about James and Charlie? Are you accusing me of something?'

'Where are you? You keep disappearing. I'm worried. I'm worried all the time.'

'Of stealing?' She was drawling. A woman's voice asked her a question that Claudia couldn't make out.

'Where are you?'

'How c'n ye?' Gina's voice changed to a nasal drone when she was using, her accent thickened and dropped four social classes. When people knew her as a drug user they were always amazed to find out where she came from and that she had a fine arts degree.

'G – would you get your shit together and help me a bit?'

Gina considered her plea for a moment and then held the mic close to her lips. She whispered, 'You're a cunt.' And hung up.

Claudia blinked back tears and nodded and lit another cigarette. Gina had a point. That's exactly what she was.

She lit a cigarette and picked the feeling apart. It was self-pity, comfortable, familiar and paralysing. She sat and smoked, watching people come and go, pigeons fluttering near benches and bins, the gardener opening up and disappearing into the half-timbered black and white hut in the middle of the square.

Gina was going to die if Claudia didn't do something. But did she have the right to force sobriety on her? Should she respect Gina's bad choices and stand by and do nothing? Suddenly, she recalled an interview she had read with a trans man. He talked about taking testosterone and said that after the very first injection he stopped questioning himself all the time. He just decided things and did them. In this frozen, terrified moment that decisiveness sounded luxurious.

Gina was going to die and Claudia was just sitting here smoking and whining.

Claudia looked up the number of a rehab Gina had been in before over in Richmond, hanging on until she could speak to someone about an admission. Someone hadn't turned up for their detox admission yesterday, they said, and they could take her but Gina would have to agree to come.

She texted Gina the question, keeping it as short as she could, less an offer than a proposal, then sat, fighting off the tsunami of self-doubt, squeezing her phone so tight she had to check a couple of times to make sure she hadn't turned it off by mistake. This was a huge mistake. It was the wrong time. It was her agenda. She was selfish, pushy, domineering. How could Gina ever get clean with her pushing all the time. When the phone buzzed in her hand she almost fell off the bench.

'Hello?'

Gina was crying. 'Gonnae come and get me?'

'Where are you?'

Gina said a street address and Claudia told her not to move. She ran to Tottenham Court Road and hailed a cab.

The driver was young and chatty, said traffic wasn't bad at this time of day but give it an hour and it would be rammed. His eyes read her face in the rearview mirror, saw that she was upset but not keen to talk. She was courteous though: Gina might be in a bad way and the driver might not let her into the cab if she was visibly intoxicated.

So she asked him where he was from, how long his shift was, did he own the cab or did he rent it? He talked too long, as if he knew she needed him to fill in the gaps for her. Eventually she said she had to pick someone up and take them to Richmond. Was he able to do that?

Sure, he said, his eyes flicking to her, yeah. Anywhere special in Richmond?

Just a clinic to the east of the park. Lighthouse clinic.

They arrived at the street in Camden, at the address Gina had given her, but it was a junction of several roads with a tube station nearby, busy. Gina wasn't there.

The cab pulled up at a small supermarket near a pedestrianised street of cafés and shops. It was busy and she watched the faces, hoping every moment for Gina to materialise from the crowd. She might have changed her hair, it had been bleached and growing out and she tended to shave it when she was using, it was a kind of self-harm thing she did, so Claudia watched for her face. She was holding onto the taxi window sill, anxious as a dog looking for its owner to come home.

'Any luck?' asked the driver.

'Not quite yet, no.'

But then she saw her. The shame was so intense it felt as if someone had stamped on her ribcage.

Gina was on the pavement outside the supermarket, skinny legs folded up tight to her chin, a hand out to beg, forehead resting on her knees. Someone had placed a full dog poop bag in her outstretched hand and it balanced there. A teenage boy was passing by and smirked at that and then doubled back to take a surreptitious photo of her and scuttled off laughing to himself.

But then the supermarket's automatic doors swept open and a man stepped out. He looked at Gina as if he'd seen her on the way in, checked the street to see if he was being watched. He wasn't and this pleased him and his mouth dropped open a little. Inside his tongue convulsed, flashing wet with pleasure at what he had planned or anticipation or both. He crouched quickly down next to Gina, taking a packet of sandwiches out of his shopping bag. He was too close to her, his face tilted away from the street, and his other hand reached out to touch her face.

Claudia was out of the cab and across the pavement. Batting the bag of dog shit out of Gina's hand she grabbed her roughly by the shoulders, yanking her up onto her feet, unaware of the twist in her arm until she felt the snap.

The man staggered back, shocked at the sudden assault. 'Hey!' He backed off, astonished at the ambush, pointing at Claudia and shouting at the street. 'She broke her arm! She broke her arm!'

Gina's eyes were animal wide as she lifted her right arm and saw the shattered bone. The skin was not pierced, but her forearm began to swell up. The sight made Gina's knees buckle. 'You've broken my fucking arm.'

Claudia lifted Gina off her feet and dragged her to the open cab door, shoving her into the taxi.

'Oh my God!' said the driver. 'Her arm!'

'Help me,' Gina held her arm up to show him and then the pain hit her. The sight of it was sickening. Gina's face slackened as if she was going to vomit.

'I'm sorry,' Claudia climbed in and did up Gina's seatbelt. 'I'm so sorry, I panicked, I just lost it.'

'She's broken her arm,' said the driver again.

'Look, this is my wee sister. If she makes a mess of your cab or anything I'll pay—'

'I know you will. Don't worry. We need to go to A and E.'

Gina groaned, her left hand hovering around the broken bone, panting.

'If we stop at A and E she'll never – I'm trying to get her to Richmond.'

'Lighthouse Sober House in Purcell Road?'

She hadn't told him the address. He had been there before.

'Okay,' he said and pulled out into the traffic. 'Put your own belt on as well.'

The sandwich man watched them leave, mouth still open, eyes full of hate.

Claudia knew what she had witnessed as surely as if he had written his ill-intent down and had it notarised. There was no proof. She wanted so badly to be wrong. She didn't want the world to be like that, men to be like that, for people to walk past ignoring it while that happened. She wasn't the first woman to see her sister being preyed upon, being ridiculed, being in danger. She wanted to doubt herself because it would be easier to be wrong. But she wasn't.

It was a long, grim drive over to Richmond.

Gina couldn't speak, she was finding it hard to breathe for a lot of the journey. Dried white saliva had crusted at the sides of her mouth and she was all bone. She smelled of piss and stale spunk, of pavements and rotting food. Every time Claudia looked away from her she saw the man with the sandwiches bending down to touch her face, his furtive glance around the street and his sneaky little smile.

The Lighthouse clinic staff brought a wheelchair out for Gina and took her in through a side door. Gina had detoxed there before so they had all their details on file, both medical and financial. They asked Claudia to leave and said they'd phone her tonight with an update.

She didn't trust herself to navigate public transport and took a cab over to Philip's address in Fitzrovia.

All the way over she found herself trying to parse a useful life lesson from what had happened – she should be more decisive, people were awful, never trust a man with sandwiches, but there wasn't anything useful or good to be learned from this. There really wasn't. It was just sad.

16

The Fitzrovia address that Philip had given her was not the great white-washed townhouse she had expected but a pleasant block of Edwardian flats, neither showy nor grand apart from the location in Central London. White marble-clad steps led off the street, the top step inset with a lovely brass number three.

Through the doors she found a welcoming wood-panelled hall, heated through brass grates on the skirting. A wooden concierge box was manned by what looked like a child with a beard.

The baby-man asked her who she might be here to visit. When he heard it was Philip Ardmore he corrected her discreetly. *Sir* Philip's apartments are on the fourth floor, he said and directed her down a passage to a corridor and a carpeted lift at the back of the building. Floor four, he advised, second door on the left.

As the lift rose Claudia's mood sank further. Philip had heard about her fucking up the lunch, Elena had called, Amelia had called, Lorna Coole had called. He'd heard about the sandwich man. He'd heard about Kirsty's evidence and was being kind, inviting her here to tip her off before her work was publicly torn apart by the Ethics Committee. She wouldn't be able to stay on at ForSci. She was going to lose the house. She wouldn't be able to pay for Gina's rehab and they'd both end up begging and humiliated outside a mini Sainsbury's.

Her catastrophising reached an absurd pitch as the lift reached its destination.

She was too tired to think straight.

The door opened out into a high corridor papered with vertical stripes on purple and gold. The modesty of the place surprised her. It wasn't beautiful or showy, just an ordinary corridor with walls papered to hide lumpy plasterwork. She found Philip's door, pressed the bell and Philip answered it himself.

'Claudia,' he said solemnly. 'Thank you for coming.'

He hadn't dressed up for her coming. He wore an untucked dress shirt, pale slacks and tan loafers with no socks, a leisure suit for formal men. It was ominous.

The hall was small and low ceilinged, oddly devoid of the detritus of normal life: no opened letters left on a sideboard awaiting a decision, no shoes hurriedly kicked off in the hall or coats dumped on a chair. A lone pale linen jacket was hung on a hook and that was it. The first door led into a bedroom. The door beyond opened into a sitting room.

Philip ushered her in there.

Three big windows in the bright and airy room overlooked the roofs of small buildings. The Post Office Tower loitered on the left, filling the window like Godzilla sneaking past an office block.

The room was painted matte black. A faded pink antique rug covered the floor but was tucked under against the far wall, too big for the room. All of the furniture seemed to be from a larger house. Leaning against the back wall, reflecting the light around the room, a huge gold-framed mirror sat on the floor and an antique brown leather sofa and matching armchair, large but low, faced a carved Chinese rosewood table with a red clay teapot sitting on it, clear steam snaking from the spout, and two small tea bowls.

He smiled, 'Green tea?'

'Lovely.'

'Please, sit.'

Claudia sat dutifully in the middle of the sofa and put her bag on the floor at her feet.

This would be over soon and then she could smoke more cigarettes. She knew she would. She could feel the nicotine draining from her body, making her twitchy. She just had to suffer through this disgrace without showing any emotion.

Philip perched on the edge of the armchair and poured for both of them.

'What a lovely room.' She sounded nervous.

'I'm afraid my circumstances are somewhat reduced until my divorce is settled. Mary is being quite unreasonable.'

Looking around, Claudia guessed that the money in the marriage had been hers.

'She was at that lunch I left.'

'Drunk?'

'I'd say tipsy.'

'Very drunk, then.'

He handed her a cup and took his own. They sipped. It was earthy and hot and not very nice at all. She put it down.

'Philip, can I just ask you, who funded ForSci when it was first set up?'

He looked confused, 'When what?'

'Who gave you initial funding to set it up?'

He looked away, ran some calculations through his mind and then turned to her, 'Mary and Rob. Mostly Rob.'

She was stunned. 'Rugby Rob? My assistant, Rob?'

'I don't think it was all his own money but he was the face of a group of about ten investors. I thought you knew, I thought that's why you kept him in the office.'

'No. *You* recommended Rob as an assistant.'

'Did I?'

'Well, you and several other people. I'll ask him about it.'

'Don't. Really don't. He'd have told you if he wanted you to know. His father-in-law needed a tax write-off and Rob needed a new career. It's a bit of a sore point.'

'His father-in-law?'

'Hm.'

It sounded like a lie to her but she didn't want to pry. She felt protective of Rob. He was a good man.

'Hm. He doesn't have a science degree. How did you think he came to be working there?'

'Just because everyone likes him?'

Philip smiled at her tenderly. 'That's not really how things work, Claudia.'

'Oh.'

It was very quiet in the room.

She looked up at the facing wall. There were a lot of paintings hung there, small but well spaced. The frames were gold, all different styles and sizes, and somehow the arrangement came together into a harmonious whole. A small one caught her eye. It was a still life in the manner of the Dutch Masters: a dark background with bright details carefully picked out. She looked more carefully and smiled: it was of an iPhone and an open roll of Fruit Pastilles. The detail was amazing, the iPhone screen was beautifully realised with dark but greasy finger smudges, swiped and tapped, and the sweets spilled joyfully out of the ripped silver wrapper, glittering with tiny sparkles of sugar. It was dated in yellow paint next to the initials 'AD '.

'That's clever,' she said. 'A nod to Albrecht Durer.'

'It's by Amelia Dibden; it's from her degree show at Saint Martin's.'

She didn't want to mention her lunch at Claridge's again, 'I didn't know she was at Saint Martin's.'

'Yes, with Francesca. They were friends. That's how Francesca met Jonty. Through Amelia.'

'I wonder why she gave William a false alibi.'

'It's a very complicated relationship. You saw the mess he was in that night? That's what he's always like but she was letting him stay in her house. She's too loyal.'

'She's deeply codependant,' said Claudia, remembering Amelia in the booth, sitting with her hands on her lap, turned towards her erratic mother, keeping her eyes down as Mary drank and slurred and swore. 'She was trying to help him. She's fairly practised at trying to save people, I think.'

'She meant well, I suppose.'

Together, they looked at the painting. Claudia asked how much it cost but Philip didn't know. 'She's a talent, though, isn't she?'

'I could stare at that for days. Does she have a gallery?'

'Well, she's in a group show at the Hawes . . .' He looked out of the window and one side of his face twitched in a cringe. He didn't like talking about the Dibdens, she felt.

'Good for her anyway,' she said and Philip nodded.

Claudia sipped her tea.

He cleared his throat. 'Claudia, I've always kept our friendship on a strictly professional basis but, I don't know how to say this really. You've been struggling a little, with the boys.'

Claudia's heart sank. He was going to suggest spending more time with them. 'Been busy, you know . . .'

'Well, I think I understand how you feel and how hard losing James has been. I have known Jonty all my life and I've been a little lost since he died. I'm sorry . . .' He shook his head. 'Anyway, look, I spoke to Elena. She told me about asking you to lunch with Lorna Coole and Fairchurch offering the boys places. Is that what you want?'

Disarmed, she nodded. 'Mary was at that lunch.'

'I know – the lunch for Francesca.' He dropped his eyes. 'I don't quite know how to broach this but if your reservations about Fairchurch are about cost, I have to tell you that the company can pay the fees for both boys. It's a standard condition of employment. You're the star employee. I'm telling you because I know you come from a, you know, a family that – you know – but I thought you wouldn't necessarily know or think of it yourself.'

'That would be quite a raise.'

'Yes, it is a benefit, but you can take a salary cut. ForSci can't afford to lose you, it's entirely justified and it's a tax write-off.'

'Well, that's great . . .' She didn't know what to say but Philip heard what she wasn't saying.

'And of *course*,' he jumped in, 'then there are the uniforms and everything else. But you'd have so much more free time and I, well, look at this.' He handed her a large white envelope.

She looked inside. Documents. She pulled them out. A letter offering her a lucrative board membership for a west London scientific research company. Under that was a second letter and a university prospectus with a letter asking if she would accept a visiting lectureship with an annual fee that was more than generous for the effort the contract entailed.

She looked up at him.

'I know the Vice Chancellor. I called and asked. I hope I didn't overstep.'

'Philip . . . I don't know what to say but I don't want the boys to board. James wanted that but I don't.'

'The boys will thrive there. You've mentioned that Bernard is a bit chaotic but they'll channel that, they'll do something with that.'

She looked at her shoes. She had been expecting a completely awkward different conversation and found herself relieved that she hadn't done anything to incur Philip's disapproval. She pressed the envelope to her chest.

'I'll talk to them about it,' she said, her voice high and strained. 'Thank you.'

'You're incredibly welcome.' He sipped his tea and smiled up at her.

'I thought you were going to ask me about Kirsty Parry.'

'No, not that. Just some good news,' he said and sipped again. 'Finally.'

She had the feeling that he was drinking tea so that he didn't have to meet her eye. But it was marvellous that this had happened.

She sipped hers and flattened her free hand over the envelope on her knee.

'Did you hear about Kirsty Parry on the stand for Hamilton Analytics this morning?'

Philip hummed and nodded sadly, 'She crashed and burned, I heard.'

Claudia nodded.

'Kirsty's inclined to overreach, I think. She had an article knocked back by the *Oxford Forensic Journal* about the BSPS. The peer review feedback was brutal.'

Claudia was shocked to hear that. She hadn't been told about it or asked to do the peer review and she should have, it was her scale. 'She wrote an article about the BSPS?'

'Yes. She has quite the bee in her bonnet about it. Thinks this oppositional position is how she'll make her name. Upstart.' He sounded sad about it. 'I'll talk to Andrew Hamilton.'

He meant he'd tell him not to give Kirsty any work.

Claudia spoke quietly, 'She did make some good points.'

'Oh? She did?'

'Badly, but she's right to say that some parts of the scale are, well, they were right at the time of design.'

'Hm. Perhaps you could tweak them? Otherwise all the old cases will have to be reopened. A bonanza for criminal lawyers.'

Roland Garret might be able to appeal, she thought. But just then her phone rang loud and clear and she reached down to her bag. Her hand was closing over it as Philip's phone began to ring too. It was in the breast pocket of his shirt. He put his hand on it as if he was swearing allegiance and they locked eyes. A profound unease settled in the room. They answered their phones at the same time.

It was Nick Heely's office.

17

The emergency services had shut the road to traffic at either end. The sun was setting over Horsenden Hill, light failing, the woodland was breathlessly quiet. Claudia and Philip got out of his car and Maura Langston walked over to them.

Sorry, she explained, sorry that they called both of you. They ran the licence plate but the details were wrong, the owner sold the car several months ago. They did notice that a search for the plates had been done recently by DI Nick Heely on the night William Stewart was brought into Paddington Station. They called him to see if he'd identified the owner and he had.

It was Charlie Taunton.

Neither Claudia nor Philip had a family contact for him but Heely's officers couldn't stop them coming to the scene.

Nothing could have stopped Claudia coming to the scene.

Claudia stared down into the dark, at the tail lights of a yellow rescue vehicle and the slow-moving hoist dangling over the break in the trees as Philip spoke to Maura.

Maura offered to walk them down to the site. She explained that the car had been spotted by a passing driver. They'd noticed headlights glowing under the water and slowed down to look. That was when they saw the tyre tracks gouged through the muddy verge.

The wind picked up as they started down the road and Claudia felt as if she was walking back through the fabric of time.

They passed an ambulance with paramedics standing to attention by the open back doors. In the oven-warm glow of the van's interior a stretcher lay ready to receive.

Down at the crash site it looked as if the car had swerved and left the road at just the wrong place, mowed down a bank through a tangle of bramble bushes and ploughed straight into the water. It was wetland, wild, not a lake or pond so much as a deep depression in the clay that had filled up with still water.

'This is a crime scene,' said Claudia to no one in particular. 'It has to be preserved. It's a crime scene.'

Maura nodded at her. 'We don't even know if he's in there yet. Give us time.'

The roof of Charlie's Ferrari stood proud of the water, a red metal island in the flat expanse of brown, the top of the windows visible. The passenger door was open and the car had filled up.

Deep under the brown water orange hazard lights pulsed, irregular, flashing twice then pausing, then flickering frantically, deep down in the muddy earth as a hazy sun set over the hill.

Maura told Philip that look here, see? The Ferrari had swerved sharply, coming off the straight road and going down this bank straight into the water. Charlie drank a lot, didn't he?

Philip said no, not really, well, not always. But it sounded defensive and they all knew it wasn't true, that he was reluctant to admit Charlie might be entirely to blame at the site of the crash.

Of course, Maura said, let's reserve judgement though until we're certain that Charlie is inside. There was always a chance that the car had been stolen. There was definitely someone in there though. They'd just have to wait until they got the car out to see who it was.

Claudia took out her phone and rang Charlie's number. Maura shushed everyone to listen and they all stilled, tipping their heads to listen as the water lapped at the bank and Claudia's phone connected.

A plaintive sound came from the water, a distant xylophone, notes ascending, as if the phone was wishing itself up and out of the water.

'Oh,' said Maura, 'Oh gosh. Let's see, well, I'm sorry . . .'

Around them the emergency services were conferring about how to get the car out, quietly wondering why the fuck the head of the Met was attending a traffic accident.

The arm of the towing crane dangled impotently out over the water. It couldn't reach the car. They lowered the truck stabilisers onto the road but still the car was too far away for the arm to reach it. One of the men from the rescue vehicle pulled on waders that came up to his nipples. The plan, they told Maura, was to walk out to the car, fit the tow line in through the open passenger door and window.

'It'll take a while,' said Maura. 'Why don't you two wait in the car, or better yet go home and we'll call. You might not want to see this.'

But Claudia wouldn't leave. Philip said he was cold and going back to the car. He walked away and Claudia looked at Maura. She was watching the wader, standing with her arms crossed.

Claudia whispered, 'You know this is a murder?'

Maura pinched her lips, 'We'll see.'

'And if this is murder, you know . . . ?'

Maura nodded, deep and heavy, humming noncommittally. She pretended to have an urgent need to talk to a member of the tow truck team and moved away.

Claudia stood in the dark by the side of the quiet road alone, looking past the tangle of trees and bushes to the watery bog. Cold ebbed up through her shins, coming in at her toes. Her heels were on asphalt but her toes had sunk into the soft mossy soil at the road's edge. She watched the filthy day fade and darkness slide across the open ground, tainting everything in its path.

She knew this road, knew every bump, where the rim of the tarmac dropped suddenly into the mud. She knew the road surface and the average speed of traffic. She had been up and down it many times. It was straight, two lanes, carefully marked. Drivers were considerate on it, slow. There were no swerves or blind summits, no potholes, no reason for anyone to crash.

The man waded out into the water, hands held high, a torch in one and a hammer in the other.

Carefully and slowly, he made his way to the car, now knee deep, now waist deep, back up to thighs and then a sudden plummet into the deep dip the car was nestling in. Men on the bank shone a light at him but they were holding it at the wrong angle and the wader turned back and shouted that he couldn't see anything, go over there, move down the bank a bit. The light operator turned the spotlight off and moved down the bank, switching it on again. Crisply lit now, the wader raised his hammer and struck the back window of the car.

The crack hissed out across the water, the safety glass crumpled like a sheet of foil.

He waddled awkwardly around to the passenger door, his hands still up in surrender, opened the door further and shone his torch inside.

A cold lick of light on a big head resting on the steering wheel.

He turned to the bank, held up a single finger and shook his head. At the signal the waiting paramedics turned to the open back of their ambulance and began quietly to tidy their kit away.

Charlie was dead. Claudia took a deep breath and looked beyond the dark hills to the glow of the houses beyond.

One of the paramedics was at her side, a woman with a melodic Derry accent, and asked Claudia if she was cold.

Claudia was but said she wasn't.

Well, said the woman, how about we just put this wee foil blanket over ye, can't do any harm, eh?

The silver crackled around her ears and the woman tucked it under Claudia's arms, rubbing her upper back, asking if she was feeling dizzy as the tow line was fitted and they started dragging the car out.

The Ferrari lifted an inch from the deepest part of the water to the edge, nose down, but the wheels got jammed in the mud and the hoist wasn't strong enough. A conference began on the bank about what to do now.

The paramedic kept talking.

Claudia didn't catch much but she was aware of being spoken to softly, kindly, someone was bringing her back into the world with an insistence she found equal parts touching and annoying as the car was dragged backwards up to the road, sloshing water out of the windows as it rocked back and forth. Charlie was not wearing a seatbelt. His forehead was caved in, the skull above his eyebrow broken like an egg. The investigation would find that he had hit the steering wheel and passed out before he went into the water. But his face was marked by vertical streaks of blood. It had soaked into his collar and the water had washed off the pattern of it.

The paramedic stepped between her and the sight of the car, took both of her cold hands in hers and rubbed them. Claudia was overwhelmed with emotions she was too tired to process, conflicting, euphoric and desolate in equal measure. She was in shock, barely able to formulate a coherent thought.

The world as she understood it shifted tectonically around her.

James had been murdered. He didn't kill himself, he didn't mean to leave her. He loved her. He loved her as much as she loved him.

And Charlie was dead.

'How could this happen?' Claudia said, 'How?'

'Look at me, now,' said the paramedic. 'Don't look at that car, look at me here for a wee minute, now. I'll tell ye, this road is deceptive. It looks safe enough but there's foxes running across the road or mibbi just maybe some wee boys shining laser pens in driver's eyes, something like that. We were out here at another fatality not too long back, ten months or so ago.'

'Eight months and three days ago,' whispered Claudia. 'The fourteenth of September. It was a Monday night.'

The woman stopped rubbing her hands, 'That's absolutely right. And how would you know that? D'you live around here?'

'It was James Atkins. He was my husband.'

Same place, same way. They were goading her. They weren't even disguising it now because they thought they were untouchable.

Claudia felt her anger fizzing up from her feet to her chest and hands and neck. She was going to find out who did this. She'd burn the world down around her to find out. She'd use herself as kindling if she had to.

18:49

Kirsty Parry was standing in the mouth of the corridor, blocking Claudia's escape. The maroon Issey Miyake dress was supposed to be ankle length but it had bunched up around the waist, making Claudia think of someone who had just come back from peeing in a bush on a camping trip.

'You bloody well blackballed me.'

'I didn't, Kirsty. I disagreed with you.'

'You ordered Andrew Hamilton not to use me. Your peer review of my article in the *OFJ* was brutal but I was right. My crits were right and you altered the scale to accommodate them and never gave me credit.'

'I'm in no position to order Andrew Hamilton to do anything and I didn't do the peer review. They didn't ask me to.'

Behind Kirsty, through the double door, all the way across the courtyard and the wide-open space, she could see Maura Langston talking to Philip. They were underneath a patio heater, lit by flickering flames, and Maura was telling him what she'd seen in the bathroom. There was something wrong with Claudia's speech. Something about Maura, accusing her of something, crazy stuff. It was handwritten and she shook her head, angry and baffled. They had to do something, tell someone.

Philip looked around and saw Rob telling a jolly anecdote to an adoring audience. Philip waved over to him and Rob raised a hand to say he'd seen him, he was coming. He finished the story and headed over to the pair at the heater.

'You did so review it.'

'I didn't. They're anonymous but it wasn't me. I never even saw the draft of the article.'

'I was told it was you.'

'Who told you it was me?'

'Andrew Hamilton said it was you.'

'How would he know? It's supposed to be anonymous.'

Kirsty stalled. Peer reviewers of academic articles were always done blind, they had to be or no one would tell the truth, and of all the people Claudia might have confided in that the crit of Kirsty's article was hers, Andrew Hamilton was the last person. He was a commercial rival and admitting that had commercial value.

'Oh.' Kirsty nodded as she realised she might well be wrong. 'I was told it was you. Maybe he guessed? He said you'd never let me publish that.'

'Well, I wasn't even asked.'

'You should have been.'

'I know. But I wasn't. Did Hamilton invite you tonight?'

'No.'

Rob was over with Philip and Maura now, getting the story. Maura was pointing angrily back to the toilet.

'I don't know. It was just an official invite from the college.'

'Look, I didn't blackball you but I know you were treated really badly. And I did adjust the scale but not because I read the draft of your article. I saw you give evidence in the Old Bailey, about volumising drip velocity and height estimations and I realised you were right and I changed it then.'

Kirsty looked horrified. 'The Old Bailey?'

'You were in the dock.'

'Oh I know,' her head dropped. 'They made mincemeat out of me.'

'We've all had those days in the dock.'

Kirsty sighed, 'Not me. That was my only day and I blew it.'

Philip was coming towards them, crossing the path and heading for the doors. He looked very concerned. Rob tried to follow him but he snapped at him and Rob fell back.

'I've got a fucking doctorate from fucking Oxford,' Kirsty slumped on her hip, defeated. 'And we can't get any work in this country. We had to go and live in our fucking holiday home in France. We're in the middle of the fucking Auvergne, it rains all the fucking time and we're the youngest people in the village. Once a week I have to help a neighbour who's fallen over and can't get up. I'm basically a home help except I get paid in wine.'

Claudia nodded over her shoulder to warn her and Kirsty spun around to see what she was looking at. Philip was storming over to them, coming through the door.

'They're going to throw me out, aren't they?'

Claudia held onto Kirsty's arm, 'No, it's not you.'

But Kirsty turned and bolted towards the ladies' room.

Philip was storming over to her, coming straight for Claudia, coming so fast she thought he was going to walk straight through her.

'Claudia, I just had a conversation with a very panicky Maura. She said your speech seems off.'

'Maura said this?'

'She did. Can I see it?'

She stared up at him. 'See what?'

'Your speech. Can I see the transcript?'

Claudia gave a soft laugh. 'Because Maura said it seemed *off*? Is she my editor now?'

Philip looked at her, found her calm and friendly, seemed re-assured by that. Claudia opened the documents folder and took out the printed transcript. She gave it to him.

He looked at it and read the title out loud: '*Chester Terrace: The Case Against William Stewart*. She said it said the case against *her*. And that it it was handwritten. Why did she say that?'

'I really don't know,' said Claudia, faking concern. 'Is she okay?'

Philip turned to look at Maura and waved the speech. Maura frowned at him and started over to them, bringing Rob with her.

Maura was a cop. She would not flinch from searching the folder and she would find the handwritten version in there and she would show Philip.

'May I?' Claudia took the speech back from Philip's hand. 'Is Maura having a breakdown, do you think?'

Maura was twenty feet away, bowling towards them, and Rob trailed after her, unsure what was happening but too affable to walk away.

Philip frowned, 'She's certainly having a very hard time.'

'Hallo, all! Ha ha ha ha!' It was Sir Evan Evans, blindsiding them both by coming around the corner. His hollow laugh sounded like a warning siren coming from a mouth downturned at the sides, teeth yellow and brown, his gums receding. 'Claudia and Philip! My dears! How marvellous to see you!'

Scattering like skittles at his arrival, Claudia reeled and Philip rolled away towards the open door, stopping Maura on the step with a hand, turning Rob away.

'Oh . . . off so soon?' Evan Evans called after them.

He turned back and looked at Claudia. She was stuck with him. 'Sir Evan, how are you?'

'Oh! Call me Evan. Honestly, I don't use the old honorariums. Anyway, I'm terribly well, terribly well!' He tipped towards her, 'And your good self? How are you?'

'Oh, I'm fine. I'm speaking in a minute, I should go for a sound check, maybe.'

'Well, now, then . . .' He dropped his voice conspiratorially, 'I was looking for the lavatory. Any clues?'

She pointed him to the corridor. 'Round the corner there.'

He looked back to the corridor, nonplussed. 'They've taken all the signs down, hahaha, expecting the Germans. Rather awful, getting old, you know. Having to avail oneself of the facilities every ten minutes.'

'You should get a check-up, Sir Evan, that doesn't sound right.'

'Oh, call me Evan, please. Ah! And I believe you're suppering with us at the Albemarle later on? Splendid. More ladies, that's what I say!'

Claudia pointed down past the auditorium doors to the bathroom sign. 'The loo is just down there.'

But he didn't seem anxious to go to the bathroom now. As if making an important point he turned his back to the corner, blocking her in just as Kirsty had. His demeanour changed. 'And of course James suppered there on the evening he died.'

Evan Evans laid his hand on her forearm and looked her in the eye. He was more serious than she had ever seen him.

'Where?'

'At the Albemarle, at my club.'

18

Today would be the end of a lot of things. She was taking the boys to safety and then she was going to hand herself in.

She had hired a flashy Bentley to drive them up to Fairchurch, the most expensive one she could find. She was pantomiming prosperity for them, so they would fit in, performing to an audience who probably weren't watching and really didn't care. She just didn't want the boys to stand out.

They were going up for a short induction stay, organised to give boys who were especially trepidatious or had never boarded before a bit of experience before the term began.

She drove through a suburb of grubby houses with bricked-over front gardens cluttered with wheelie bins and mini skips, windows grimy from exhaust fumes from the busy road that ran in front of them. She took a roundabout and then a left, up the long sweep of Fairchurch Hill towards the school.

Bernie had bagsied the front seat and wouldn't stop whining. He looked at the trees. 'What if I get really fucked off here?'

'Bernie.' She stopped at a set of lights, 'You cannot say "fuck" in front of these people. And you need to give it a chance and start minding your manners a little bit more.'

She had made them turn their music off and take their earphones out when they left the M25 so that they would be capable of civil conversation by the time they arrived. She regretted that now. She just wanted them to shut up.

It was coming up to the hour and she put the radio on.

'Oh, God,' Sam groaned, 'not the news again.'

'It's not the news *again*.' She turned the radio up. 'It's just the news.'

The newsreader spoke in a monotone, delivering disaster and war and famine to the ears of the concerned multitudes and then –

'Questions are being asked in Parliament today concerning the Met's handling of the case. MPs are demanding a response from the Met's CI Maura Langston over what is perceived as an unreasonable delay in bringing charges against William Stewart. His lawyer, Laurence Beecham issued a statement—'

She punched the radio off. She knew what Larry would say, that the trial wouldn't be for a long time and when it eventually happened the truth would come out. Some standard way of saying nothing at all. The fact that William hadn't been cautioned wasn't public yet but she knew Nick Heely had his defence ready and he'd be keen to play it. Maura was cornered.

The boys knew something important had happened but not what.

'Was that one of your cases?' asked Sam.

'I can't really talk about it but the police officer in charge of that case is who we bought the nice biscuits for. He's coming over to the house at lunchtime.'

They rarely had biscuits in the house. She'd been play-wrestling Bernie out of the cupboard all morning. He'd eaten half the packet already.

'Is he coming to talk about William Stewart?'

'No, just . . . another case. Something he's working on.'

Heely was coming to talk about Charlie. She'd put him off until today so that she could be certain the boys were out of the house. They didn't know any of the details around Charlie's death other than that he had passed away. She told them nothing about the parallels with his death and their father's. She wanted them tucked away somewhere nice and safe before it came out. She didn't want them to feel a fraction as afraid as she did.

Since Charlie died she had been poring through the boxes in the attic, had fitted cameras to the front and back of the house and sat up most nights, smoking, unblinking, in the dark.

Bernie was interested now and he hadn't been interested in anything but biscuits for a while. 'Did they try to let him off because he's an earl?'

'He isn't an earl, Bernie.'

'Still, wow. Did you meet him?'

She took a tight roundabout and they all three swayed in concert, 'Yes. I was at the house on the night of the murders. I had to take William to the police station in Sir Philip's car. He went to this school.'

'If I hate it I'll run,' smiled Bernie.

'Please don't,' she said.

'Yeah, don't,' said Sam. 'They'll chuck me out as well and I actually want to go. I'm brainy, not a fat thicko like you.'

Bernie grinned unhappily, 'Well, I've already looked up the train times home.'

She yanked the car over to the side of the road, her foot hard on the brake, tossing the boys forward in their seats. The car behind her honked its horn; the road was narrow and it had to veer out into the oncoming lane to avoid back-ending her.

Claudia sat staring at her hands clutching the wheel. She was panting. She wanted to scream at them so hard that her knuckles were white. Your father was murdered. Your father was murdered. You are in danger and I am terrified.

'Mum?' Sam leaned forward from the back seat, 'Mum?'

Claudia looked out of the window at the traffic passing in her side mirror. She wanted to reach across the chasm already opening up between them and explain why her moods were so volatile, why she was sending them away when she should be refusing to ever let them go, why she had become James.

She turned and looked at them.

Do you know how hard it has been for me to lose your father, she wanted to say. But it had been harder for them.

Do you know how hard I work to support us all? But they worked hard and Bernie didn't even like school, the school didn't like him and he still had to go in every day.

Do you see how fucked up I am? But they were more fucked up and she was their primary carer and she was staring at them, her face fraught and angry, looking as if she'd happily punch the shit out of them.

Bernie stared out the window, blinking rapidly, afraid to look at her. Her chin crumpled as she looked at him. The white fluff on his chin was starting to darken. His nose was suddenly too big for his face. Soon the hormones would hit harder and things would get even messier. Boarding school was the right choice. James had been right. They'd be safe in there and they'd be away from her.

She pulled out and took the turn to the narrow street that led to the school.

Sam said quietly from the back seat, 'This is hard for you, isn't it?'

She nodded.

'I won't run away, Mum,' said Bernie. 'I'm only messing with you.'

She nodded at that as well. 'You can put your earphones back in if you want.'

They both scrambled to get them on and cut her out.

Fairchurch was on a high hill overlooking London, an English idyll of small Georgian villas, whitewashed and cherished, with neat front gardens of lawns and flowers. They passed green lawns and borders of red dahlias and white lilies and messy clusters of loud pink sweet peas. The narrow high street was built for carriages and handcarts and was pockmarked with traffic-calming measures, speed bumps and give-way pockets.

They found the uniform shop easily, parking across the road next to a vertiginous village green with grand views over London and an old pub.

As she turned the engine off and they put their earphones away she unclipped her seatbelt buckle. Sam asked her nervously if she was feeling better now?

The seatbelt hissed across her chest.

'I'm fine,' she curled her hair behind her ear. Her voice was shrill, 'Absolutely fine. Bernie, could you get my handbag for me? It's in the footwell. It's by your feet.'

Bernie looked at her, his eyes brimming. 'Did I say something wrong?'

'No.'

'Because you've been acting funny for weeks and Gina won't speak to you and suddenly we're going to this school you said we'd never go to. You're not going to kill yourself, are you?'

She could hear what he wasn't saying, what he and Sam must have talked about: that maybe their father had killed himself.

Now would be the moment to admit it all, why they were here, about Charlie, about their father, what she was doing in the attic every night. She could confide in them. This might be the fulcrum of the rest of their emotional lives. But if she did they'd want to stay home with her and they wouldn't be safe.

'I'd never, ever do that. Ever.' She smiled wider and looked out of the car. 'How lovely. Isn't this lovely?'

She got out and waited on the pavement for them to get out. Then she locked the car. She knew she'd fumbled the moment. She felt deeply sad, as if she'd never be close to them again.

They walked up the steep hill to the Fairchurch School Outfitters, Claudia in front and the two boys walking close together, trailing her, further behind every time she looked.

A brass bell rang at the opening of the shop door. An attendant stepped out of the back room and bowed. He was unctuous but pleasant and explained what they would need and what was optional.

'We'll take that as well,' said Claudia.

He measured the boys' arms, legs, chests, feet, chattering all the time – here we go, let's just see. She saw him notice Bernie's chubbiness, how his trousers tucked under his belly, how his collar dug into the puppy fat on his neck.

She wanted to muscle in between them, stop the man seeing that and leave her son alone, but she made Bernie choose the trousers with the smaller waist, the size that dug in a little. It was a nag in absentia, a reminder not to eat too much. Or maybe she was trying to remind him of herself and replicate her own perpetual discomfort.

The shop assistant gathered the order into two separate tidy piles for the boys: straw hats and flannel slacks, sports kits, jackets and laundry bags, the crested socks for sports only. And yes please, she wanted both boys' items tagged with their names and school number and the two silver trunks with black trim to be filled and sent to their dorms at Bowes for the start of term.

The inside of the shop was warm and the odd-mannered man very tiring. When they finally arrived at the till and he presented Claudia with the itemised bill she flinched and hoped it didn't show. He offered her the discount that they gave to every new boy.

She froze. Should she refuse it and show that she had money or accept it and show that she had money. Did considering the implications of a discount mean that she looked poor or did it make her seem rich. She was playing a part, the part of someone who knew this world her boys were moving into, but she didn't know it or understand it at all.

'Thank you,' she said and took the discount.

This was the right answer. The man instantly warmed to her and tilled it up, let her pay and then suggested they set up a tab for the boys, for when they came to school, so that they could reorder anything they needed and she agreed to that as well.

Outside the boys said they were hungry and they went next door to an empty café. Fairchurch was a ghost town in the summer.

They ordered food and the boys ate, Sam stopping when he was full, Bernie eating his pepperoni pizza and then finishing off Sam's and the crusts from Claudia's.

She watched him overeat and thought of Charlie sitting there, armouring himself. She was scared for them.

Her phone rang and, relieved, she took it out and saw that it was Larry. She stood up and told the boys, 'I need to take this.'

Bernie looked up at her, 'Can I have another Coke?'

'Only if you have a Diet Coke,' she said, answering the phone as she walked out to the door.

A waitress at the counter glared at her.

'And ice cream?' He shouted after her, knowing how much she wanted to talk.

'Yes, yes, yes,' she said, slipping out of the door to the street. 'Mr Larry Beecham, how are you?'

'Mrs Atkins O'Sheil, how are you?'

'Very well.'

'You've called me one hundred and fifty times this morning. What is afoot?'

It was closer to four times, 'Larry, can I come and see you this afternoon? I'd like to talk to you about something a bit personal.'

It wasn't personal but she knew how to get Larry's attention.

'Oh my God, of course. Where suits you? Late luncheon? Chambers? I'm at the Old Bailey for William Stewart's arraignment at two thirty, that'll wrap up super quick.'

'Before?' she said. 'I'll come and find you. It'll take five minutes.'

'I'm agog.'

She had decided to do something potentially career-ending: she was going to tell Larry point-for-point what to refute in her streamlined forensic report. It was unprofessional and if he told anyone then she would lose her reputation and her job. But she knew Larry. He was vain. He'd be happy to take credit for all her startling insights. He wouldn't pass up the opportunity to look like a genius in a high-profile media case.

'See you there, Larry, thanks.'

She looked in the window and saw Bernie ordering something more than a Diet Coke. He was smiling up at the waitress, a woman of about her age, and the woman was smiling back and Claudia wondered how anyone managed to summon that sort of warmth. It seemed like a magic trick that she had lost the knack for.

She watched Bernie's face brighten, his eyes wide as the waitress put a bowl of strawberry ice cream down in front of him. It had a sparkler in it and an upside-down cone on it like a dunce hat. It wasn't a big or fancy ice cream and didn't warrant the fuss the waitress was making. She was savouring Bernie's delight at the silly display.

Claudia went back inside. As she approached the table Bernie glanced up guiltily, dipping his head down, ashamed.

Sam was grinning, 'Mum, look, the lady gave Bernie free ice cream.'

The sparkler burned itself out and spluttered to a stop. Claudia looked back for the waitress and found her standing behind the counter with her arms crossed, watching her with hooded, disapproving eyes. She didn't like Claudia. She made Claudia think of Gina, of James, of herself in the mirror.

She smiled warmly to spite the woman, 'Thank you,' she said.

'For him,' said the waitress quietly. She sucked the front of her teeth at her, as eloquent a put-down as Claudia had ever received. Then she turned away to wipe the clean counter top.

Claudia sat down.

'Who was on the phone?'

'Larry Beecham. He's the KC defending William Stewart. Remember when Dad was called to the bar? You know how hard KCs work?'

'Yes.'

'Well, Larry doesn't. He's a lazy pig.'

'Is he terrible?'

'No, he's actually quite brilliant.' She had them on her side for a moment, interested in a lazy man who was brilliant. To keep them on side she told them the story of William Stewart, a clean story about a terrible crime and how she was going to help solve it with her eagle eyes and calm demeanour. It was nice to think about someone else's tragedy for a change. She left it on a cliffhanger with justice bound to triumph in the end.

'But if he didn't do it, who did?' asked Sam.

'I think it's someone we don't even know about. I think it was a stranger who's left the country.'

'Why?' asked Bernie.

She started to answer but stalled.

'Maybe he's guilty?' suggested Sam.

'No blood on him. Not a drop. Impossible.'

Sam accused Bernie, then Bernie accused Claudia and they laughed as if two people dead was nothing more than a parlour game.

They would always remember today and that ice cream in the café. For that moment they were together and she was theirs, trying to entertain them, trying to connect. The drift began as soon as she paid the bill.

They went back to the car and drove along the road to the boys' house, Bowes, and she took them to the door. When it shut she turned away and felt a sudden cold clarity.

She drove back to the house in Gerald Road.

19

Claudia had been expecting them for half an hour but when they knocked on the front door she was still startled. She stood behind it and cleared her throat, straightened her shirt, stepped forward and looked through the fish-eye spy hole.

DCI Nick Heely and DI Gupta, officers she'd met at Chester Terrace. They were both in plain clothes but recognisably police because of their tidy hair and prim attire. They squinted at the gritty breeze carrying dust from the perpetual renovation works of central London. Heely smoothed his hair and stared into the spy hole as if he'd like to fight with whoever was in there, making him wait. Gupta was young and sturdy, square shouldered, her fists tight at her sides.

Claudia opened the door.

'Claudia Atkins?' asked Gupta.

'Atkins O'Sheil.' Claudia heard herself say it in the wrong tone of voice. She had meant to be honest, as if she had nothing to hide, but it came out of her mouth sounding pedantic and correcting.

Gupta looked at Heely, checking they were at the right door. Heely nodded at her. She took out her warrant card and showed it, sliding a shoulder in front of Heely to make the point that she would be doing the talking, not him.

'Can we come in?'

Claudia said of course, please do, opening the door wide to welcome them.

Gupta asked if it was a shoes-on or -off house and Claudia insisted they keep them on and come through to the kitchen.

'We're not a shoes-off kind of family,' she assured them.

'Well, you never know,' said Gupta. 'It's nice to ask.'

She led them through to the kitchen and saw that they were impressed with the lovely old house, the staircase that circled around the well at the back of the hall, the green-stained glass letting light in on the turn. They passed the door to the front room and looked in, then they came to the kitchen with long windows looking onto a neighbour's garden. It was old-fashioned. Philip's grandmother must have had the plain oak cupboards fitted around the free-standing stove, but it had been well made and cared for, the wood oiled and cleaned regularly. A big dark table sat just in front of a draughty window with six chairs around it and room for more.

Gupta's mouth was open slightly and Claudia felt she had to excuse herself.

'It's not my house. The company provides it.'

'Very nice,' said Gupta. 'I'm out in Billericay near my family. Takes forever to get into town.'

'Anyone else in the house today?' asked Heely.

'No. You might hear banging but it'll be the pipes.'

She invited them to sit down at the table, offered them tea or would they rather have coffee? They said no thanks. She knew cops didn't generally take tea or coffee when they were interviewing people in their homes but she'd hoped they might from her. It was a matter of trust. In this context though, she had gone from a fellow professional to the dread role of 'family member'. She knew how police and law-yers talked about the families, especially ones with 'theories'.

They weren't explicit about it but there was a wariness in their attitude, an othering of her. She was one of these outsiders getting under their feet.

Claudia would have expected that to bother her but she didn't care what they thought. Any lingering respect she'd had for the Met had evaporated. She was staggered at how badly Charlie's case was being investigated. She'd emailed all the information she had to the 'Officer in Charge' but the named recipient kept changing.

Then, for a week or so, no one was in charge.

She thought briefly that they were abandoning the investigation entirely. She called Maura Langston but couldn't get beyond her assistant. Philip had called her shortly afterwards and explained what she already knew: that there were legal issues that had to be sifted through and that was why there had been a hold-up. Investigating

Charlie's death as a murder meant that James's case would have to be reopened. By 'legal issues' they were investigating the possibility of them having messed up James's investigation and the likelihood of her making a complaint against them for it.

She assured them that she would not and was very keen for James's case to be reopened. Charlie was not close to his family, they were unlikely to be involved and there was no insurance policy on James. No one would sue them for doing their job and she was sympathetic: she could see how James's accident looked odd but not super suspicious. It was an easy mistake to make, she assured them.

And now Nick Heely was sitting at her kitchen table with DI Aisha Gupta.

Claudia made herself a cup of tea, put the rest of the packet of Malted Milk biscuits on a plate and set them on the table. They were unexciting biscuits but a family favourite.

'Please,' she said, fanning her hand around the plate like a master chef presenting her greatest creation. Even she thought the way she did that was odd but it was strange to have people in the house and give them nothing, not even a glass of water.

'So,' Gupta took out her notebook even though her bodycam was working. 'You saw Charles Taunton on the day he died?'

Claudia told them she was there because she'd been called as a witness in Roland Garret's case but there was a last-minute continuation and said she was already there. It wasn't really true but they sympathised. Poor notification of continuations ate up a lot of police time.

In the long hard nights after Charlie was murdered she had admitted to herself that the BSPS was not fit for purpose, Charlie was right, Kirsty was right. It was profitable, had made her reputation but she would have to admit it before someone more credible than Kirsty Parry denounced her. She was saving it for William Stewart though, to honour the memory of Charlie. She was going to gift wrap the defence case and hand it to Larry Beecham.

'And you just bumped into Mr Taunton there?'

'No, we went to see a case in Court Seven, briefly, and then we went to a café.'

'What was on in Court Seven?'

'Defence's forensic expert was doing a critique of a test I devised. We watched that and then we went for a coffee.'

She told them which coffee house it was, the vegan one, and what they had and where they sat.

'And what did you talk about?'

'Charlie was investigating a case. It was the last one my husband was defending before he died.'

'He defended a lot of fraud cases, your husband, didn't he?'

'Yeah. Money laundering. Companies asset management, that sort of thing.'

'Why was Mr Taunton investigating it? Did he think your husband had been killed?'

'I don't know. He said that James was trying to find the beneficial owner of the company he was defending, that he had found them and that was unusual. I remember Charlie used that term because I didn't know what it meant.'

'I don't either.'

'Charlie said that the named owner of the company isn't always the *beneficial* owner, they don't get the money at the end of the day. Off-shore companies operate under different laws. They can name a bartender head of a multinational oil company but actually the money's all going to, say, the head of the Nazi Party in Germany. Usually lawyers just defend cases through the named owner but, for some reason, James was trying to identify the beneficial owner, the end of the chain, the person who owned everything. You can see why that could be dangerous.'

Gupta's eyes had glazed over a little bit. Claudia sympathised but carried on.

'The company he was looking into is called RS Trusts. They're owned by a Jersey company called Viscount Court Associates and they, in turn, are owned by another company in the Cayman Islands called Tontine.'

'Wow,' said Gupta and wrote '*companies*' in her notebook. 'So, Charlie said that it was while tracing this person that James died, and then Charlie died in the same spot?'

'Yes, there.'

'In pretty much the same circumstances?'

'Yeah.'

'Charlie lived in the Cayman Islands?'

'Briefly. James went there to find out who owned all this stuff. He told Charlie about it but he didn't know who it was then.'

'If they usually deal with just the named owner, why did James care who it actually was?'

'I really don't know.'

Gupta was asking the questions but she was monitoring Heely's responses very carefully, glancing at his face, twitching when his hands moved on the table.

Heely's jaw was clenched, his leg juddering furiously under the table, his shoulders set tight by his ears. He had delegated his social skills to a female colleague but Claudia did not feel that Gupta was subordinate to him or doing anything that would make him angry. It felt as if she was asking the questions Heely wanted asked but couldn't risk asking himself.

Gupta hummed a little and listened to the house and then she asked again if there was anyone else in the house?

'There's just you and me and the ghosts,' she said.

Gupta smiled. Heely bared his teeth. Gupta asked if she could use the bathroom and Claudia said it was on the first floor but her boys had used it this morning so please excuse the mess. Gupta turned off her bodycam and walked away.

Heely waited until she was notionally out of earshot before he spoke. 'Charlie Taunton was a friend of mine.'

'I know. He said you called him about William Stewart and Chester Terrace.'

'I trusted him.'

'So did I,' said Claudia. 'I really trusted him.'

They locked eyes and she understood that Heely was asking if he could trust her too but she didn't know. She didn't know what he was asking to trust her with and because she didn't reassure him he hesitated.

'Why don't I just tell you everything I know?' she said and he relaxed a little.

So she told him about James and the case against RS Trusts, how it was just an average fraud case, they were suspected of money laundering or something like that. But the case changed James. He became paranoid. He had never investigated a case so intensely. Suddenly he wanted to send the boys away to boarding school – for their safety he said, which was weird because they both hated the idea of boarding school and he'd been and hated it and they'd just had a historic sexual abuse scandal which made it seem even less safe. Anyway, they couldn't afford it and it was quite bizarre. He was so determined they'd go that he got the boys to sit the entrance exam behind her back.

She could hear herself and knew she just sounded like a disgruntled wife. 'It was so out of character, Nick, I'm telling you, and he didn't want me to work any more.'

'He didn't want you going out of the house?'

'No,' she tried to remember what Charlie had said. 'He didn't want me working in that area.'

'Specifically in a legal context?' asked Heely.

'Very specifically. I didn't realise at the time. I thought James didn't like me working or having my own money or something. I just wish he'd explained.'

'Maybe he didn't think it was safe to explain,' Heely said.

His angry edge was gone now. He seemed a little afraid and Claudia liked him.

'Why would it not be safe?'

Heely shrugged, 'Why did two men die in the same accident on the same safe road?'

'Gov?' This was Gupta shouting from the top of the stairs. 'Have I finished washing my hands?'

'Give them another rinse, Gupta, if you don't mind.'

The bathroom door shut and Claudia heard the lock slide shut again.

So she told him about Gina and the boxes of documents from James's work, about the missing papers and how Gina had given them to Charlie that day and then he died.

'There were no papers in the car,' Heely said. 'Not one. Even Charlie's briefcase was empty when they pulled the car out of the water. He went to confront the beneficial owner on the day he died, did you know that?'

'Charlie did?'

'No, James. He left a note in his office: he'd identified his client and had been invited to meet them but he wanted to leave a note telling someone in case anything happened to him. And then it did.'

She wished she'd known that all along. It changed everything. 'Who was he meeting?'

'He didn't specify the name. Client–lawyer privilege. Charlie was looking for the name but you know he'd have blurted it out to someone half on purpose if he'd found it.'

They looked at each other, remembering Charlie.

'God,' she said. 'He was some man.'

'He really was,' smiled Heely.

'You'll never meet another. What's happening about Chester Terrace?'

She had hit a sore point. Heely's eyes registered something, fear or despair, she couldn't quite read it. He pressed his lips together and looked away, raised a shoulder. Dropped it.

'Does that answer your question?'

'Nothing happening?'

He didn't want to talk about it. 'That's about it.'

'Mary Dibden's DNA was a partial match. Did you ever look into who else the sample might match?'

He shook his head. 'Amelia, you mean? She's on the doorbell cam. She has an alibi.'

'No, she isn't. If William's alibi fails so does hers, doesn't it?'

Heely gave her a blank, belligerent stare that ended with a slow blink. He was asking her to drop it.

'Is that above your pay grade, Nick?'

'Look, you have to trust me.' His mouth twisted in a sad smile, 'It's probably above *yours*. We've got enough going on here with Charlie's crash. Let's just stick to this case.'

Gupta called again from the top of the stairs, 'How about now?'

Heely shouted back, 'Wait there, Aisha, we're coming up. Would you show us the boxes?'

So Claudia took them upstairs to the attic room, pointing out which documents on the floor came from which boxes as they packed them back up, looking for some clues to what was missing.

Gupta found some dot matrix printouts with perforations down the side, 'Woah, remember these?'

Heely smiled at it, 'I do.'

'Yeah,' smiled Claudia taking the folded paper from her hand. A string of numbers was printed on it, account details for a Luxembourg bank account in the name of the company Tontine.

Heely said they had traced Charlie's phone records and her sister was on there. They would need to speak to her about Charlie's last day because they'd been calling each other back and forth and they seemed to have met in the afternoon. Could she tell them where Gina lived? Claudia cringed as she explained where Gina was now. Gupta touched her upper arm, trying to comfort her, assuming she was ashamed about Gina being in a rehab. But it wasn't that. Claudia didn't want Gina telling them that she had broken her arm, that it hadn't healed properly because Claudia took her to the Lighthouse instead of getting her medical attention, that Gina hated her and wouldn't talk to her.

She gave them the address and asked if she could visit Gina first, to explain why they were coming.

Reluctantly they agreed but said they'd have to speak her today because, as far as they knew, Gina was the last known person to see Charlie alive.

'Of course, of course.'

They took the lids off more boxes and looked into them, showed each other things, moved boxes out of the way and looked into other boxes. Shoved them around. It was cursory. Claudia had seen more careful examinations by people picking up free furniture listed on Gumtree.

They picked three boxes with papers that they thought might be relevant and asked if they could take them away. Claudia said of course they could and Heely gave her a receipt and helped Gupta carry them downstairs.

Gupta left them alone in the hall while she went out and hailed a black cab, waving it into the street. She opened the door and put the three boxes on the floor before climbing in.

'What did you do about the school in the end?' asked Heely.

'I sent them,' she said, feeling defeated.

'Good move. They'll be safe there, he was right about that much. We don't know who's involved in this but we do know they're dangerous. Promise me one thing: you won't do any investigation into this yourself.'

Claudia assured him that nothing could be further from her mind.

'Promise me you'll be kind to my sister?'

Heely didn't answer that because he wasn't in the habit of lying. He told her to take care and tripped off down to the cab, climbing in after Gupta and shutting the door.

Gupta raised a hand at the window, waving goodbye as the cab drew away along the street.

As Claudia waved back she realised what had just happened. Gina was the common thread. She knew Charlie. She knew James. She was occasionally desperate for money.

She had just made Gina their prime suspect.

20

The lobby was overheated. Claudia stood in the visitors' queue and saw steam rising from the wet coat of the woman in front of her signing in at the desk. It was raining heavily outside, a sudden summer downpour, loud enough to bring the shoulders to the ears, as if the world was hissing at the residents of the rehab.

The decor in reception was muted: dark walls and lilac plaid chairs, an outsized hearth and boxes of paper tissues everywhere.

Bill tipped his chin at Claudia to call her forward.

'Nice to see you again.'

'You too, Billy.'

Bill was square jawed with a nose as straight as a pencil. He had overdone the lip filler this time but was treating the stretched skin with Vaseline. It looked as if he had just eaten something very greasy and hadn't had time to lick the oil off. A large TV flickered above him on silent, a sun-bleached couple in their sixties dressed for a casual church service. Subtitles ran along the bottom of the screen.

Morris and Tabitha have always wanted to live in France and now that they're retired –

Bill gave her a form to sign and she did it dutifully, handing it back over.

'They'll come for you.'

She knew her way to the visitors' waiting room next to the detox ward. It was beyond the locked doors and Billy buzzed her through. A windowless room with a grey and pink sofa and a coffee table that had never seen a coffee morning.

Waiting rooms are liminal places. Beyond the windowless walls anything was possible. The surgery had been a success or a disaster. The police were bringing charges or they were going to send you home.

A man in ripped Levis and a grey hoodie appeared at the door. 'Someone called Claudia, visiting Gina O?'

She got up and followed him down a corridor. 'You know Gina?'

'Aye.' He smiled back at her. 'Cannae pump each other in here but she says I'm on a promise.'

A shocked laugh erupted from Claudia and he laughed too. 'You're Scottish?'

'Naw, I'm fae Airdrie. We're our own thing.'

'I've heard that, aye.'

'Special.'

'Special brew.'

'Ha, I'm only kidding ye on about Gina.' Then he gave a look that suggested very strongly that he meant every word.

He was ragged but tall and finely muscled, walked like a sprinter, leading with his toes. She looked down and saw that he had the same Nike trainers that her boys had for school, expensive and new. This man either had money or was bad with what little money he got. It was a very expensive private rehab facility with few subsidised places.

He led her through to the corridor for the counselling rooms and knocked lightly on a door, grinning back at her before opening it and calling in, 'Delivery for O'Sheil.'

Then he pushed the door wider and she saw a female therapist and Gina sitting at a small table with a box of tissues in the middle, awaiting her arrival. It did not bode well.

'Hi Gina,' she said and went in.

The man said goodbye and shut the door.

'He seems nice,' she said to Gina. 'He your boyfriend?'

'No,' said Gina, sucking her teeth and looking away.

It did not look as if it was going to be a good session. Neither woman would meet her eye. She sat down.

The therapist had a long face, long brown hair and an exceptionally long top lip. The dress shirt she was wearing was unbuttoned too far, giving an alarmingly frank view of her breasts, which were also quite long. She looked as if gravity had a grudge against her.

'So, I'm Elizabeth Middleton,' she said in a breathy voice so soft and velvety that Gina and Claudia had to strain to hear her. 'As you know it is very painful for Gina to see you and we only agreed to this session because, as part of her recovery, Gina has to clear the air about her behaviour, about her character defects. She wants to make amends to you for the damage she has caused—'

Claudia held up her hand. 'Look, I know I've done wrong to her as well but I really need to talk to Gina about something. Is there any way we could put this off to another time?'

Gina shook her head, 'No. We've been working towards this, for me to make amends to you.'

'Can you make amends by listening to me?'

Middleton and Gina caught each other's eye. 'It doesn't really work like that,' said Middleton gently. 'We're here for Gina to own her behaviour and take responsibility. You'll be welcome to speak freely at the end.'

So Gina lifted a pad of paper from the table, opened it and began to read.

She was sorry for the hurt and worry that her drug taking had caused. She was sorry for her erratic behaviour and for stealing from Claudia. She was sorry for leaving the boys and going off when Claudia needed her. She was sorry for punishing Claudia and taking her own pain out on Claudia. She knew that Claudia was not responsible for Charlie dying and she wished that she hadn't said that. She was sorry for not being kinder when Claudia was grieving for James and she should have been kind to her. She was sorry. She was sorry for being jealous of Claudia and Auntie Ray, jealous that Auntie Ray was calm and emotionally stable, she was sorry for blaming her for things she was not responsible for. She hoped that Claudia could forgive her.

She was sorry. She was sorry. She was sorry.

She didn't sound like Gina at all. But what did Gina sound like? A drawling mess calling at midnight from a police station to call her a cunt and ask for money? Was that Gina? Claudia liked that Gina better, in some ways, because she was conflicted and Claudia was conflicted too. But she looked at her sister, at how calm she was, how centred. The scars on her arms had cleared up and faded. She'd had an open weeping ulcer on her inner elbow when she came in and it was healed now, dry and clean. Gina was going to get on with her life and her life didn't include messy people like Claudia.

She put the paper down and looked at Middleton. Middleton nodded her approval. They both looked at Claudia.

'Great. All is forgiven.'

This was not enough, or was too much, or did it sound sarcastic? She didn't know what she'd done wrong.

'What?'

'Well, I think Gina feels that, maybe – is it all right for me to speak for you, Gina?'

'Yes.'

'That's okay with you?'

'Fine.'

Middleton turned to Claudia and explained that Gina felt she was owed an apology for Claudia breaking her arm. It was symbolic, she felt, that her ability to make art was literally damaged by Claudia's attempt to change her. Claudia was overwhelming. She was swallowing Gina. She had no boundaries. Gina's life was swamped by the drama of Claudia's life, by her needs and the boys' lives.

'Okay.' Claudia sounded brisk, 'Well, I'm really sorry about that.'

Middleton nodded, 'Will you try to work on boundaries?'

'Yes.'

'Thank you. Gina?'

'Okay.'

Everyone nodded unhappily. They looked at Claudia.

Middleton asked, 'What was it you wanted to say to Gina?'

'Okay,' said Claudia. 'Well, thanks for apologising for all that stuff. I didn't mind most of it, I don't remember much of it and I'm sorry you feel I'm suffocating.'

Gina looked miserable, 'Everything's too dramatic with you. I can't breathe around you.'

'Well,' Middleton leaned towards her, 'that's done now. Do you have something you wanted to say to Gina?'

Claudia took a breath. She didn't want to tell them what was happening because she was bringing the drama, making the case against herself. But then she went for it.

Gina knew Charlie died in an accident, yeah? Well, it was a carbon copy of James's car accident. It happened in the same place and he was alone in the car, passenger door open, no seatbelt, massive head injury. It was suspicious and the police were going to come here today and ask Gina about it. Sorry if that was upsetting. She hadn't said any of that when she first told her that Charlie had died because she knew detoxing was rough, she could see that, but now the police were investigating both deaths as murders and they thought Gina was the last person to see Charlie before he died. They'd want to know about the papers she gave Charlie from James's files. Claudia emphasised that she hadn't told them that Gina stole the papers or that she sold them to Charlie.

She thought she was delivering a dramatic, emotive story in a monotone with no intensifiers or dramatic details about being at the roadside in the dark, seeing Charlie's body, campaigning for the police to take it seriously, none of that. She thought she was doing quite well until Middleton interrupted loudly.

'Are you making this up?'

'No,' said Gina softly, half-smiling. 'She's not. This is what it's like all the time.'

'I'm not making it up. The police are coming here today.'

Gina sat back and put her hands behind her head. 'I gave Charlie papers from the boxes but I don't know what was in them.' She sat forward, rubbing her fingers together, remembering. 'Thick paper? Formal letters, like stamped at the top with colours on it. "Letters of Incorporation" is what he asked me for.'

'And that's what you gave him?'

'Think so, yeah. It's a bit of a blur. Should I tell them that?'

'Please do, yeah, tell them the truth.'

'Thank you for sending me here,' she said, as if it was something she had really thought about. 'You've saved my life. I'm going to make it matter. I'm going to try and do some good.'

'I'm sorry I broke your arm. I didn't mean to.' She remembered the sandwich man, the sights and horrors and started to cry. She'd never tell her about that. 'Gina, will you move back in with us?'

'No.' Gina stood up. 'I cannot stay sober in your orbit.'

And Claudia, still thinking about the nameless threat of what could have happened with the sandwich man, sobbed and stood up to meet her. '*Please*? Come back, *please*?'

'No.' Gina was cold and held her eye, 'Look. As a mum you're warm but you're totally chaotic and absent. I can't watch it any more.' She slapped her chest and she was crying now too. 'And I'm, like, the fuck-up sidekick. I don't work for you, I need to be in my own life. You need to raise your own kids, teach them a value system that's worth a fuck, it's not my job.'

'But the boys would hardly even be there.'

'How?'

'They're going to boarding school.'

'You're sending them away?'

'They got in to Fairchurch. They wanted to go. And you're right, I am chaotic but I'm working on it.'

'Claudia, *we* got sent away. Look what it did to us.'

'They'll get good exam results and go to university—'

'What are they learning there? That life isn't fair and they need to make sure it stays that way?'

'They'll be safe, Gina, someone killed their dad. I don't know why or who but I need to find out and I can't keep them safe on my own.'

Elizabeth Middleton stepped between them, 'Now, I think Gina might be finding this quite intense—'

But Claudia grabbed her sister, wrapped her arms around her and hung onto her skinny shoulders. Gina smelled of cheap soap and clean water. She was wearing a soft T-shirt.

She saw herself suddenly, coming here, doing this, bringing all of this mad stuff to her sister's rehab. She felt toxic and damaging. Gina stepped away and shook her head.

Claudia nodded. 'Is that it then?'

'Yes. I'll contact you if and when I want to see you.'

'*If* and *when*?' said Claudia, picking up her bag and standing up. 'Fine. I'll just pay the fucking crippling bill for the treatment that brought you to this conclusion and fuck off then, will I?'

'Look, I'm sorry,' said Gina. 'Maybe bringing me here was an overreaction but I'm very grateful.'

She didn't remember how bad she was, how vulnerable, she didn't remember the sandwich man.

'I'll be moving into the sober living house next door and I can apply to work as a residential assistant. I'll be supporting myself.'

'Good for you. So. *If* and *when* I find out who murdered your brother-in-law and your old pal, Charlie, I'll drop you a postcard. Keep you in the fucking loop, you smug cunt.'

They were all standing up and they all knew that Claudia was wrong. She looked up at Gina and saw pity in her expression. 'Do that.'

'I have to go.'

They saw her out. Dr Middleton hung out of the room and asked her if she could find her way to the car park and she said she could. Thanks so much, for everything. Really.

She walked back to the reception and sat down heavily on the sofa.

She was alone. The boys were gone, Charlie was gone, James and Gina. It was just her now. No one needed anything from her but her earning potential and that would be severely dented after she unburdened to Larry.

She had to get to the Old Bailey in an hour. She booked an Uber. Eight minutes away. It was raining outside.

The aircon growled above her. A door slammed in the distance and someone shouted.

Seven minutes.

Billy had gone for lunch and left a plastic sign notifying anyone with a parcel to ring this bell.

The TV on the wall was showing a documentary about something royal. Race days or something.

The footage was of the procession at Royal Ascot several seasons ago. Four horse-drawn carriages seen from a long shot and respectful awe in the lingering camera shot. Her Uber was six minutes away. Claudia read the subtitles.

There they are, her Majesty, looking lovely in a summery yellow ensemble. How graceful she is, how marvellous, with the Duke of Edinburgh in his splendid top hat and tails. And there, in the second carriage, with Prince Edward and Sophie, Countess of Wessex, is the very lovely Lady Amelia Buchanan-Dibden.

Amelia's hair was tucked up under her hat and her neck was bare and long. She wore a white linen dress with tiny yellow roses appliquéd to her neckline, tumbling across her shoulder, and she was smiling.

It was only because she saw it in writing that she noticed: Lady Amelia Buchanan-Dibden.

L.B.

21

The Hawes Gallery was in a modern building tucked in tight behind Paternoster Square. It was an outlier. Most of the London galleries showing new and exciting works were further west, clustered around Mayfair, occupying grand Georgian showrooms. Claudia didn't hang out in galleries but had glanced in the windows when she was in town, aware, like everyone else, that these works were outside the scope of her wallet, on display for an audience she would never be part of.

This gallery was in a brand-new office building of concrete and cladding, the showroom straight off the street. The double windows on either side of a large steel door made it look a little soulless, as though they were ready to sell anything to anyone with money.

A slim young woman was sitting at a small desk, typing softly on a laptop. She looked up as Claudia stepped in from the street, caught her eye, waiting until the door shut and they were alone in a weighty silence.

'Hello,' said the woman in softly accented English. 'Can I help you?'

'Hello,' said Claudia, 'I'm just having a look, thanks.'

The woman nodded her into the large room and went back to her screen.

The room was very big with a hollow centre and small paintings on the plain walls. Claudia turned to the left, facing away from the desk, and looked at a grouping of pastels on canvas. They were abstracts, it seemed to be the theme of the show, blues and greys fading in intensity towards the centre. They did nothing for Claudia. She moved along, looking for Amelia Dibden's work.

She took it slow, looking at a couple of other artists' work on the wall. Many had red dots underneath the title card denoting that they had been sold; some prints had a line of red dots. The work was bland

and saleable, nothing offensive, just watered down mimicry of better artists from twenty years ago, images that could hang on a wall and not scratch the eye.

Amelia had three canvases in the show. These were nothing like the appealing still life she had seen in Philip's flat. These paintings were big, wild swirls of colour and yet they were somehow familiar. The dominant colours in the first were a deep matte black on a pale-yellow base.

'Seurat,' breathed the gallery attendant.

Claudia turned back to her, 'Sorry?'

'These are pointillist paintings. You have to let your eye rest when you are looking at them. The image is on the canvas but resolves in the viewer's eye.'

'Ah,' said Claudia as if she knew what that meant. She stepped back and suddenly saw something that made her feel sick.

Blood on a wall. She blinked. Blood on a yellow wall. Black blood hitting plaster and running down, trailing all the way down to the bottom of the canvas. Then a space. Next to that a splat of black and a trail, starting lower than the last and then another, a repeat of the pattern, down and down as far as the edge of the canvas.

Claudia felt panicked. She looked accusingly at the attendant. The woman was smiling innocently, keen to help.

'Can you tell me about this work?'

She said she could, of course she could. The artist was Lady Amelia Dibden, a young artist, recent graduate of St Martin's. Her work was already in the collections of a number of prominent collectors and galleries. Her work used to be more figurative but she had lately developed into more abstraction.

'Are these works recent?'

'Yes,' she smiled, 'done this year. Quite new. Absolutely up to date on her style. You like it?'

'Yeah. I saw her earlier work, a Dutch-Master-style still life from her degree show.'

'Ah? I don't think I've seen that. So, these are quite a change of style and temperament.'

Claudia nodded and squinted but could not unsee Francesca's

blood trail as she had turned left, her hot blood hitting the wall next to her before she realised that there had been a knife, that this was the end.

Amelia hadn't seen this in the crime scene photos. She had been there.

The next painting had more texture in the background to the black marks: vertical planes that could only just be made out but they were less tonal than textural. These black marks were short and tear-drop shaped, clustered at the top of the canvas and at the bottom. Jonty.

Swallowing uncomfortably, she stepped further back and saw the first canvas: it was an abstract portrait of the dead dog, Bixby: a huge mess of black spray in the upper right corner and a trail down to the lower left. The background was pale pink.

'From the titles of these works we can see that these are part of a substantial series of images.'

But Claudia did not think that's what Amelia meant when she chose the titles 'Seven Fifty One', 'Seven Fifty Two' and 'Seven Fifty Three'.

Those were the times on the clock when the murders happened.

22

Flanked front and back by uniformed prison guards, William Stewart shuffled down the narrow wooden gulley between the high-sided dock and press benches. Cuffed at the wrists, he was led up two steps and the guard behind him shut the little door, completing the wall around the dock. The trio sat down on a bench facing the glass wall in front of them.

Court One in the Old Bailey was confrontational by design. The judge and the accused sat higher than everyone else so that they faced each other across the room, looking over the heads of the barristers and all the court staff in the well below them.

William Stewart had been tidied up as much as a rake-thin wastrel could be. His face was thinner, cheeks sunken. He looked broken, a physical expression of a squandered life. But Larry or someone working for Larry was trying with him. His hair was buzz-cut short enough to look unstylish and he wore a black suit that neither suited nor flattered him, the kind an unambitious man might go to an interview in. It hung from his bony shoulders as if from a wire hanger and the sleeves undershot his hands, definitely one of his father's. Larry Beecham would have chosen it and she thought that maybe Larry wanted him to look pathetic, to dilute his air of entitlement and make him more sympathetic than he would be in a fancy new suit that fitted.

William kept his eyes on the floor, his shoulders rounded in front of him.

The press benches were right next to the dock. The four pews faced the judge, each with a shelf like a hymnal rest for the journalists to prop their notepads or laptops on. They were separated from the dock by the narrow wooden passageway William had entered through. The glass wall that ran all the way around the dock was partly there to stop the journalists speaking to the accused or passing them notes.

But the press benches were quiet today. Only five people were sitting there and they were all young and inexperienced. This arraignment was a dull bit of procedure that would last no more than twenty minutes. Once William entered his plea the judge would set the date for his trial to begin. This was a trailer for a very big case and, when that happened, the important journalists would take over, people with careers and reputations and their byline on the front page.

The skinny trainees looked like children from up here, not much older than Sam. They sat typing and looking around, the overload of perceiving and writing at the same time making them look slack-mouthed and vacuous.

The Clerk of Court, seated below the judge's bench, sorted through her papers and chatted to her nearest colleague as they waited for the judge.

As an expert witness in the case Claudia was entitled to sit in the body of the court but she had arrived too late for admission and went upstairs instead. She wasn't alone there. A smattering of members of the public sat together at the front of the gallery. They seemed like law students, with their good skin and smart-casual clothes, and an older woman was quietly explaining to them who everyone in the court was.

None of William's family were watching, there were no friends or supporters up here. Charlie would have stacked these benches even for a cursory hearing like today's. He knew visuals mattered.

William looked around the room, at the clerk consulting her screen, at the lawyers on the benches. Finally, he looked up at the public gallery and spotted Claudia.

He observed her, expressionless, as coldly as the journalists on the press benches were observing him. One young journalist followed his eye, looking up at her, and the people in the public gallery turned around to look but found no one of any interest, just a woman, possibly Italian, dressed in black, watching.

She nodded a hello and William nodded back, giving her a confused little smile as if he couldn't place her.

The court was called to please rise.

William stumbled to his feet, eyes wide, a sudden espresso shot of adrenalin ripping through him. The rest of the court, personnel and press and public, stood up.

Claudia wasn't usually here for this part. She generally came in for the trial and stayed in the witness room, reading through her notes and checking her teeth for lipstick. Witnesses, even expert witnesses, were not permitted to watch trial proceedings before they gave evidence in case they were swayed by something they heard.

With great solemn dignity, the judge walked along the wooden platform and took his seat. Everyone sat down.

The judge, in his powdered wig and gown, glanced up and sagged a little. He turned on his computer screen and read the screen. His wig was off centre. He looked like an exhausted actor trapped in a long-running role. He used a mouse to click on something on the screen. He let go of the mouse. He looked up at the clerk and nodded at her to proceed.

The clerk stood and looked over at William.

Flanking him, the security guards signalled for him to stand and he did, nervously resting his hands on the brass rail. The clerk cleared her throat, straightened her papers and, in a clear, emotionless voice with perfect diction, she read out the charges against him.

First degree murder. First degree murder. Attempted perversion of justice. Threatening a witness. The journalists tapped furiously as she asked William how he pled to the first charge.

William looked at Larry. Larry nodded encouragingly. William lifted his chin and spoke in a soft voice: 'Guilty.'

Next charge: 'Guilty.'

Next charge: 'Guilty.'

Next charge: 'Guilty.'

The room convulsed. The young journalists sat to attention, mouths open, fingers twitching fast on keyboards, their eyes skittering from William to Larry to the public gallery to the clerk.

One of the journalists turned to his neighbour and smiled openmouthed. They were not meant to get this story, it was meant for their betters.

The law students bridled, their guide struck dumb by the moment. Even they understood what was happening.

Claudia squeezed the back of the seat in front of her, digging her nails into the oak, watching the back of Larry Beecham's head for a sign that he was going to intervene. But he wasn't. He watched William, nodding along as if William was a child in a school play he had rehearsed lines with: guilty, guilty, guilty, guilty.

No one moved. A breathless pause gripped the room.

William Stewart had admitted to the murders at Chester Terrace. He'd admitted to killing his father and his fiancée, he'd admitted to lying about the doorcam footage and trying to intimidate Amelia to lie about it.

The judge announced languidly that he would grant no continuation in the case and sentencing would be immediate.

One of the young journalists gasped so loudly that they could just hear it in the public gallery.

The judge shot him a disgusted blink, watched him for a moment until the young man dropped his head in supplication. The judge continued: an agreed narrative of the case would go into the records and be available this afternoon but, having taken into consideration the social work reports and the risk assessment carried out over the past few months, and the reduction of sentence at such an early stage in the proceedings, the sentence was to be two life terms to run concurrently for a minimum of twenty years with a further two years and eight months for the two lesser charges, again to run concurrently.

Then the judge thanked everybody for their fine and timely work, got up and left. The door slammed shut behind him.

William Stewart was on the move too, shuffling down the stairs, a guard in front, a guard behind, and then he was lost to sight behind the wall. An unseen door slammed shut and it was over.

The clerk nodded sadly to everyone around the table and they began gathering their stuff. The journalists watched, stunned, as the court staff fell out of character, chatting and waving to each other across the room.

The journalists were delighted at being present at the unexpected finale. The case that had everything: money, blood, drugs, powerful people brought low. The expected not-guilty plea was the only reason they had been sent. It was Christmas in July. One of them slapped his laptop shut, grabbed his pens and scrambled for the door. Others followed him, racing to get their stories in.

Slowly, Claudia gathered her belongings and stood, reluctant to leave, unable to believe what she had just witnessed.

Larry Beecham looked up at her and pointed to the exit of the public gallery. He mouthed, 'Wait? Wait outside.'

She was too late. She had been so curious about Amelia Dibden, so sure she had enough time, and so certain she could manage Larry, that she was far too late. She should have admitted her mistakes on the phone, in a letter, but her vanity wouldn't allow her. She had come here thinking she would be a martyr and admit her mistakes. But she was too late. Because of her William had two life terms.

Claudia took the steep stairs up to the door and waited in the shabby corridor, watching the law students leave, chatting excitedly, asking questions of the woman who was explaining everything. No, she said, that was the end of the case, that was the last hearing there would be, he pled guilty so no, there would be no appeal.

He'd admitted to it all.

Larry Beecham hung out of a side door and waved like a child on a roundabout. 'Hello!' he said. 'Sorry I missed you beforehand.'

She walked down to him. He let her into the back corridor. It was part of the court, plastered grey with a wooden bench sitting along a wall.

'You didn't miss me, Larry, I got here late. I got distracted.'

'Well, so nice to see you up there with Joe Public. Let's sit,' his smile evaporated abruptly when he saw the expression on her face. 'What?'

Claudia fell onto the bench, 'Why the fuck did you let him plead guilty?'

He was taken aback, 'Because he's guilty as fuck. It was his choice to plead guilty.'

'To *everything*?'

Larry sat down and thought about it. 'More or less. Why are you surprised? Your scale said he did it. He knew he was going to be found guilty as fuck. At least this way he gets a sentence reduction. It was your scale that swung it.'

'Charlie was going to fight the BSPS. Point by point, he was going to fight it.'

'Oh, of course: Charlie. So sad.' Larry took hold of her hand and looked her in the eye, concerned for her, 'But Claudia, remember this: Charlie Taunton was a nutter. And I say that as a man who has been hospitalised with depression. Charlie was bonkers. William did it and he deserves to go to prison and he knows he does. End of.'

'End of?'

'End of.'

He stood up and she stood up. He held her shoulders and tried another smile.

'Clauds: lunch soon?'

She said oh yes, yes, lunch soon, she'd call him soon and Larry walked away. She watched him saunter off down the corridor, his black gown swaying side to side, off to submit his expenses, the laziest man she knew.

William may have wanted to plead guilty but Larry should have challenged him. He had not seen the healed scars on William's arms and chest, he wouldn't recognise that his client had a compulsion to hurt and harm himself, to side with the world against himself. And William had no money. Larry had no motive to question William or explore the BSPS or ask if the whole case was flawed. Charlie was dead and no one would bother now.

There was only her.

23

George Farrell was sitting at an outside table in Caffè Nero next to a busy road in King's Cross. They weren't far from the current scene he was managing, an assault in a night-club toilet, multiple actors, one dead on arrival at hospital. The traffic was busy, interwoven with mopeds and cycles. A van farther down was parked in the cycle lane and everyone was having to take their chances in the slow-moving stream of cars and buses. Pedestrians bustled by, coming from or on their way to the Tube or the train.

George had bought her a pint of nice, strong tea and she had brought him two large pouches of Golden Virginia rolling tobacco coloured yellow and black with dire health warnings and matching shock-tactic photos of a wizened tar-bound human lung lying on a steel autopsy table.

George looked at them, 'Well, that's fantastic. There's a TikTok superstition that if you get the same health warning on consecutive packets it means you're going to win money that day.'

She grinned and sat down. 'Nice to see you – that's me keeping in with you for a share of your soon-to-be riches.'

'Your tea's getting cold.' He took out his tin and offered her a rollie, 'I can't stay long. I've left a forensic science graduate in charge and he's a bit rigid with access to the scene. If anyone left a glove in there and tries to go back for it he might have them hog-tied, hooded and in a car boot by the time I get back.'

She lit her cigarette, 'Overly keen?'

'Could say. Watches too much TV. Actually brought a torch with him on the first day. He's good though.'

'I was just at William Stewart's plea hearing.'

'Oh yeah?'

'He pled guilty.'

'I know.' He looked away. 'I heard that.'

She couldn't take much more today, 'Fucking hell!'

He looked tired, 'I know.'

'He gave that plea because my BSPS came out at 92 per cent.'

George leaned forward across the table and examined her face. He could see how upset she was and touched the back of her hand with his fingertips. It was the George equivalent of a warm hug. 'We're all doing our best here, kid.'

'Are we just giving them excuses to do what they want, George? Is it all a load of shite? Roland fucking Garret got twenty-five years. William Stewart's fucked. I don't think the BSPS is worth a tuppenny damn any more but the Ethics Committee is going to make it the gold standard in forensic testing. What should I do?'

'Hm mh, hmm.' George took a long draw on his cigarette as he held her eye. He exhaled and sucked a tut in through his teeth, whistled, hummed, then he smiled at her. 'Hope that clears things up.'

She tore the lid off her tea, 'What does that mean?'

'Yes.'

'What?'

He leaned in, 'D'you know why I left teaching?'

She didn't.

'I didn't want to leave. I was chased out of that job because I told the Ofsted Inspector that our headmaster was shagging the deputy and skimming the budget. And I said he's never in. And he's a lazy git. I'm doing all his paperwork. And they said *thanks, mate* but what they meant was *you'll never teach again, mate*. I loved that job. I was good at it. But my contract wasn't extended and then they got rid of me. There was an invisible black mark on my file, I was awkward. Couldn't even land an interview. Couldn't even get a maternity cover job and they'll take a fart in socks for that. I should have fido'd.'

George's eyes were red and damp and sad as he turned his cup around and around on the table.

'What does 'fido'd' mean?'

'F.I.D.O.: Forget it, drive on.'

They'd never had a frank conversation before. She didn't really know how to handle it so she nodded and said nothing.

'What I mean is this: don't run straight at them. They can see you coming and they're ready. And never say anything that can be quoted. If they can't quote you they can't sack you. See what I'm saying?'

'You don't have to say anything if you don't want to, George, I understand.'

He looked at her, 'About what?'

'William Stewart.'

His eyebrows bobbed another prompt, 'Try again.'

'Ninety-two per cent?'

'Try again.'

'The BSPS?'

He held up a finger, 'I'm *not* going to tell what I think about that. Ever. Not going to tell you about the science moving on or your numbers being so convincing that they're getting used for cases where they shouldn't. If this comes up again, this convo, I'll deny saying anything. Understand?'

'I do.'

'I won't say anything. Remember Camden Council's CCTV coverage?'

'Of where?'

'Chester Terrace.'

She had to think back to her Streamlined Forensic report. 'No sightings of William Stewart that night?'

'Yeah. Well, the neighbours four doors down came back from Dubai a couple of weeks later. Had their own cameras on the lane at the back. Their security camera caught someone looking a lot like Amelia Dibden walking out of their back door just as we pulled up outside number twenty-nine. She must have walked along the roof and got into their empty house, walked down the stairs, and left out the back as calm as you like. She knew how to get in, that they were away, all of that.'

They looked at each other.

Claudia had breathed in a lungful of smoke and found she couldn't breathe out for a moment. Finally she spoke. 'Does that footage still exist?'

'Yeah. They're at number twenty-six. Nice couple. Go ask them.'

'Why didn't the Met tell Larry Beecham that?'

'They must have. Discovery. They're legally bound to show him the evidence they have.'

'But Larry just let him plead guilty. Why would he do that?'

George shook his head. 'Did he mention it? Did he read everything? He has to submit the plea his client wants to anyway, doesn't he? He might have known but did he tell his client? No way of knowing.'

Claudia sat back. 'If Amelia killed them why did she try to give William an alibi?'

'Did she? You know, we didn't call in that doorcam footage. She couldn't wait to send it in. He hadn't even been charged yet. I heard she nearly shit herself when they went back and asked to see the time settings. She wasn't giving him an alibi, she was giving herself one. You don't seem surprised to hear any of this.'

'I wondered about the fragments of DNA. The cops don't always differentiate between fragments and partials. A frag is Mary but we can't prove it. A partial is who shares her DNA.'

'Like ancestry DNA in cold cases.'

'Yeah.'

George shook his head, '*Why* would she do it though?'

'Don't know. She's not what she seems. Lot of secrets in that family. I think she's been fucking Philip Ardmore all this time.'

'Has she?' He wasn't shocked but he wasn't saying anything quotable. 'Did he tell you that?'

'Quite the opposite. He used to hint at it, as if he might tell me one day, but now he's actively lying.'

Claudia had worked it out and Philip was even smarter than her. He was almost certainly either turning a blind eye or actively covering up for Amelia. She could be blackmailing him. Having a relationship with his stepdaughter would ruin his reputation and that mattered to Philip very much.

'Well,' said George, 'she's off scot-free.'

'I have to do something. What should I do? Could I have a private word with Maura about this?'

'Too late for Maura, she's face down in the water and doesn't know it yet.'

She knew he was right. 'Could I speak to Nick Heely?'

George shrugged vaguely and shut his tobacco pouch. He didn't want to talk about this any more. He checked his watch and gathered up his lighter and cigarettes, 'Heely won't touch it now they've got a conviction and a guilty plea. They're not exactly having an internal inquiry to work out what went wrong. He's not stupid. He's not nasty but he's practical. He does his job as well as he can. He makes mistakes. Sometimes he even notices.'

She sighed, 'That's depressing. He's not going to do anything about Charlie Taunton's death either.'

'Of course he isn't. Langston has given him that to fuck him up, he knows that. Is he gathering evidence?'

'Yeah.'

George laughed bitterly and she saw suddenly that the three boxes he and Gupta had taken away would never resurface from wherever they put them.

'Oh,' she said. 'Oh fuck.'

'Yeah, welcome to real life. Try not to get caught.'

She pushed the tobacco pouches over to George. He tried to give her one of them back but she said two lung cancer pouches in a row was almost more luck than she could handle.

He looked down at her, her hands curled around the paper cup, feeling small and defeated and tricked.

'Don't talk to anyone else about this,' he said, patting her shoulder. 'There's nothing you can do. You lost. Fido.'

'Yeah,' Claudia sipped her tea. 'Cheers, George.'

'Take care of yourself, kid.'

18:54

Sir Evan Evans had Claudia trapped in a side corridor. He was acting strangely, uncharacteristically serious. Usually, he was just an amiable buffoon, a haw-hawing bore, a clown that everyone envied for his money and position but no one wanted to talk to. But he was solemn now. His ice-blue eyes, whites tinged yellow with a touch of jaundice, were trained on her and he was telling her that James had been in the Albemarle Club on the night he died in the car crash at Horsenden Hill.

The cold from outside was creeping in at ankle height, despite the roaring patio heaters. The January sun had set and the party was winding down, people clutched their jackets closed, clustering together as they filtered into the building, getting in position for the auditorium doors to open.

Claudia was almost inaudible in the rising burble of the crowd making their way inside. 'Was James there to meet you?'

'No, I wasn't there, dear, I was holidaying in Switzerland.' He remembered himself, pulled the hawhaw mask back on. 'Monkey gland injections keep me spritely.' He laughed joylessly, his eyes still serious and steady. 'When you come in this evening you'll have to sign the visitors' book, just as James did.'

'Visitors' book?'

'Hm. Famous. Historic. The names in there . . . Lord Byron, Carnarvon, the previous Lord Mosley, Ribbentrop . . . Of course, they can't rip out a page, it's an historic archive. Can't alter the visitors' book but they're all in there. No guest can enter unless they sign in. James signed the visitors' book.'

Evans took out his phone and opened it to an image in his photo library. 'Would you like to see?' He handed her the phone.

Judging from the shadowy focus and jaunty framing, the photo had been taken surreptitiously.

The guest book was large and heavy, leather bound with ruled pages of pale green paper, red-margined into four equal columns. She saw the column headings written out in a beautiful longhand at the top of the page:

Name   *Member Visiting*   *Date and Time IN*   *Date and Time OUT*

James's signature was near the top of the page. His handwriting was so familiar, she found herself tearful at the sight of it, this tiny relic, proof that he had existed, once.

She wanted to kiss the face of the phone but instead she read along the page.

James Atkins   Philip Ardmore   14ᵗʰ September 3pm.   ----

It was the day James died. The last column was left empty.

'He didn't sign out?'

'Left in a hurry.' Evan Evans took the phone back and pocketed it. 'They had rather a falling out, I heard.'

He presented himself as a fool but Sir Evan Evans knew exactly what he was doing. He had been trying to tell her this for a year but she was so poisoned towards him that she wouldn't listen.

'Thank you,' she squeezed his hand to show that she understood.

'I loved James. I loved his papa. The Atkinses were as sweet to me as any couple I ever knew.'

'I never knew them. They'd passed away before I met James.'

'They were very nice people. Kind. Decent people.'

Claudia could hardly breathe in.

Sir Evan Evans looked at her, his expression pitying but kind. He blinked but when his eyes opened he was full buffoon again.

'They can't change the pages, even the one with Mosley Senior on it.' He let his mouth fall open and said, 'Ha ha ha ha ha.'

There was a whole language in his hollow laughter and she could hear the words now that she was listening: he was saying that he was grieving for James too and he saw her struggle and he knew how hard it was.

'Ha ha ha ha ha,' echoed Claudia flatly.

A voice from the overhead intercom announced that everyone was invited to take their seats in the auditorium where the first Ardmore Inaugural Address was due to begin in just a few minutes.

Around the corner the doors were opened to the auditorium and the queue began to form.

Evan Evans nodded and hawhawed as he turned away and made his way through the gathering to the bathroom.

James had gone to meet Philip on the day he died and he'd left so angry that he didn't sign out. It was a confrontation. The meeting could have been a meaningless detail but for one thing: Philip had never mentioned it.

She looked up and saw him outside, listening to an unseen speaker, agreeably nodding as he looked back at her. He raised a hand to tell her he would come to her, wait there, one minute.

Philip had given her one of his precious guest invitations to the Albemarle that evening, knowing that she would have to sign the visitors' book, knowing the risk, that she might see James's signature if she just turned back a page or the porter on the desk offered to show her the historic signatures. But that would be after this talk, delivered to their peers, on this evening that would affirm his position and her loyalty to it. The trap had been set for her and, step by step, she was walking into it.

He must have known there was always a danger that she'd fit the pieces together and tell someone. This evening was his insurance against that. He was setting her up, a public display of her faith and fealty, before she found out, a seal on her loyalty, binding her to him. He did it with all his favours, giving her the house, the places at Fairchurch, even the clinical directorship.

But asking her to speak tonight was shutting the trap door.

Claudia wasn't even nervous any more. She was so angry she felt cold. She was certain that this was the right thing to do. Nothing would stop her.

Philip was coming towards her and she walked to meet him, smiling as she joined Larry and Amelia and Maura and Rob, all standing together listening as Kirsty ranted at them.

'Who drew up the guest list for this? Who invited me?' demanded Kirsty, touching her hair to make sure it was still nice and flat.

'Rob, you did the invites, didn't you?' said Larry.

Philip joined them and smiled at Claudia, 'Ready to go in?'

'Who the hell invited me?' Everyone looked at Kirsty as she sing-songed accusingly, '*Anyone?* Hello?'

Philip slipped across to Claudia and cupped her elbow, guiding her out of the circle, 'We have to get to the side of the stage now. We need our mics on.'

'ANYONE?'

Kirsty was not letting it go.

Rob stepped forward. 'I sent out the invitations.'

'Well,' Kirsty was surprised. 'Who told you to invite me, Rob?'

Rob raised an arm. For just a moment, everyone looked at his huge, square hand rising up in the middle of them, wondering. Was he going to hit Kirsty? Was he going to reach up and pull the ceiling down?

He did neither. His fingers curled back into his palm, all but the index finger, and he pointed at Philip. 'He asked me to put you on the list. He reserved a seat for you in the front row.'

Philip's cheeks flushed. He didn't want them to know that but Rob was there, standing right in front of him and he was enormous, had been violent for a living, and was not a man to contradict.

Kirsty Parry, true to form, said the thing everyone else was thinking, 'That's a hell of a surprise to spring on O'Sheil. I mean, everyone knows we're rivals.'

Sir Philip Ardmore looked down at them both, a thousand calculations running through his brilliant blue eyes. He chewed his cheek. 'Oh dear,' he said, which might have meant anything. 'A bit of confusion.'

Claudia looked at Philip and suddenly saw his posture mirroring Amelia. They were standing together, a handsome couple. They were slim and tall and matching, Philip and L.B. looking at the world with a joint line of vision. Philip saw her look at them and his eyes widened just a fraction, as if he saw that she knew that they were together and Larry, poor sweet lazy Larry, was their cover.

'Mix up. We can sort this out at supper,' said Philip and led Claudia away down the corridor, through a heavy fire door, and into the bare back corridor.

A man in a red T-shirt waved at them to come down to him. They walked over and Claudia smiled happily up at Philip, giving him no cause for concern.

But Philip knew something was wrong so she asked him again, 'Why did you invite Kirsty, Philip?'

'I thought Rob had.'

It was a blatant lie, a test, a bigger question altogether. He was asking if he could trust her to see this lie through.

'Maybe he did.'

He nodded. 'Yes, she's an odd little woman.'

'She certainly is,' said Claudia as she turned down the corridor towards the tech, hurrying through the door to the stage side. Philip followed her.

The tech in the red T-shirt was standing at the mixing desk. He introduced himself as Dave the Sound Man, and showed them to a table with two remote mics laid out on it. The sound packs were the size of a flip phone, each attached to a peach-coloured wire headset shaped to go over the ears like backward glasses with a mic arm that reached around to the mouth.

She watched Philip's face as Dave fitted a mic on him. His forehead was damp. There was a spark of fear in his eyes. She liked that.

Dave fitted her mic on the back of her head behind her ears and showed them where the 'on' switch was on their packs and then fitted the packs into their pockets.

He told them that they had a few minutes to go before Lord Philip would go on and do the introductions. Just let everyone settle into their seats first, yeah?

'Yes,' said Lord Philip, sounding as if he was correcting Dave's grammar.

They had three minutes. Dave went back to the sound desk and left them alone.

Philip looked at her, 'Are you all right, Claudia?'

She looked back at him, 'Honestly, I'm a bit nervous. That meeting with Kirsty was so uncomfortable.'

'You know why I asked you to give this speech?'

'Of course.'

They looked at each other, neither giving anything away.

He said, 'We can't have anything go wrong, can we?'

'Really, don't worry, I'm a tiny bit nervous but I'll be fine.' She squeezed her documents folder. Philip looked at it. He looked at her.

'No.' Philip reached around to the back of his head and pulled his mic set off. 'This has gone far enough. I'm calling this off.'

24

Deep in the thin woods of north-west London, down a long and winding road, Claudia was sitting on a hard wooden chair.

Charlie's coffin was on a roller bed with blue velvet curtains hanging from a motorised track, waiting to be drawn around him. On the floor in front of it sat a small Bluetooth speaker the size of a Coke can. Someone had neglected to turn off the disco lights option and a lazy ooze of changing colours spilled along the floor, keeping time with Pachelbel's Canon in D.

The slow music sounded simultaneously virtuosic and like a child practising scales. It was sad and happy, calm and frantic, speaking to the ineffable indignities of life and the inevitability of endings.

This was the smallest room at the crematorium complex with seats for just thirty, a shallow rectangle of wood-lined walls and mottled glass windows. To the right an open double door looked out on a carport where mourners could be dropped off and picked up.

Claudia was alone in the last row.

The row in front of her was taken up with Charlie's friends from the Cayman Islands. These people were sun-bleached, dressed in bright colours under heavy coats, as if September in Ruislip was Moscow in March. She'd overheard them talking. They'd come back in someone's Learjet but were going to be stuck in bloody England overnight now because the pilot had a mandatory rest period of ten hours, which was ridiculous.

In front of them were lawyers, successful men in expensive suits, bellies battling buttons, jolly boys all. They were alert, chatting cheerfully, watching the door for old friends. Tweedledum and Tweedledumber were there, moving as one, sitting close.

Taking up the very front row were what seemed to be Charlie's relatives. They were a military family, upright men in dark dress uniform, white belted, hats tucked neatly under their arms, and their tidy, featureless wives.

None of the school friends from Jonty Stewart's service had turned up. Philip wasn't there. There would be no school songs at Charlie's send-off.

Claudia reached down into her bag and checked her emails on her phone. Nothing. She was waiting for a search result from Companies House. A financial history for ForSci. She hoped they didn't send it to Rob first or address it to the company. It was due in today.

A car drew up outside and the room darkened. The sound of a car door slamming shut was followed by Gina appearing in the doorway. Her face was obscured behind big round sunglasses and her black dress was cut indecently low for a funeral. She looked at the coffin, at the front row, at the second, at the third and, seeing Claudia, sashayed across the front of the room, down the side aisle and sat next to her. She sighed and held her lumpy right arm in her left like a broken umbrella.

'Still hurts.'

'Sorry.'

'Place is a cunt to get to.'

The Cayman Islanders heard her and one man turned around to look her up and down. 'You Gina?'

'You boys the Cayman crew?'

He nodded and smiled and turned away. No one had acknowledged Claudia when she came in but they'd heard of Gina and she'd heard of them. It was nice.

Gina took her glasses off. She had a lot of eyeliner on. She looked fantastic.

'Shipped the boys off to paedo island yet?'

'Drop it.'

Gina shook her head but reached over for Claudia's hand and held it, looking away from her, loving and hating her at the same time.

She was doing well and staying sober but still refusing to see Claudia. Claudia had to accept that but she missed her all the time.

'Seen the article?'

'Which one?'

'The first one.'

'What do you think, Gina, I live in a cave? Of course I've seen it.'

Events had moved apace since William Stewart's conviction. An article about the murders at Chester Terrace had appeared in a New York magazine and went viral. Soon there were articles about why the article had gone so viral, why true crime was hot right now and, inevitably, what was wrong with young people today. Old interviews with William Stewart were republished and now a film about the case was being made with fading film star Jessica Ronay playing Claudia.

'Ronay is too tall to play you.'

'Yeah, and good looking.'

'And rich.'

'And thin. But what we do have in common is our long marriage to Bruce Willis and being nepo babies.'

'That's right,' Gina warmed to the game, 'and Ronay's had a load of work done on her face.'

'Well,' Claudia flattened the back of her hand to her double chin, 'we have that in common because I need a lot of work done too.'

It was like the old days, their mutual sensibility, thin jokes curling around each other like puppies tumbling over each other in a box. But they couldn't go back. Gina wouldn't go back. They looked at Charlie's coffin and both began to weep.

'Fucking hell, Charlie.'

Claudia dried her face with a hankie. 'Charlie.'

Gina slapped the tears from her cheeks, her make-up miraculously unmoved.

'The cops asked about the certificates of incorporation again.'

'They came to see you again?'

She nodded heavily at her knees. 'They tried to be nice about it but the suggestion was that he'd be alive if I hadn't given the documents to him.' Her intonation rose at the end in a question and Claudia didn't hesitate.

'That's a hundred per cent bullshit. Whoever killed him killed him. If I'd stayed with him that day instead of storming off in a huff and going off for a stupid fancy lunch he'd be alive. If a parking attendant had his car towed he'd be alive. He came back from Cayman to find those documents. You were just one of the ways he tried to get them.'

'What about the cops?'

'They're doing nothing. They don't fucking care. It's up to me.'

Gina was staring at the side of Claudia's face, drinking in the sight of her. She had been carrying a terrible weight around and now with every exhale she seemed to shrink a little. Claudia couldn't look back at her. She didn't trust herself not to cry and cause a drama. She squeezed her little sister's left hand but Gina pulled away.

'I'm going to find the fucker that did it. I'm going to bring them down. I'm going to tell you and you're going to come and stand by my side while I kick their face in.'

'Nah,' Gina nodded sadly. 'We're done, hon.'

Claudia looked at her sister and knew she meant it. There was no point in disputing it. They had tried so hard but they were done.

The doorway darkened again.

A black taxi had pulled up outside, a Hackney cab. The passenger door slid back on unoiled runners and filled the room with a high metallic screech.

The fare for a city cab all the way out here from London would be exorbitant. Everyone turned to see who it was and were rewarded by the sight of a very beautiful woman in a black cashmere coat, her straight ash-blonde hair framing her slim shoulders like ermine on a cloak. It was Amelia Dibden.

Regal, young and tall, Amelia stepped into the room and looked, first at Charlie's family, then the lawyers, then the ragged Cayman Islanders, richer than the rest but dressed like beach bums. Finally, she saw Claudia and her face brightened. She walked across the room, every eye trailing her, and sat down next to Gina.

'Hello again,' she whispered, leaning forward to shake Claudia's hand. 'Thanks for letting me know about this.'

'Of course,' said Claudia, astonished that she had come, wondering why she was here.

She had used Charlie's service as an excuse to get Amelia's contact details from Larry Beecham and approach her. She had been trying and failing to forget about Chester Terrace. She couldn't let it go. She'd been stalking Amelia on social media, her own and other people's. She was obsessed with her being out here in the world, painting records of her deeds and putting them on show, going to parties and weddings, conspicuously never pictured with Philip.

'I'm surprised you came all this way though. I didn't think you knew Charlie all that well.'

'Oh, no,' she gave her knees a cold smile, 'Charlie was so kind to William though.'

'He was kind.'

'Larry Beecham wasn't as good to him, not like Charlie.'

'Yeah, Larry's . . . not Charlie.'

Amelia smiled. 'Handsome, though.'

It was an odd thing to say. Larry wasn't especially handsome. He was bland and emotionally blank because of his medication. He was ordinary and Amelia was extraordinary. 'We're actually kind of dating. Meeting for lunch after this, later. He's such fun.'

It was an odd way to describe someone battling depression. It sounded like someone else entirely. Claudia tried to think of something positive to say. 'He did his best for William, I think.'

Amelia held out her hand to Gina and introduced herself. Gina looked at the hand, sneered and nodded.

They sat quietly for a moment. Claudia hadn't anticipated the two of them meeting. She didn't quite know who was in more danger.

The lawyers in front of them were giggling about something, shoulders bobbing silently. One of the Cayman Islanders had nodded off and was snuffling as his chin bobbed on his chest. Amelia reached into her handbag for a handy pack of disposable tissues and sat, holding them loosely with two hands, waiting for a chance to offer them. Claudia leaned behind Gina and whispered, 'I saw a painting of yours.'

Amelia looked up, eyes wide with alarm or excitement or both, 'Yeah?'

She was wondering whether Claudia meant the blood spatter painting. It excited her.

'Yeah. The one with the iPhone and Fruit Pastilles. Oh, I loved it.'

It took a moment for Amelia to remember that one, 'From my degree show?'

'Yeah. Your stepdad had it in his flat.'

Amelia shook her head a little, 'Oh no, Philip, well, he's not really my stepfather.'

'Oh?'

'I'd left home by the time they met.' She kept her eyes down.

'He said you introduced Francesca to Jonty Stewart?'

Amelia's cheek twitched anxiously at the mention of Jonty so Claudia said it again, 'Jonty and Philip were quite close, weren't they?'

Amelia shook her head, less a negative than a rhythmic back and forth. 'I don't know . . .'

'Well, he was the one who bought Jonty the dog, wasn't he? The guard dog? He was a good friend.'

She kept her eyes down, 'I suppose so,' she said, a slight blush on her cheeks. 'A good friend.'

Claudia watched her face and knew then that Amelia and Philip loved each other. Poor Mary. No wonder she moved abroad. Poor Larry Beecham, so numbed and passive he was the perfect place to hide. And she wondered again why Amelia was here at all. Did she think it would look suspicious if she didn't come? Or was she here for the same reason that she had done the paintings and put them on public show. She was gloating. She had taken a gamble and won but she couldn't crow openly.

'You a painter?' asked Gina.

Amelia sat tall, responding to the change of subject. 'Yes, St Martin's. Seems a lifetime ago now.'

Gina said, 'I was at GSA.'

She looked at Gina. 'You did fine art?'

Gina nodded vaguely. Claudia compensated for her, 'She did fine art, yeah.'

'Oh, Glasgow's such a great school. I had friends who went there.' Amelia tried to catch Gina's eye, keen to engage.

'Yeah,' Gina sucked her teeth. 'I remember a big bunch of rich twats sucking the oxygen out of the place.'

A momentary spark of anger flashed in Amelia's eyes. She blinked and when she opened them her expression was soft and passive. 'And are you still working?'

Gina turned her head to Amelia like a haunted doll coming to life. She growled: 'No. Why? Are *you*?'

Amelia looked a little scared, 'Yeah, I'm only asking because we have studios available at Westbourne and you might like to come and view them.'

Gina twitched with undisguised disgust, 'How much is that? Five fucking grand a month? Who's got that sort of money? I hate you rich cunts and your mimetic culture.'

'Oh,' Amelia had been trying to be pleasant and wasn't expecting that. Her chin twitched as if she was about to cry but her eyes were dry. 'Sorry.'

Claudia intervened, 'Gina, you can't blame her for the entire class system.'

'No, that's . . . she's right, studios are much too expensive,' said Amelia.

Gina put her sunglasses back on.

It was interesting to watch the effect Gina was having on Amelia. While Amelia's body said sorry there was a shimmer in her expression, a turn of her top lip, a shallowing of her breath as her lips drew back, exposing her teeth like a dog about to bite. Amelia was a moment away from losing control. But then she took a breath and smeared a smile across her face and the murderous mood was hidden behind a thin veil.

Amelia was a gambler. She had come here quite brazenly to face Claudia again, putting herself in needless danger because she knew they could not touch her. William pled guilty. It didn't matter what they knew. Evidence was unimportant.

Claudia had doubted the evidence of her eyes, the paintings, the potential DNA match, the CCTV, but she didn't now. She knew who Amelia was and what she was capable of. Amelia blinked and turned away and Claudia found her heart racing in her chest. Amelia found it thrilling to be here, near Claudia, to blatantly get away with it. She was here to relive her triumph.

Quite suddenly the congregation stood up and turned to watch a short man processing solemnly from the back of the hall. He walked as if his left hip was determined to dance, twisting his left foot a quarter inch with each step. Dressed in a dark shirt and slacks, he carried a plastic binder, stepped onto the rostrum and turned to face them, put a hand on Charlie's coffin and sighed. Then he slut-dropped down to turn the speaker off in the middle of a bar of music.

Bobbing back up, he opened his binder and a sheet fell out, sliding down to the ground in front of him. He smiled nervously.

Two of the lawyers giggled.

'I've never actually done this before,' he said meekly. 'But Charlie meant so much to me. He was my hero.'

One of the lawyers heckled, 'You're doing ever so well!' His neighbours nodded sweetly.

'Go on, darling!'

The man brightened and spoke directly to them, saying that they were all gathered here to celebrate the life of Charles Hawthorn Taunton. This would not be formal or serious or sad because it was for Charlie and anyone who knew the man would appreciate that.

The Cayman Islanders and the lawyers nodded. The army officers didn't react at all. They had mastered impassive.

He cheerfully gave the broad-strokes story of Charlie's childhood in Somerset, only child, military family, clever boy with a scholarship to Fairchurch, a *very* prestigious school.

Now, none of his classmates were here and some of those present would know why. Charlie went on to study law for one reason: he had a mission. Single-handedly, Charlie gathered the statements of his schoolmates and sued two masters from the school, sexual predators, at a time before historic sexual abuse cases were being prosecuted. It was not a popular thing to do and Charlie became something of a pariah, accused of fabricating the claim for money or revenge, because he had a grudge. But it was the truth, said the celebrant, and he knew that because he was one of those boys. Charlie Taunton saved his life. He paused, misty eyed, and nodded at his feet.

'I will always be grateful to him. I will never forget.'

He moved on to talk in a muted way about Charlie's later years, about his marriage to Kiki and her lifelong struggle with depression. He finished up with the Tale of the Tooth.

When Charlie was called to the Bar he had to attend a formal dinner in the Great Hall where drink was imbibed, teams were chosen and each nominated a champion from the other side to chase a live chicken in New Square. Charlie was chosen. Somehow, chubby and plastered, Charlie managed to catch the bird but, just as he did, he tripped on a kerb and landed on his mouth, knocking his front tooth clean out of his head. He held onto the bird as he leapt to his feet, holding the poor thing up high as the blood ran down his chin. He said it was his proudest moment.

The lawyers were laughing. The Cayman Islanders were roaring and wiping tears away. But Claudia was watching Amelia, her pretty little chin tight, her lips rolled back again, baring her teeth. She wasn't listening to the story, she was looking at Gina's arm, remembering the slight, rolling the resentment around her head. She was a terrifying creature.

The pompous men giggled and laughed, a fleeting lunatic ecstasy, looking around at each other as the vapour trail of joy and connection Charlie had conjured in life slowly burned away.

The celebrant grinned, waiting for them to settle down, and then turned to the coffin and raised a hand as if introducing a variety act, 'Ladies and gentlemen: Charlie Taunton.'

The laughter turned to cheers and applause, a rapturous whooping that brought everyone to their feet. The military front row stood to attention as the rest of them clapped, hands over their heads, tears streaming down their cheeks, cheering for Charlie with shouts of 'bravo' and 'go on, my son' as the blue curtains closed on Charlie Taunton, tidying him away for posterity.

The celebrant bobbed down to the speaker and Pachelbel's Canon in D started again mid bar as the side door was opened to the day.

The military family left swiftly but everyone else waited for the celebrant to step down and followed him out, Caymanites and lawyers all smiling and nodding at each other.

Claudia fell into step with Tim, Tweedledumber, when she saw

Gina power-walking away across the car park. She ran after her until she caught up.

'Gina? You not even saying goodbye?'

'Goodbye. I've got an Uber taking me back to Richmond.' She pointed at a white Volvo idling in the driveway.

'I need to get across town.'

'D'you know,' Gina wrapped her fingers around her sunglasses and yanked them off her face, 'after what you've just heard in there, I can't fucking believe you're sending the boys to that school.'

Claudia whispered, 'Gina, we're in danger. They'll be safe there.'

'Your arse, they'll be safe. You're a bootlicking cunt.'

Tearful, Gina turned away.

'Can I write to you?'

'Fuck off,' she said and walked off to the waiting car, slamming the door and staring resolutely forward as the driver pulled away.

Claudia walked back over to the Tweedles and Tim offered her a lift into town. She asked if she could bring someone.

'Sure.'

Amelia was standing alone, holding her handbag in front of her with two hands. She looked very subdued. Claudia offered her a lift.

'That's so kind but I don't want to suck all the oxygen out of the car.' She gave a sullen smile.

'Please don't let my sister make you feel bad, she says things—'

'It's fine. She's right. Fine art is full of dilettantes.'

'She's rude, Amelia. I'm sorry. She loved Charlie.' She turned to Tim, 'You taking the Westway?'

Tim nodded.

She turned back to Amelia, 'They're passing your studio anyway.'

Amelia said she didn't want to impose but Tim and Abir wouldn't have it. They insisted that she come with them.

25

They were in Tim's massive Range Rover, Amelia in the front seat, Claudia in the back with Abir. From outside they must have looked like a grotesque double date, with their mismatched ages and personal styles. Abir and Tim were young, fit, the hypercompetitive, fastest-runner-in-the-school types. They married slim and pretty women who stayed slim and pretty. If they didn't they were replaced with new slim and pretty wives. Claudia looked like a fertility goddess and Amelia a Goth wood sprite.

Tim reversed the huge car and drew out quickly before they all had a chance to get their seatbelts on, cutting up a Mini on his way to the exit.

'Fuck off,' he murmured cheerfully.

'Quite right, mate,' said Abir.

They took the turn through the narrow gates recklessly but it felt very safe sitting so high up above the other cars, as if all the peril on the narrow country roads was someone else's. Tim drove fast, tilting on corners and flying on the straight roads, staying at a legally defensible four miles over the speed limit. When they reached the dual carriageway his driving style changed abruptly, tempered by the threat of traffic cameras to cautious.

As they drove Tim and Abir chirruped about what a great service it was, how like Charlie, how fitting that it was a bit mad. Claudia asked about the Fairchurch case and Tim and Abir laughed about it. They had been at a rival school. The rugby team at their old school made up a song about paedo teachers and sang it at matches when they played Fairchurch. Even they seemed to realise it was distasteful but only as they were telling the story.

'No rapists at your school, then?' murmured Amelia. 'Are you sure?'

The mood in the car dropped.

Peace-making, Claudia asked after Abir's wife who was a lawyer as well. She had walked out on him and took the kids, said Abir, but don't feel sorry for him, he had a new wife now and she was training as a therapist. He told them how he felt about that, sad and betrayed, then wise and happy. As personal journeys go it was pretty dull because Abir's emotional register was as flat as a fenland. But Claudia nodded at the right places and congratulated him at the end and Abir seemed pleased.

They chatted intermittently on the drive, about Charlie, about his family and Kiki, who they had both known, and the Cayman crew who were all ex-lawyers. The group had formed around a particular London barrister who'd retired there at forty with a big cash win from a famous tort settlement. He invited some friends to visit and they all fell in love with the climate, the income differentials and the day drinking.

They were on the Westway, a three-lane flyover that swooped over Notting Hill and Paddington before slaloming down into central London. Tim was taking it at a smooth fifty-five in the middle lane and the road curved wide around Westbourne Studios.

It was a warehouse abutting the carriageway, matte black with huge silver lettering on the side. Tim suggested dropping them off at the next slip road and Claudia said that would be great.

'Hey,' he said, 'why did Charlie come back from the Caymans?'

Abir answered, 'He was investigating Tontine, wasn't he?'

'Tontine?' asked Claudia innocently.

'Some megabucks trust. William Stewart's trust money sank into it after Jonty petitioned for an alteration. Where the fuck is all that going now, because Stewart won't get tuppence?'

'I'd stab my dad for less and I love my dad,' added Abir. 'And there's the Francesca of it all.'

'God, she was a total fucking pleasure model—'

'Guys,' Claudia cleared her throat, 'Amelia is William's cousin . . .'

'Oh,' Tim glanced at her. 'I'm sorry. Didn't mean to . . .'

'No, no,' Amelia spoke very quietly, 'it's fine.'

'Guilty though?' asked Tim, embarrassed. 'I mean he pled guilty so . . .'

'So he was guilty,' said Abir.

'Yeah,' said Amelia, wary. 'He's guilty.'

But Tim was still uncomfortable, 'Just, you know, so sorry for the whole . . . you know, Jonty was such a good bloke. So sad. Hey Abs, remember the party in Cannes?'

'Oh my god!'

'Bang fest,' smirked Tim.

'Nero-standard.'

'Nero would blush.'

Amelia was staring at the side of Tim's face, the cold hard smile on her face again and an odd atmosphere crackled in the car, uncomfortable, electric until, between the two front seats, Claudia saw Amelia's small hand dart across to Tim's groin.

She didn't touch Tim though. Her fingertips hit the red button on his seatbelt. The metal belt clip whipped out of the buckle and up, smacking Tim's jaw, as Amelia's hand yanked her side of the wheel straight down.

The huge car staggered sideways on the motorway, jolting across lanes, barely making it into the space between a white van and a saloon. Claudia and Abir were thrown sideways as Tim's bum slid off the seat. He grabbed the wheel, overcorrecting as he tried to straighten up. The car careened wildly back across the lane.

Amelia was perfectly calm. She reached out with one hand and took the wheel and pulled it straight. She didn't blink. Her thin smile did not falter.

A chorus of car horns sounded around them and the seatbelt alarm rang loud in the car.

'What the fuck!' Tim shouted, his voice an octave higher, 'What the actual fuck are you doing?!'

'Oh, sorry,' she said smoothly, 'I must have pressed the button by mistake.'

Tim glared at her, 'You shoved the wheel down. What the fuck is wrong with you, you fucking mental bitch?'

'Mistake,' she said softly. 'I made a mistake.'

Tim saw his chance and sped down the slip road, breaking hard as soon as he reached the bottom.

'Get out of my fucking car! Get out!' He leaned over and threw her door open, 'Get out. Out!'

Amelia smiled at Tim, she smiled at the back seat, 'Sorry everyone. For the mistake.'

Traffic was backing up behind them. Someone was sitting on their horn.

Claudia took off her seatbelt and opened her door, staggering out to the side of the road and clinging to the railings. She didn't think she'd ever let go.

This is what happened to James. This is what happened to Charlie. She looked up and watched Amelia turn gracefully in her seat, slide both legs sideways and step daintily down to the verge like a fairy godmother on strings landing on a stage. A nasty little smile was nestled on her face.

'Gosh,' she said softly. 'That was frightening.'

Tim slammed the door behind her and drove off. The drivers behind them followed, rubbernecking the two women at the side of the road.

'Wasn't that frightening?' she said to Claudia but she didn't look frightened. She looked excited and a little vacant, a gambler on a winning streak.

Claudia could hardly breathe. 'What the fuck happened?'

'I pressed the button by mistake and his seatbelt came off. So frightening.'

'Why did you grab the steering wheel?'

'To steady the car.' She leaned into her, their noses almost touching, 'Why else?'

As if nothing at all had happened, she hooked a finger into Claudia's sleeve, tugging her down to the end of the slip road and across to the pavement on the street below. A bus rumbled by, lifting dust from the road surface, making them narrow their eyes.

Claudia was on the kerb side and lurched backwards, suddenly convinced Amelia was going to shove her into traffic.

Amelia giggled, 'Whoopsie. Did you take a little tommy tumble there?'

Claudia managed a dumb smile, 'My ankle went over.' But she

stayed back from the roadside because she knew who she was with. It was the paintings all over again. Amelia was showing her workings, in plain sight, and enjoying it.

Amelia had made that move on James, on Charlie, veering them off the road into the water, her own seatbelt still on, got out of the car somehow and left them both to drown. Neither accident was investigated properly and there were no cameras up there. Injured or not, she could easily have walked away across the short heath in any direction and caught a taxi or called someone for a lift. She knew everyone James and Charlie knew, would have named dropped any number of mutual friends to make them feel safe. Neither man would have refused her a lift if she gave them a sad enough reason to let her into their car. A slip of a girl. A drunk mother. A rich family. She was rubbing her nose in it, knowing there was nothing Claudia could do.

Claudia couldn't look at her.

'What a morning,' said Amelia, as if they'd had cross words with a taxi driver. 'And where are you off to now?'

Claudia hoped to God she didn't know about Thamesmead and shrugged, 'Work?' Her mouth was so dry that her throat felt sandy. 'You?'

'Might go for a swim.'

Claudia stiffened, trying to read her face, wondering if she was hinting about James and Charlie drowning. But Amelia didn't seem to be making an oblique comment about anything. She was just thinking about going for a swim.

'Well, I'm going this way.' Claudia peeled off, backing away. 'Say hi to Larry for me.'

'I will.' Amelia watched her walk away, flashing her teeth in a taut smile. 'Bye bye, then.'

'Bye bye,' echoed Claudia, nodding and walking and nodding. 'Bye bye.'

She scurried off, walking faster and faster until she reached the crossing under the flyover. When she looked back she saw Amelia watching her and smiling.

Then she raised a hand at Claudia and waved and Claudia waved back like a big dumb fool with no cards left to play.

26

The waiting room was a dreary grey passage between two locked doors. The visitors were all female, mostly older, one with a couple of excitable small children. It was a school day and the bigger kids would visit at the weekends. The tiny agents of chaos jumped around, singing and hanging off their adult's hands.

A bank of CCTV screens took up one wall and the officers watched the visitors carefully, alert and suspicious, attempting to welcome the children and frighten the adults at the same time.

Claudia was asked to stand aside and let the exasperating children go through first. They were winding each other up, getting weepy, their mother starting to raise her voice and issue threats. The officers wanted them out of there.

She was asked to wait again as they queued the families up at a heavy door. They let them out to a brighter place. The heavy door was shut immediately.

When her turn came Claudia set her keys in the plastic tray and got through the metal detector without setting it off. But they weren't looking for guns or bombs or knives. They were looking for drugs. Wordlessly, a stern woman in an ill-fitting uniform opened a side door and nodded Claudia through to a cupboard room with no windows. The camera up high on the wall buzzed like an aggrieved wasp.

The officer shut the door so they were alone, told Claudia to take her shoes off and then asked to see her photo ID again. She patted Claudia down as she asked her what it was she did for a living.

'I'm a forensic examiner.'

The officer nodded but her face betrayed no opinion.

She lifted Claudia's shoes and felt inside with her gloved hands, tried to pull the heels off, tapped the sole, listening for cavities.

Satisfied, she put them down on the floor in front of Claudia and nodded her back into them. 'What is a "forensic examiner"?'

'Forensic reports on crime scenes for the courts.'

The officer hummed with interest, watching as Claudia stepped back into her shoes.

'Good job?' She glanced guiltily up at the camera on the wall.

Apparently being a junior prison officer charged with conducting body searches wasn't that satisfying.

'Sometimes. Wears you down though.'

The woman looked tired as she opened the door back into the lobby. 'It's the stories that haunt you.'

Claudia knew exactly what she meant, 'I know: the stories.'

They all said the same. This was the real wear and tear. The Roland Garrets and other vignettes, knowledge of lives that spiralled out of control, of the banal brutalities and failures of well-meaning state interventions. It was exhausting to hear about them day after day. Living them must have been devastating.

They walked back through the heavy metal door to the room they had come from, standing together now as they looked up at the camera, waiting for the lock to be remotely undone.

A heavy click sounded like Gina's arm breaking. It made Claudia feel sick. The door in front of them sagged a fraction and the woman officer raised a weary hand to thank the camera. She stepped forward and opened the door, waving Claudia through and saying goodbye. She sounded like a depressed mother dropping her kid at nursery, heading outside to weep silently in the street.

The Thamesmead Prison visiting room was warm and cavernous, a school assembly hall filled with the smell of piss and bleach. High, bare ceiling girders were thirty feet above them. The room was lit by a wall of scratched Plexiglass that looked onto a brick yard with a muddy patch of dead plants. Attempts had been made to mitigate the harsh environment. It was furnished with purple and pistachio plastic chairs and tables all nailed to the floor and a mural of outsized cartoon flowers ran all along the wall.

At each table sat a lone man, all dressed identically in grey sweatshirts and joggers. Some already had visitors and some were still waiting, their eyes trained on the door, willing their person to arrive.

There were more men waiting than visitors being processed. Someone was going to be disappointed.

The small children who had been jumping around in the lobby were sitting at a table with their mum across from a man so untouched by the sun he might have been a ghost. The kids seemed cowed now, concentrating intently on their crayons and colouring-in sheets as the woman talked and the ghost nodded. He kept his hands flat on the table as if he had been warned to do so.

William Stewart was at a far table over by the window. She hesitated, shocked at the change in him. He had gained weight in the last four months; even his eyelids looked swollen, a sort of watery puff. He didn't have broad shoulders and the weight sat badly on him. She hardly recognised the young man from the memorial service.

She walked over to him. 'William?'

He looked vacant.

'Do you recognise me?'

He didn't seem to. He nodded in a way that might have meant yes, or no, or whatever. She wondered what medication they had prescribed for him. She'd heard he was disruptive when he began his sentence. But drugs weren't hard to find in prison, they might not have been prescribed at all.

'Can I sit down?'

'Yeah.'

She hesitated again, guessed he meant it was okay for her sit down and she did.

'I was at Charlie Taunton's funeral this morning.'

'Charlie? Poor Charlie.'

'Do you remember me, William?'

He shrugged. Prisoners had to agree to a visitor coming in. Whether he knew who she was or not he had agreed for her to come. She tried a little small talk.

'I was surprised to get a slot. I thought you might not remember me. I'm Claudia O'Sheil, I was in the car with you outside the house that night, with Philip, do you remember? Then I was at your arraignment. In the gallery. You looked at me.'

He looked at her then, his bloodshot eyes tracing her face, remembering. 'Oh, yeah. That's where I know you from?'

'You didn't know my name? Why did you agree to let me visit then?'

'No one else comes. They send money but they don't want to come.' He sat slack in the chair, lips parted, breathing heavily through his mouth.

'They let me charge a card to buy snacks with,' she pointed back to a vending machine. The window display of goodies was bolted to the wall with a thick metal belt.

William nodded.

'What do you like? D'you like chocolate?'

He nodded again.

She walked over and bought a family bag of chocolate Minstrels with her card. They weren't allowed to use coins. Claudia had seen case photographs in forensic journals and knew that coins could cause terrible injuries if they were thrown hard enough at someone's face.

The machine belched out a bag and she bent down to reach in for it, aware of being watched by cameras and a room full of men with murky pasts. She took the bag back to the table and split it open, sitting it on the table between them to share.

William leaned forward and pinched the corner of the packet, dragged it over to his side of the table, smiling cheekily as he did it.

'Greedy guts.' She smiled.

He gave a gusty little laugh at the milquetoast insult. 'What d'you want anyway?'

'Have some chocolate, William.'

'You called me son that night.' He closed his fist over the pile inside and put his hand to his mouth, cascading the sweets into his mouth while he watched her.

'Yeah. We talked about tattoos. You told me why you had the Gordian knot tattooed on your chest.'

He almost smiled, 'If only I had known how much worse things would get . . .'

'You said you would slice through it all.'

'I was deluded. I remember you calling me son and saying I needed a lawyer. Then Charlie Taunton arrived.' He chewed vacantly and swallowed. 'Liked him.' He blinked. 'Good man.' He inhaled, exhaling through the side of his mouth so that he didn't spray chocolate everywhere. Each movement looked tiring, as if he was having to talk himself through the business of breathing. He crammed more sweets into his mouth, holding the full hand close to his chin as if they might get lost on the way. He put more sweets in his full mouth. Some of them tumbled down his chest to the shelf of his belly. He noticed but didn't bother reaching for them.

'That's why I came to visit. I wanted to ask you why you pled guilty.'

He chewed for a bit. 'I am guilty. I deserve to be here.'

'For that, William? Why did you say you did *that*?'

'I'm responsible.' His face remained unmoved but his eyes were narrowed, bitter and wry, as if everyone else was in on a joke and she was the only one who didn't get it.

She shook her head. 'Even if you did kill them that night, this is what gets me: the case was defendable. There was reasonable doubt. All of the evidence, *all of it*, was circumstantial. Why didn't you fight it?'

He ran his tongue across his dry gums, smearing oily chocolate across them. 'I was poorly advised.'

'By Larry Beecham?' Claudia craned forward. 'Did he advise you to plead guilty?'

He didn't want to answer that.

'Look, I love Larry, I've known him for years but he is famously lazy. Did he tell you to say you did it? Did he tell you about the sentence reduction?'

William snorted a laugh but stopped and looked at the table, digging in his molars with his tongue. 'One third off.'

'What did he tell you?'

'Well, I was not exactly open to reason at that particular time. The whole thing was a little bit of a dream.' He took a greedy handful of sweets but lost interest and just held them, looking into the middle distance.

'I know you didn't do it, William.'

He smiled widely, 'Really?'

She nodded.

'How do you know?'

'You should have been covered in blood and you weren't. It's that simple really. It was a mess in there, you didn't see what happened to them. It would be like walking through a shower and coming out dry. Did you stab your dad in the bollocks thirty times?'

'What?'

'He was stabbed in the cock thirty times after he was dead. Are you claiming you did that?'

He blinked, shocked. 'Where?'

'In the genitals. Cock and bollocks. Post mortem. Why don't you know that, William?'

He was moving faster now, agitated at what she was saying. He sat forward, took another handful of sweets and tried to fill his mouth with them.

'Plus: the opiates. Even cut with coke or meth, I can't see you focusing on something for that length of time, managing to sneak out across the roofs to number twenty-six, which you've scoped already and know is empty, breaking in, sneaking down through the house and going out the back. My sister has a problem and when she's using she can hardly be bothered to finish a fucking sentence that isn't related to getting off her face.'

He looked her up and down sceptically, 'Your sister?'

'She was in the Lighthouse.'

'Oh, I've been in there. A lot of Dutch people go there. They call it Alki-traz. I liked it in there. Rehab's good training for being in here.'

She waved a hand at the grimy room, 'Great. Glad she's retraining for something with a future. That's fifty grand of my money well spent.'

He smiled at that. 'Is she doing CBT or the Twelve Steps?'

'Twelve Steps, I think. She can ask me for forgiveness but she's giving out none.'

'She eighth stepped you?'

'Is that when she apologises for the things she feels bad about and refuses to listen to the things that actually hurt me?'

He snorted.

'She doesn't remember them, I suppose. She has a lot of blanks.'

'She's checking out of life. In French an orgasm is a "*petit mort*": a little death. That's what it feels like, checking out of life. Overwhelming. It's too much for some of us.'

'But then you come back and it's worse?'

He gave a sad nod. 'Time moves on for you. For us . . . it's dipping in and out, it's caring too much and then not at all. My dad, I mean, I could have done it.'

'But the blackouts are chaotic, aren't they? Not tidy. Not around events or anything. Did you think you might have blanked out and done it by accident? Because I've watched her try to open a packet of crisps for half an hour and I can assure you, you didn't.'

He put some sweets in his mouth and chewed once but then left them there to melt, his mouth open, his eyes watering.

'Did you know you'd lose everything if you pled guilty?'

He nodded and hummed. 'Yeah, almost why I did it.'

'Self-harm takes many forms.'

'That was self-preservation. My whole life was controlled by the money and what's an inheritance anyway? None of it was mine. What would I do with it? Kill myself in a bigger house? On a massive grouse estate in the Highlands?'

Claudia swallowed. For the first time since she sat down she felt she had something to lose. She reached across the table and took two sweets, sat back and ate one.

'Who gets it then? Mary? Amelia?'

He shrugged.

'No. They're rich but not *us*. Just rich.'

'Philip Ardmore?'

'That sad-eyed old fucker? No, wouldn't do him any good even if he could get it. It costs a lot of money to run those properties and estates. Philip doesn't have the money to run a car park, not until Mary bestows it on him. She is very rich though.' He smiled unkindly, 'The way it works is that the wealth gets concentrated, down and down and down, until just three people own the whole world. All the titles and the money and the land and the castles. The rest of us – we're just fodder.'

'You were in line to be one of those three people.'

'I can't change the system,' he looked down at the cheap sweets in his hand as if they were his children. 'But I can pick a side.'

She ate her last sweet and they sat together for a moment as the noise of uncomfortable encounters swirled around the room and heat throbbed through the scratched windows.

'Does Amelia visit you?'

He smiled at her, his mouth twitching at the sides. 'Doesn't have to, does she?'

'You grew up together, I thought you were close?'

William watched her vacantly, but it wasn't hostile or unkind. He just wasn't feeling anything and, in that moment, she envied him. 'She used to be around a lot. I depended on her too much, maybe I shouldn't have done that. I made her stay with me, come on holiday.'

'Cannes?'

He breathed in hard and held the breath for a long time. 'Cannes . . . she was thirteen. I was twelve. She came because I begged her. Jonty drank a lot. He liked to party . . .'

'Did your father assault Amelia?'

A deadness came over his eyes. 'Rape. Call it what it was. Just say rape.'

'Sorry. Did your father rape Amelia?'

He didn't answer. He didn't need to.

'I'm sorry, William. I'm sorry for her and for you. Thirteen is very young.'

'Ami couldn't stand it when Francesca started seeing him. Another betrayal. She told Francesca what he did to her that summer but then she got engaged to him. She's doing her best, Amelia. She's . . .' He seemed to lose the thread of what he was saying. 'She only came to Cannes because I was so lonely.'

'Have you seen a twelve-year-old recently?'

'In C block?'

'Oh, yeah, fair enough. Well, they're children. They're not old enough to be responsible for things like that. You've let everyone off the hook but yourself.'

He shrugged one careless shoulder and picked up the escapee Minstrels, putting them in his mouth one by one, a monkey eating his fleas.

'William, I know you're innocent.'

'Everyone is innocent.' He looked around the room. 'Everyone in here claims they're innocent. It's pathetic.'

'Everyone out there claims they're innocent too. All the wrong people feel guilty and all the wrong people are ashamed.'

They smiled sadly at each other until Claudia broke off eye contact.

'Yeah, anyway.' He trailed off and looked suddenly exhausted.

'Can I send you anything in?'

'No.'

They sat in silence for a moment and she wondered, 'Hey, you went to Fairchurch, didn't you?'

'Yeah.'

'Was it all right?'

'Some people hated it but I had nowhere else to go. I left in the middle of the final year, just walked out. Jonty didn't care.'

'My boys are there. I don't know if I'm doing the right thing.'

'They'll be all right,' said William. 'The safeguarding is Stasi-like now, I hear. No one will touch them in there.'

She was comforted by that for a moment but then looked past him and saw the bigger picture: he was in prison, his life over at twenty-two and maybe not the best source of advice about personal safety.

27

She was on the Metropolitan Line train, looking out across the passing roofs and roads to the giant arch and edifice of Wembley Stadium when her phone rang out. It was a redirect from the office phone so the caller ID was disguised. She let it ring and checked her work email.

The financial history of ForSci Ltd was in from Companies House. She opened it. Initial funding for the establishment of the company came from Luxembourg. From Viscount Court Associates, a company situated in Jersey. No more information was available because of international legislation.

She shut her eyes.

Her body remembered the sensation of the Range Rover jolting sideways and she sat up, gasping for breath as she saw the image of James, dead, slumped, seatbelt-less, his orbital bone smashed and his bloody eye hanging at a wild angle on his cheek. The steering wheel had caved his chest in, ripped his heart from its mooring arteries. His circulatory system had emptied into the sack of his body. He was dead in minutes.

She understood what had happened at Chester Terrace and why, but Amelia killing Charlie and James made no sense. There must be some reason, some common theme. James and Charlie hadn't seen each other for years. Charlie would have defended William but James was no threat.

She thought her way through the forensic evidence from Chester Terrace. The misattribution of DNA to Mary. A flawed BSPS. William's DNA on the gun and nowhere else. None of it was useful for an appeal anyway. With a guilty plea they would only appeal on a point of law and Larry had been meticulous. Amelia would get away with all of it.

She looked around the carriage.

The Metropolitan Line was an old branch of the London Underground. The carriage was low and the bench seats were upholstered in itchy material. A couple further down the carriage looked as if they were heading in to Fairchurch for Home Supper too.

Home Supper was a tradition that stretched back a hundred years. Boys in their first term were allowed to wear their own clothes and their families or friends could come and take them out for dinner, if they were nearby. The couple were dressed formally as if they were presenting themselves for interview, but they were excited. The woman had a shopping bag at her feet, probably full of goodies and fresh underwear. One child, guessed Claudia, some adored, clever child they were pouring all their love and resources into. They could have been Charlie Taunton's parents.

The phone rang again and she took a deep breath and forced herself to answer it. It was Sir Philip.

'Oh,' she said. 'Hello, how are you?'

'Claudia? O'Sheil?' He was surprised to hear her voice. 'Is that you?'

'You called me.'

'No I didn't, I called the office. I'm trying to get hold of Rob. Is he there?'

'No, sorry. He's off today and the phone's been redirected. I'm on the train.'

'Ah. Oh, well.'

She didn't know he and Rob spoke to each other. 'Can I help you, Philip?'

He hummed and hesitated. 'Well, I wanted to ask him about these forms I got from Companies House asking about the financial history of ForSci. It says Rob requested a search on the records, which seemed odd. I just wanted to check. It's not a scam, is it?'

She had requested the search in Rob's name. 'No, that was us. We need it to re-insure the company because we've changed clinical director. For the registration to be finalised, you know, to show that we're not owned by Pablo Escobar.'

Philip said oh, yes, of course, of course. Insurance. But he stayed on the line. He had something else to ask her. 'Of course. Of course. All well with you? Why are you on a train?'

'Home Supper.'

'Of course! Metropolitan Line?'

She said it was and Philip said he loved that journey, how it hadn't changed much since he was a boy and he dreamed about it often. Did she hear the news? An investigation was being launched into Maura Langston's conduct of the Chester Terrace investigation and why William Stewart was allowed to be out on bail for so long. Langston had been suspended.

He would hear that she had been to Thamesmead, she knew he would, so she shut her eyes and forced herself to tell him: 'I went to visit William today.'

'In Thamesmead? Today? *Really?*'

His voice was too high, friable. He already knew, she could tell. William wouldn't have told him. He must have someone there, a spy in the prison keeping an eye on him.

'Yeah,' she said. 'Well, it was Charlie's memorial service this morning and Amelia was there and I spoke to her and she said how kind Charlie was to William so I thought he'd like to know about it.'

'Did you?' He didn't believe that was why she'd gone.

'Yeah.'

They were lying to each other, they both knew it but neither was prepared to break cover.

'Yeah, William was pleased it went well. Thought he'd like to know . . .' She was talking too much.

'But you have to request a visiting slot weeks in advance, don't you?'

He was calling her out. He knew she was having doubts about Chester Terrace. He knew it.

'Yeah,' she blustered. 'Surprised he agreed. I didn't think William would want to see me.'

'He's a sorry mess. Dear old Charlie Taunton. How was the turnout?'

'Tremendous,' she lied. 'Caymanites came over in a Lear jet together.'

'Nice.' He stayed on the line though, listening, waiting for her to break.

He waited quite a long time and then finally he said, 'Yes?'

'Yes,' she said.

They listened to each other again. This was the inflection point, the moment when she would either break ranks or join him.

'Hm. Did you receive a special letter this week?'

'I did, yes.' She had been offered an MBE in the upcoming New Year Honours list and had written back to say she would accept. She was sworn to secrecy. 'Did you know anything about that?'

'Yes. I nominated you. What did they offer you? An O or an M?'

'An M.'

'So well deserved! An M! That's lovely, good for them. Actually, Claudia, there's something else I wanted to ask about. January is the anniversary of the College Building opening and last year was so awful that I wondered if it mightn't be rather a nice thing for us to rechristen it, put it all behind us and have a proper party this time with a special speaker, viz *you*. There's great interest in the Chester Terrace case with the film coming out next summer and it would be a good idea to nail your name to the mast. You could talk the audience through the case, through the evidence, lay it out. Honestly, it doesn't really matter very much what you do or don't say, just that ForSci and the college are mentioned so that the tie-in is forged before the movie comes out. Otherwise, I'm quite sure Andrew Hamilton will be giving interviews about it for the next five years.'

'With his mad hair.'

'Yes, his home-grown toupee.'

They laughed longer than the joke deserved.

'You know what, Philip, I'd love to put it all behind us.'

'Is that a yes to the talk?'

'Of course it is.'

'Wonderful! That's wonderful. Great. You know, once the film comes out, after this talk and so on, well, you might well be sent another lovely letter with an offer of a D. This is so exciting. I'll have Rob draw up a guest list. We'll fill the main auditorium. And afterwards, to celebrate, perhaps you would like to dine with me at the Albemarle?'

'Really? Does the Albemarle even allow women inside?'

'Oh yes,' said Lord Philip. 'Yes. For private dining, yes. By order of the committee we're limited for numbers now. Members were being bribed with summer stays in Tuscan castles or yacht parties for supper invitations. We're only allowed five guests a year now.'

'Did that stop the bribes?'

He sighed, 'Honestly, it just pushed the price up. The food isn't even that nice but the venue is terribly exclusive.'

'Are you sure you want to waste one of your five on me?'

'I'd be honoured. Would you like that?'

'No, I wouldn't like it, Philip. I'd absolutely love it.'

28

The Old Etonian restaurant was opposite Fairchurch School. It had the air of a very posh school canteen with starchy linen and steel cutlery. From the street it looked modest enough, a two-storey cottage with nets curtains on rails to fend off the eyes of passersby. The décor was mock Tuscan with plain plastered walls and a stone floor, lots of tables and a dessert trolley of tasty cakes and trifles idling by the bar. Further into the building, though, it opened up to a terrace looking out over the high hill, past the roofs of the little houses to the playing fields below. The name of the restaurant was a joke, the boys said, the two schools being bitter rivals in all things, chiefly self-promotion and cricket.

Sam and Bernie sat at the table with Claudia in their home clothes, uncomfortable and a little formal, as if she was a social worker who had come to assess them. There had been a showing of rooms, of friends, of a new gym in the basement of Bowes house: the resident boys had all voted for it but it didn't look as if anyone had used it much. They were showing her things she didn't need to see, filling in time with noise.

But they were here now, at a small table in a very full restaurant of other parents and other boys going through the same busy charade of closeness. The boys sat close to each other and left Claudia across the table from them like an interviewer.

The food was French with touches of Italian, dated but done well, as if it was catering to grandparents from the 1980s coming back from the Cote d'Azur to visit grandsons at the school.

Bernie ordered spaghetti Bolognese and garlic bread, double carbs. Sam ordered steak and haricots verts. Claudia went for the trout to set a good example.

'Can we have wine?' said Bernie.

'You know you can't.'

'We have wine at home.'

'Do you want the lovely family who own this place to lose their licence?'

Bernie said he didn't care much for the family. One of the masters' daughters, Sally, worked here at weekends and said they didn't share the tips with the staff.

When he said her name he glanced at Sam who blushed and seemed to tremble a little. There was a fraught teenage subtext here. Sam liked her or she liked him.

'Is she working today?' asked Claudia.

'No,' said Bernie, and he was blushing too now. 'She's not working here now.'

Sam spoke suddenly, his voice too loud, 'Dad was in trouble all the time here.'

'Was he?'

'He carved his name on a very old wall. We saw it. He got a technical suspension for a week.'

'What's a technical suspension?'

'It means your parents are away and you can't go home but you're suspended. They only give it for something really dastardly. Black mark on your record.'

They sat for a moment in the clack and clatter at the other tables. Claudia told them about James complaining that his parents were never there for him. He'd been left to deal with these adult disputes alone, against powerful authority figures, and had told her how he thought that's why law appealed to him so much. She trailed off tearfully at the end.

'I find Dad very hard to talk about,' she said, her voice choked.

Bernie reached over to her hand but the table was too wide for his little arm to reach. His fingertips bumped hers. 'We know, Mum. It's all right.'

The food arrived and saved everyone but an understanding had been established and it made the meal much nicer.

While they ate Claudia told them about the cheering at Charlie's funeral and the Caymanites. She left out Gina being there, it hurt too much to think about.

'Plus, and you mustn't tell anyone this, at the New Year Honours list this year there maybe a little something for a certain someone you know . . .'

They looked nonplussed.

'Sir Philip?'

'No, not him again. No. Try again.'

'Rob!' guessed Bernie, 'Services to rugby.'

'What *are* you talking about, you idiot,' sneered Sam. 'They don't give honours for services to rugby.'

She told him not to talk to his brother like that and eat his steak before it got cold but the antagonism lingered. She was worried about Bernie. She'd insisted the boys be in the same house to protect him but even Sam seemed to have turned on him a little. Bernie was awkward and defiant, moon-faced with red cheeks that showed his emotions like a mood ring. She hoped he wasn't getting a hard time from the other boys, that Sam hadn't decided it was too much work to stand up for him and given up and taken their side.

She gave them another clue, pointing at herself, and they finally realised that she was getting an honour.

'Woaw,' said Sam, and Bernie nodded along. They clearly didn't care too much but wanted to be nice. They were sweet kids.

The food was delicious, salty and buttery and the bread was served warm. They all got very full and Claudia warned them to stop eating the bread and leave room for pud. They could have two if they wanted, of course they could. The joy of the dessert trolley was that they could pick as many as they wanted and be served a little bit of each.

As they were coming to the end of their meal a family of three sidled past their table and the boy nodded at Sam, 'All right, Atkins?'

Sam nodded back, 'Yeah, good.'

The parents looked like bit-part players in a film about Hampshire, the moustachioed father dressed in a double-breasted blue blazer and slacks, the mother in an ugly-expensive flowery dress cinched at the waist with elastic.

'Hello,' said the mother to Claudia and Claudia reciprocated and asked if they'd had a nice supper.

'Terribly nice,' said the woman, smiling apologetically. 'I believe you know the Earl of Strathearn?'

Claudia froze. She'd only seen William a couple of hours ago. She was surprised word was out so soon. 'The Earl . . . ?'

'Of Strathearn?' Surprised by Claudia's reaction the woman turned stiffly to her husband for reassurance, 'Am I wrong?'

'No, no,' the man assured her and stepping forward, said loudly to Claudia, 'The *Earl* of *Strath*earn. You know him, yes?'

A more likely scenario occurred to her: they must have seen her at Jonty's memorial. 'Ah, yes,' she said as if she had just remembered. 'Of course.'

The woman nodded warmly, 'We were at a little house party with him last weekend. Terribly nice man. Invited us shooting on his estate next year.'

'He hasn't any parties going up this year, of course, a bit early,' smiled the man, sliding behind Bernie's chair to get past the table.

'Early?'

'Well, he's been out of remainder for less than a fortnight. Lovely news for him though.'

'Oh, yes.' Claudia suddenly wanted them to stay. 'Pass on my regards?'

'Oh,' the wife smiled modestly down at her shoes as she moved away, 'I'm sure you'll see Philip again before we do.'

Claudia watched the departing couple take their coats from the hooks at the door and leave, passing the window outside as they walked away down the street with their son.

She took her phone out and googled 'Earl of Strathearn' as Sam and Bernie excitedly told her who the couple were, who their son was, how good he was at rugby and how the family were massively rich and never spoke to anyone but of course, because of the film and Jessica Ronay, she was famous too.

Sir Philip Ardmore was next in line for the Earldom of Strathearn, making him a lord. The title came with large tracts of land in the Highlands around Ullapool and two substantial farms in Wales and a castle she'd never heard of in Aberdeenshire. But he didn't have any money. William said he had nothing but his settlement from Mary. He couldn't run a grouse shoot or have parties. He didn't have any money.

She could barely hear the boys' chatter as they finished their meal and she walked them back to their house, night falling softly on Fairchurch on the hill. Gusts of warmth from the valley below blew up at them with the smell of the flower-heavy gardens and exhaust fumes.

She thought of the urgency around installing all those CCTV cameras in the courtyard of the new college. It wasn't because of a zombie army of Ginas. The footage was needed to place Philip in the courtyard when Jonty was killed. She thought of the party being held in January, all those witnesses and of course, when the time stamp on the doorcam could be twelve hours out and it would still be dark outside.

They had planned it so intricately. They'd thought of everything. Philip knew what Amelia was capable of and he'd used her. It was him all along.

As they approached Bowes House Claudia's step quickened but the boys' slowed. When she came to visit before she was reassured by how keen they were to get back and gossip with the other boys, exaggerate what they had to eat and boast about their plans for the holidays but not now. They were reluctant to go in now.

They walked quietly, weaving between one another, growing quieter as they reached the corner and their house. A double-decker bus crawled past them, taking care on the narrow street, lighting up their faces. They both looked sad and resigned. It was hard to look at.

She expected to leave them at the gate, was looking forward to getting away, but Sam stood to the side of the path and waved her in, his face very suddenly very serious.

'I thought I was leaving you here?'

Sam wiped his nose with his palm, 'Miss Coole wants to see you.'

Bernie had already scuttled up the path to the door.

'Bernie,' she called after him, 'Bernie, what have you done?'

Bernie opened the front door, 'Nothing.'

'Bernie . . .' He'd done something terrible again. Last time he was in trouble he had gone missing with the Nigerian ambassador's son. They found them sitting in the Waitrose café. He almost caused an international incident.

Bernie ducked into the hallway, letting the door fall closed after him.

'Bernie!'

She hurried after him into the house but he was gone when she opened the door. A small boy in a blue track suit was standing there, pre-pubescent, a small child with thick black hair in a side sweep. His eyebrows shot up at the sight of her.

'Can I help you?' he said, a polite but firm challenge.

''S all right, Moony, it's my mum.' Sam was behind her. 'Mum, it's not about Bernie.'

'What is it about then?' she asked, instantly worried that it was about money or a Prince of Qatar wanting two spaces in Bowes. Someone had been bumped for her boys and they might be bumped for someone else's, someone more connected.

Sam turned down the corridor, expecting her to follow. She did, jogging down a small set of wooden stairs to Lorna Coole's office.

The door slide declared Miss Coole 'IN'. Sam rapped the door with a knuckle and Lorna called 'Come.'

They seemed to be working Claudia together, sitting her down, offering tea, Sam moving his seat nearer to hers, Lorna carefully shutting the door so that they wouldn't be overheard.

They had discussed this without her, how best to put it to her, how to handle it.

'Can you just tell me what's going on?'

Lorna sat down and sighed heavily before she told her.

Sally Donaldson, the Modern Languages master's daughter, had made a complaint against Sam. It was not yet formal and the hope was, of course, that it could be kept informal and the matter could be dealt with discreetly. She claimed that Sam had assaulted her at a party in one of the rooms. There was absolutely no point, no earthly point, in jeopardising a promising young man's future over some loutish nonsense that got out of hand. No one was actually hurt. There was no damage done. But what they absolutely had to be sure of, going forward, was that everyone was fully informed of the circumstances and that it did not happen again.

Lorna Coole sat back in her chair and fell silent. In the absence of noise, an affable little smile flitted across her face but she caught it and stopped it and stared at Claudia.

She looked at Sam, bent over, elbows on knees, hands clutched together. She looked at the concave curve of his belly, his red cheeks and his long brittle neck.

'Is Sally okay? How is she?'

'Well . . .' Lorna didn't seem sure.

'Sally told you this?'

'As much as . . .'

'What the hell does that mean?'

Lorna was not going to tell her anything else.

'Mum, I didn't do anything.'

Lorna clucked her tongue. 'Sally is in Australia, she's taken a year out and that's the best thing for everyone, I think. She has signed a notarised statement making these allegations against Sam.'

'What evidence is there?'

'Evidence?' Coole looked confused. 'By which you mean . . . ?'

'Mum?' Sam looked at her pleadingly, 'I didn't do anything. We kissed and then she left. I'd never hurt her. I don't know what's going on.'

She looked at him and she believed him.

But all mothers must feel this way when their sons are accused, she told herself, and she was already a master of denial. She had refused to look at things, refused to stand up and call out lies. She would rather believe that James killed himself than question his death until Charlie.

And it was Sam. This wasn't who he was. Sam put on washes at home. Sam put tissues in the bin. Sam blushed when there was a sex scene in a film. But Sam was a bit mean sometimes. He was mean to her. He was mean to Bernie. And all mothers felt this way, surely.

No one believed it of their son.

She had a choice. She could agree to cover it up and hope it never happened again or she could hold the allegation up in public for examination, to be picked over and questioned and swabbed and measured. That was what she should do.

But in the end, all she had left were her boys.

18:59

Claudia and Philip stood in the dark, sweat trickling down her back.

'This is puerile,' said Philip. 'We can't keep playing chicken as if this was a game. Take the mic off.'

She did and handed it to him.

'It's you, isn't it, Philip? You're the beneficial owner of Tontine. You get everything. Charlie was only halfway to finding proof but James had worked it all out. He came to see you and signed the visitors' book at the Albemarle. You knew I'd find out eventually, that's why you invited me to do this because once I've given this talk I'm tied to you, to your version of events.'

He wrapped the wire around the battery pack, 'Were you going to say that out there? Denounce me?'

'Why would I do that? I'm not stupid. I'm a big girl, I know what we're doing. You've given me everything I want. I have the money and the status and the house. My boys are at Fairchurch. I'm respected. I'm rich. If the flaws in the BSPS come out I'm as implicated as you are. I'd hardly risk all that would I?'

She could see him trying to believe her. He nodded slowly but was still unconvinced.

'The story has already been told, hasn't it? We all know what happened. We all agree. Let's just move on.'

Together, they looked out to the auditorium. The seats were wide and comfortable, the audience had filled up the front rows. Kirsty Parry was sitting there, messing with her dress, pulling it down over her knees, tugging at her neck. She looked uncomfortable.

Claudia dropped her voice to a whisper, 'I know it was Amelia. I know Jonty raped her when she was just a kid and I understood why you covered for her even before I knew you were having an affair. I never blamed you.'

'How did you know?'

'A garden party in January? For fuck's sake, I've always known.'

He didn't answer her but he didn't deny it either.

'I happen to think,' she whispered, 'that you deserve everything. The girl, the titles, the estates and the Tontine money. You're a force for good in the world, Philip. I think you deserve everything. What I don't get is why you didn't just wait for William to die of an overdose.'

Quite suddenly, his knees buckled and his shoulders slumped, 'We couldn't because of James. He was being so messy about it all. He threatened to go public about my being the beneficial owner of Tontine and if he had Jonty would have moved all of the funds out of it.'

'How could Jonty not know you were the beneficial owner?'

'Daphne set it up. She trusted me and William was the named owner. Jonty couldn't know because I was a trustee. He moved Daphne's money into Tontine thinking William would get everything eventually.'

She nodded.

Philip went on, 'Look, I'm devastated about James. I didn't mean that to happen but when he stormed out from our supper I called Ami in a panic. She was coming to meet me anyway and she met him on the street by his car. They knew each other, of course.'

'Everybody knows everybody.'

'They do. She was crying, she said, and he was very kind. He offered her a lift. She did it to protect me, not for herself. He wouldn't have known anything until the very last moment. I'm so very sorry.'

'We were about to get divorced. Did you know that?'

He stroked her arm sympathetically, 'I wondered. At the time. I knew he wasn't always home. It's terrible that things happened this way, Claudia, I'm in bits about it.'

She looked up at his kind, handsome face, saw gentle concern in his eyes. But behind it, almost hidden but not quite, was a flash of steel.

'Tonight is important to you, Philip. I know that. I don't need to go out there if you'd rather I didn't. You speak. I'll stand next to you and then we'll go off and have a nice supper and we can put all of this awfulness behind us.'

'Put it behind us?'

She nodded, 'Put it behind us.' And then she added in a playfully formal tone, 'Let us never speak of this again.'

He gave a small agreeable nod but she could see that he wasn't entirely convinced. 'Come here and look at this.' He brought her to the side of the stage, 'Look out there.'

They looked out from the side of the stage at the audience gathered in the auditorium. The seat next to Kirsty was empty but the rest of the room was full of expectant people sipping their drinks and chatting pleasantly, the babble of chit chat and occasional ripples of laughter, warm and friendly, filtering up to them.

'Do you see that couple sitting there?'

Philip pointed at a couple, one in a green three-piece suit, the other in an ill-advised tight grey silk shirt stretched taut over a large stomach. 'The man in green is on the Ethics Committee with me. He has reservations about the BSPS but I dissuaded him. And the people next to them,' he pulled the curtain back a little and showed her a large group settling into comfy seats, 'The woman lives twenty feet from me, our gardens are adjoining but she lets me use her tennis court. That man with the pink trousers is on several of the same boards as me and half of us are going sailing in Cape Cod this summer. That woman behind him, the younger woman, she went to school with Amelia. Just so you know who this audience is.'

Claudia nodded.

He was right. They were his friends. But there were journalists there too, one in particular, a bald man sitting at the front with a voice recorder balanced on the arm of his chair ready for her to come on. He looked annoyed.

He whispered, 'You see, Claudia, no one here will listen to a complicated denunciation of the BSPS or believe that of me or hear ill of Amelia or any of this. It's too far-fetched. It's too complicated. It's not in their interests to hear it.'

'Why would I say any of that here?' She looked at him, 'It's being live streamed. I'm not going to jeopardise my career or my reputation or my boys' education. The boys're all I have.'

Philip's eyes narrowed. He wanted to believe her, 'You're investigating ForSci's investment history. Why?'

'You know. I want to know everything. I'm intellectually curious. I'm a little insulted that you thought I'd believe Rob was behind the company. But oh, mustn't ask Rob about that because he's embarrassed, honestly – fuck off.'

He snorted a laugh despite himself. 'I was caught off guard.'

'Well, for Christ's sake, I mean,' she stepped back as if resigned to him taking the stage without her, 'I do want to know but it doesn't follow that I'm going to burn the building down around me, does it?'

'Okay,' he nodded sadly, a touch disappointed that she was just as rotten as he was. 'Well, I'm glad we've got it all out in the open.'

'Me too. Am I still invited to the Albemarle?'

He smirked, 'You're determined to get there for supper, aren't you?'

'Honestly, yes. We can still salvage a nice evening, although this party does seem sort of cursed, doesn't it? Can you promise me you won't hold it again next year?'

They smiled at each other in the dark.

Philip stepped over to her and held out a fist, 'Take it.' He was giving her back the mic set.

Claudia fitted it to the back of her head. Philip helped her snake the wire down the inside of her jacket and dropped the pack into her pocket.

'But you know,' he muttered behind her ear, 'just for the avoidance of any . . . you know . . .' He let out a loud blustering sigh, 'Sally Donaldson. I hear she is doing terribly well in Australia. Settled in terribly well.'

The lights dimmed in the auditorium. The audience lowered their voices to hissing whispers.

They were shoulder to shoulder in the dark, standing at the side of the stage. Claudia felt herself freeze up, hardly able to draw a breath. The boys were supposed to be safe there. James was wrong. They were supposed to be protected. She had given up everything for that, Gina, their company, her family life but Philip was everywhere. He was inescapable. He was omniscient.

He would have that accusation to hold over Sam all of his life. But Sam wasn't in prison. He wasn't charged. Did he even do it, though? And why should Sally be exiled to Australia? And if it wasn't this threat it would be something else. Something on Bernie. Something on Gina.

Her hands began to tremble as a heavy silence fell over the audience.

Casually, Philip flicked his mic on and dropped the pack into his pocket. He took a first step out towards the stage but stopped and turned back to her.

'Yes?'

She thought they would be safe there.

'Yes? All well, Claudia?'

The audience was waiting. Dave the sound man was waiting. They couldn't put it off any longer.

She nodded, defeated.

Sadly, Philip nodded back, 'It's fine. Don't worry. We'll talk about it all at supper.'

Then he pulled the curtain back and stepped out onto the stage.

The audience greeted him with warm applause that gathered momentum and rose to a cheerful roar. They loved him. They knew what he had been through this year. Poor Lord Philip.

From the side of the stage she could see people rising to their feet, gurning grins, whoops and cheers. Even the cynical journalist with the voice recorder was smiling and clapping his spare hand on his thigh.

Philip raised a staying hand as he made his way to the centre of the stage, letting them know that he deserved all this fuss, really, do sit down. But they carried on clapping as he walked over to the podium and turned to face them, chuckling indulgently and keeping his eyes down, a modest man but a great man.

As though he simply couldn't take any more, he raised an insistent hand to quell the applause. The room quietened. He flattened a hand to his chest as if rendered speechless by their good regard. 'Good heavens!'

People in the audience laughed, mostly women. Women loved him.

'You're all much too kind,' he purred, taking charge of the room. They loved him.

Well, he began, here they were again.

They found themselves here this evening to celebrate this marvellous building on its second anniversary. He thanked the architects, who unfortunately couldn't make it tonight, being otherwise engaged. And to marvellous Enrique in the office, buildings manager Martin and, of course, Henry Wilde of Wilde, Kilbride and Turnbull.

Everyone applauded these names as directed by the rise and fall of Philip's intonation. He thanked a great many people, enough for Claudia to wonder if he was just going to keep thanking people to fill the time and not invite her out, but he didn't.

'And so to the business of tonight. I know you're all eager to hear from Professor O'Sheil, Emeritus of Durham, who has agreed for the very first time to talk about what has come to be known as "The Incident at Chester Terrace", soon to be a major motion picture starring Jessica Ronay.'

The audience whooped mildly and then laughed at themselves for making such a bad job of it.

He looked to the side of the stage. Claudia took a step out into the light but he stalled her with a hand.

'No,' he said firmly, as if he was training a dog. 'Not yet.'

She had misunderstood the signal and faltered, standing in full view, blinded by the fierce stage lights.

Philip pressed his lips together in a sympathetic smile, as though she was a little unstable and he had to control her.

He looked back at the audience, 'Professor O'Sheil and I have worked together very closely, as many of you know. There are a great many here who knew her dear husband James Atkins, sadly no longer with us. Now, despite her many personal tragedies and very, very difficult personal circumstances, which many of us are only too well aware of—'

He was framing her as a sad case, a tragedy waiting to happen.

Claudia chewed her bottom lip and then remembered that she could be seen. She stepped back into the dark.

'Despite these many difficulties, she has overcome so much, and risen to be one of the most respected – perhaps indeed *the* most respected in her field. She has done great work. *Great* work. What a career. Laudable. Ladies and gentlemen, lords and ladies, will you please welcome Professor Claudia Atkins O'Sheil.'

The audience did as he told them to and applauded but their warmth for her was markedly cooler than it was for him.

She shambled awkwardly out to the podium. Philip did not step aside. He turned towards her though, shook her hand and kissed her cheeks.

'Don't be nervous,' he said quietly but audibly into his mic. 'I know you can do this.'

Then he slid away into the shadow, leaving her in the blinding spotlight.

She slid her speech from the documents folder onto the podium and a bead of sweat fell from her hair onto it. She watched it seep through the paper in a perfect circle.

The audience stopped moving, she could hear their apprehension, sense her strange mood. Her shoulder twitched.

There was no point. Every exit covered. They wouldn't listen and Sam would be set up, just as William had been.

She saw Sam in the cavernous visitors' hall at Belmarsh, staring at her and chewing chocolate.

Remembering where she was, she looked up into the blackness. A red light blinked from the very back. The event was being live streamed worldwide, to the members of the college, to fans of the book, to the producers of the upcoming blockbuster film. She smiled a rictus show of dry teeth. Blackness. She couldn't see anything but the blinking red eye. She looked down at her speech. It had been shoved roughly into the folder and she watched as the top page folded slowly shut of its own accord.

Someone out there in the darkness cleared their throat anxiously. Claudia looked up.

'Good evening,' she registered that something was wrong but

carried on anyway because everything was wrong tonight. 'I am here to tell you about the Incident at Chester Terr—'

'We can't hear you.'

'What's she saying?'

'Her mic's not on.'

'YOUR MIC'S NOT ON,' shouted someone from the dark room.

She fumbled the mic pack out from her pocket. The on switch was small and fiddly and the spotlight was shining in her eyes.

Dave appeared at the side of the stage. He looked worried. He mimed turning the tiny switch.

'I can't see it,' she nodded to the spotlight. 'It's too bright.'

This was very unprofessional. The audience were restive and worried. How hard could it be? Lord Philip didn't have these problems. Someone sucked their teeth. The person with the cough made use of the pause to really go for it.

Dave reached over to the lightings board and turned the dazzling spotlight down. Claudia could see the pack now and flicked the tiny switch.

'THANKS, DAVE.'

This was the first thing the audience heard from her and it was deafening. She had been turning the volume knob by mistake.

Bad start.

From the side of the stage Dave gave her an encouraging smile and a thumbs up that looked patronising even from fifty yards away. She at least wanted Dave to like her.

'Thanks.'

That sounded normal. She turned back to the audience.

Now that the lights were down she could see every single disappointed face in the room, every single person who wished Lord Philip was giving a talk instead of this clumsy fool. Amelia, Rob, Larry, Maura, Evan Evans, everyone.

And she couldn't remember the point of ruining Sam's life, her own life. There was no point in telling the truth to an audience who didn't want to hear it and wouldn't listen. It was sheer spiteful pride on her part. There was no reason to do this. No one else cared about the truth.

She looked out and saw the first row. Even Kirsty Parry was embarrassed. Claudia looked sadly at the vacant seat next to her but a movement at the end of the aisle caught her eye. A shadow, bent low, was creeping along the front row towards Kirsty. The figure sat down in the vacant seat and looked up and smiled. It was a face she hadn't seen for a long time. The tattoos on her forearms were clear and visible in the light from the stage.

Gina had read her postcard and had come. I'm going to fuck them up, Claudia had said, I'm going to tell the truth. Come and watch.

She grinned down at her speech, touched the translucent sweat circle with her fingertip, flattened the sheet open again and looked up at the audience.

'Ladies and gentlemen,' her voice sounded clipped and unexpectedly clear, 'I'm here to tell you about the murders at Chester Terrace. As many of you know, one year ago tonight, Jonathon Stewart, Earl of Strathearn, and his fiancée, Francesca Emmanuel, were sitting down to eat their evening meal when someone came into their house. What followed was a shockingly violent attack by a single assailant and within minutes the police were at the scene. My life's work, the BSPS, was used to bring charges against the earl's only son, William Stewart, and he pled guilty. The case didn't go to trial.

'My probability scale is world famous but I know now, and have known for some time, that it is fundamentally flawed. William Stewart is innocent. He did not commit those murders. Other miscarriages of justice have occurred because of my mistakes: a young man called Roland Garret for one. The scale is wrong. Dr Kirsty Parry said so in open court and was subsequently blackballed.'

Kirsty was staring at her, slack jawed with shock. The rest of the audience glanced at their neighbours, unsure if this was what she was supposed to be saying. She was losing them. Philip took a step out into the the light.

'To quote a man I admire very much—' she gestured to Philip and the audience looked over at him, calmed by what they supposed was deference '—who once said: "So much of being an adult is resisting the urge to stand up and say: *That is a total fucking lie*."'

The audience bristled. Several people giggled because she had used a swear word and that was wrong in this sterile space. It was a signal that this was not a normal, dull speech.

The cynical journalist at the front slowly raised his voice recorder up towards her. The other journalists craned forward in their seats, biros shimmying across their notepads.

'Charlie Taunton said that. He knew my scale was wrong. He was murdered because he knew it. If you listen to me for the next ten minutes I'll tell you who really killed Jonty and Francesca. I'll tell you the truth. The absolute, total fucking truth.'

And then she did.

Acknowledgements

Several great big barrels of thanks are in a friend's lock-up and will be distributed among the following people: a rusting barrel each to Katie Ellis-Brown and Helen O'Hare for brilliant and clear-eyed editorial direction. A tear-stained barrel to Liz Foley for all her help and support as she moves up to a bigger desk. To Mia and Bethan with love and cardigans. To Sam Stocker for his patience and clarity. A subscription to a monthly barrel service for Jon Wood for all his kindnesses and thoughtful direction, and Henry Durnow for ditto. A bucket to Professor Allan Jamieson at the Forensic Institute for his time, patience and sight.

A barrel of thanks so concentrated that the council won't pick then up to Lady Nicola White for the GGs.

Credits

Vintage would like to thank everyone who worked on the publication of *THE GOOD LIAR*

Agent
Jon Wood

Editor
Katie Ellis-Brown

Editorial
Anouska Levy

Copy-editor
Fiona Brown

Proofreader
Eugenie Woodhouse

Managing Editorial
Sam Stocker

Contracts
Gemma Avery
Ceri Cooper
Rebecca Smith
Humayra Ahmed
Kiran Halaith
Anne Porter
Hayley Morgan
Harry Sargent

Design
Julia Connolly

Digital
Anna Baggaley

Claire Dolan
Brydie Scott
Charlotte Ridsdale
Zaheerah Khalik

Inventory
Rebecca Evans

Publicity
Bethan Jones
Mia Quibell-Smith
Amrit Bhullar

Finance
Ed Grande
Aya Daghem
Samuel Uwague

Marketing
Chloe Healey
Sam Rees-Williams

Production
Konrad Kirkham
Polly Dorner

Sales
Nathaniel Breakwell
Malissa Mistry
Justin Ward-Turner
Ben Taplan
Lewis Cain

Nick Cordingly
Kate Gunn
Sophie Dwyer
Maiya Grant
Danielle Appleton
Phoebe Edwards
Amber Blundell
Rachel Cram
David Atkinson
Amanda Dean
Andy Taylor
Dan Higgins

Rights
Lucy Beresford-Knox
Celia Long
Beth Wood
Annamika Singh
Agnes Watters
Lucie Deacon
Liv Diomedes
Jake Dickson

Audio
Nile Faure-Bryan
Hannah Cawse

Thank you to our group companies and our sales teams around the world

About the Author

Denise Mina is the author of twenty novels, including the Reese's Book Club pick *Conviction* and its sequel, *Confidence*, as well as *The Second Murderer*, *The Less Dead*, *The Long Drop*—winner of the 2017 McIlvanney Prize for Scottish crime book of the year—and the Garnethill trilogy, the first installment of which won the John Creasey Memorial Award for best first crime novel, among others. Mina has twice received the Theakstons Old Peculier Crime Novel of the Year Award. She lives in Glasgow.